TALES OF MY ANCESTORS

BRUCE EDWARD GOLDEN

Cover Design
Background Art: Mike Watts
Monolith Photo: Jinah Kim-Perek
Tech Support: Phil Nenna

ISBN-13: **978-1519414540**
ISBN-10: **1519414544**

Shaman Press

http://goldentales.tripod.com/

<u>Also by Bruce Golden</u>

MORTALS ALL
BETTER THAN CHOCOLATE
EVERGREEN
DANCING WITH THE VELVET LIZARD
RED SKY, BLUE MOON

FOR MY DESCENDANTS

ERIC GOLDEN

SAVANNAH PRESLEY GOLDEN

TROY CONNER GOLDEN

and all the Goldens that will hopefully follow

History is but the nail on which the picture hangs.

Alexandre Dumas

THE TALES

If history were a photograph of the past, it would be flat and uninspiring. Happily, it is a painting; and, like all works of art, it fails of the highest truth unless imagination and ideas are mixed with the paints.

Allen Nevins

Author's Note

Many years ago, I became aware of the ancestral research completed by relatives of mine, and began to learn interesting things about my various family lines. Piggybacking on the work of others, I did even more research and discovered ancestral roots that, in some cases, preceded the 11th century. However, when you go that far back, accuracy can be a problem. You are dependent on antiquated records, and you question whether bloodlines were always reported accurately. When you think about it though, a millennium isn't that far back considering the human species is some 200,000 years old.

I discovered that not only were some of my ancestors well-known historical figures, but that many of them had unique stories. That's when I decided to become the family apocryphist.

As a writer, I was inspired by the accounts I read. First by the tale of a woman descended from English kings, who grew up in exile in Hungary and returned to England only to have to flee again. Her ship, damaged by a storm, had to port unexpectedly where she met the King of Scotland, eventually married him and became a Catholic Saint. Those facts begged to become a story of some kind.

What started out as just a few tales led, eventually, to the idea of an entire book's worth of stories, each using, in some manner, one or more of my direct ancestors. This book, in fact. ("Direct" meaning related through great grandparents--no uncles or cousins or other offshoots.)

Like most historical fiction, this book is a kind of time machine, and the tales herein required extensive research. When I wrote my stories, the one caveat I adhered to, was that I would not contradict any known facts. But it wasn't just facts I was looking for. I had to research the culture of the time, the language, even what character traits a certain person might have had. I wrote these tales being true to all the historical records I could find. I dramatized what was known and filled in the gaps how best suited the story.

In addition, I added a singular speculative element to each tale--a *what if*--science fiction and fantasy, after all, being my genres of choice. For a story which took place in 17th-century Ireland, I used the Irish legend of the banshee, in the tale about the above mentioned girl who grew up in Hungary, I used a creature from Hungarian lore, and for my retelling of the Salem Witch Trials, it seemed appropriate Satan should make an appearance. I don't alter what happened, I only suggest *what if* this is *how* it happened . . . *what if* this is *why* it happened.

It's the combination of the historical, the speculative, and the characterization of my ancestors, which I believe make this book unique. This is also the first time I've ever used my middle name as part of my byline. In fact, it's the first time I've used my middle name for anything-- never having much use for the appellation *Edward*. However, it seemed appropriate here, in that the name came from my father's father and my mother's grandfather. It's also the name of the most recent king I'm a direct descendant of--King Edward III of England.

While I find it intriguing that I'm a direct descendant of Charlemagne and several members of European royalty, I take no great pride in it. If you do the math, you'll find there are likely millions of people of European descent alive today who are direct descendants of Charlemagne. In fact, as one mathematician said, it would be more unique NOT to be a descendant of Europe's last emperor. It's just that most people don't know it. They haven't been able to track their family lines back that far.

As they say in the language of the Native American Sioux, *mitakuye oyasin*--we are all related.

As to whether you should be proud of your ancestors or not, the fact is that some were good and did amazing things, and some, by today's standards, were savage barbarians, even if they were kings--probably *especially* if they were kings.

Because, famous or not, good or evil by our reckoning, they were all human. Or at least they were as far as I know.

TALES

OF MY

ANCESTORS

The very ink with which all history is written is merely fluid prejudice.

Mark Twain

The Hoodoo Incident

As I stood there, waiting, I thought about Ma and Pa, and my sister Louisa. I pondered what they'd think of me . . . though I already had an inclination. I also thought about Big Jim, since he was mostly why I was standing where I was.

When I told Louisa what I wanted to do, she thought I was plumb crazy. She told me so, then she told Ma and Pa. To say they was upset wouldn't do their anger justice. Ma was crying and Pa's face was red as a tomato. I thought he might explode. He did in a way, erupting with a barrage of cusswords that singed my ears. Some of 'em I didn't even know. But it didn't matter what he said, my mind was made up.

The man in front of me moved, so I took another step forward. I knew there was no going home now, even if'n I changed my mind--which I wouldn't.

You have to understand. I'd never been out of Rappahannock County in my whole life. My family had lived in Virginia for five generations--ever since my great, great grandfather William Deatherage and his three brothers got into some kind of trouble with the king, and had to leave England. At least that's how Ma tells it. Heck, she told me Pa's grandma came from a family who were among those who first set foot in Virginia . . . if'n you don't count Indians.

So we were dyed-in-the-wool Virginians, and Pa was as loyal to the Confederacy as Jefferson Davis--who Ma always reminded me was the grand nephew of my great grandmother. She also never let anyone forget we was related somehow to the former president, Zachary Taylor. Ma was big on family relations.

When my grandfather died, Pa inherited Horseshoe Estates, which included more than 12-hundred acres and 28 slaves. Horseshoe Estates had been handed down from father to son for more than a hundred years, and I guessed it would've been mine someday if'n I hadn't run off.

I shuffled forward again, trying to peek around those in front of me and see what they was doing. I couldn't see much.

When I was just a boy, maybe five or six, I fell into the rapids of the Jordan River. Don't ask me how I could've been so dumb, but I was. It was Big Jim who fished me out--saved my life. He'd scolded me for being so careless, then took me back to the house to dry off.

1

Big Jim had been just a little pickaninny when Pa inherited him. But full grown he was the biggest, strongest slave in Rappahannock. As I grew up, he was kind of a big brother to me. Taught me how to fish, how to hunt, how to groom a horse. He taught me other things, too, even when he wasn't trying, most times without words. He taught me a man's a man, no matter his station in life, and that good men were true to their word and their conscience. I guess that's why, when I read some of President Lincoln's words in the newspaper, I began to think about slavery, and whether it was the right thing or not. I decided it wasn't.

It was a decision that sprung out of my head so clear one day I never had to decide again. Of course that don't mean I still didn't think about slavery. I gave it plenty of thought. The more I thought, the more wrong I believed it was. It didn't fit with anything I'd read in the *Bible*--not that I was a big *Bible* reader.

I don't reckon Ma or Pa ever gave two thoughts about slavery until President Lincoln tried to abolish it. They'd grown up with slaves all around, just like I had, and thought it was the natural order of things. I tried to talk with 'em about it, but they weren't gonna listen to such talk. Thinking about ending slavery went against the grain of how they'd lived for too long. The concept of giving a negra the freedom to do whatever he or she may want was the definition of chaos to 'em. Though I reckon a big part of it was they couldn't cotton to the idea of some Yankee telling 'em how to live. I didn't bother to remind 'em Lincoln was born in Kentucky, and that his own grandfather was from Virginia.

I finally gave up trying to bring 'em around to my way of thinking. It was soon after that I told 'em I was gonna join up with the Union Army. That raised all kinds of holy hell. Ma cried that I was too young--which, legally, at 16, I was. Pa said he'd never let his son be a traitor to the Confederacy--that he'd tie me up in the barn first. I believe he would've, if'n I hadn't snuck off the way I did. I thought about saying goodbye to Big Jim, but decided against it. He would've tried to talk me out of it, and just might have succeeded. I didn't want to be talked out of it.

Those in front of me moved again and I followed. I was getting closer.

Horseshoe Estates hadn't seen hide nor hair of the war. We'd been lucky. Rappahannock County didn't have any big cities, and was off to the west of where most of the fighting was taking place, according to the newspaper. I hadn't heard so much as a single cannon blast in all the years since it had started. I guess, like any boy, I was intrigued by the idea of war. I had no idea

I'd get my fill of it before it ended.

It was two days before Christmas when I left home. I decided to head west, 'cause I heard tell the Union Army controlled most of Kentucky. I wanted to avoid running into any Confederate troops, as they might conscript me into their ranks, regardless of my age. I started off walking, but hitched a ride part way. Still it took me several days before I happened onto some Yankee soldiers who directed me. So I had plenty of time to think on what I was doing, and never once did I doubt myself. Well, maybe once.

"Next!" called out a gruff voice.

I'd finally reached the front of the line, but had gotten lost in thought while I was waiting for my turn. I almost tripped stepping forward, but tried to stand as tall as I could.

"Name?"

"Martin Luther Deatherage, sir."

"Age?"

"Eighteen," I lied.

He looked me up and down, and I saw the doubt in his eyes.

"Do you know what the date is today, Deatherage?

"January 1st, 1864, sir."

"What's your birth date, Deatherage."

I quickly subtracted two years and replied, "April 5th, 1845."

He still looked skeptical.

"Where you from, Deatherage?"

"Virginia, sir."

He raised an eyebrow at that, but just made note of it on the paper in front of him. Then he handed it to me.

"Can you read and write?"

"Yes, sir."

"This is your enlistment paper. Sign it here."

I signed my name and he put the paper onto a stack with a bunch of others.

"Alright, Private Deatherage. Go get in that line over there. Next!"

The words resounded inside my head--*Private Deatherage*. I was a soldier.

f

My trousers were too long by some three inches, and too wide at the waist. My Union blue shirt was coarse and unpleasant, too large at the neck, too short everywheres else. The cap was ungainly, and the overcoat made me feel like a nubbin of corn in a sizable husk.

3

I already knew how to shoot and ride a horse, and once they saw that, they assigned me to the cavalry--Company C of the 2nd Kentucky Cavalry.

I got along pretty well with most of the other men, and nobody made fun of me 'cause I was younger. They treated me like everyone else--like a man who'd come to do his part.

There was one big, burly feller who was always bullying new recruits--pushing 'em, hitting 'em--just to see if'n they would fight . . . to see if'n they *could* fight. He cuffed me around a bit until I suggested we get our carbines, stand 40 yards apart, and then see who was the better man. I wasn't joking, though he laughed it off as though it were somehow funny. But he never bothered me again.

When we weren't drilling or on sentry duty--which was most of the time--some of the men enjoyed playing music. Some had brought their own fiddles or banjos, but it was amazing how some men could turn anything into a musical instrument. I once saw a soldier play "When Johnny Comes Marching Home" on a washboard. I didn't play an instrument, but when I knew a song I'd sing along, or just use a barrel for a drum. I reckon the music helped fight the boredom and the homesickness.

One thing I sure missed about home was the food. The only Army food we ever had was salt pork, dried beef, beans, rice, onions, and if'n we was lucky, maybe some taters or turnips. The coffee was more like boiled swamp water, but I looked forward to it just 'cause it was warm. I didn't know it then, but I would soon miss the salt pork and beans. There would come a time when all we had to eat was hardtack crackers, which we'd soak in the coffee so they was soft enough to eat. We came to call 'em "worm castles," 'cause much of the time they were infested with weevils. Sergeant Foley showed us how to fry the crackers in grease, when we had it, so as to kill the weevils. He called it "skillygalee." As hard as it may be to believe, that became a real treat for us.

At first there was a lot of drilling, a lot of sentry duty, a lot of waiting, but then our regiment got its orders. Our company commander, Captain Lower, called assembly and told us curtly in that raspy voice of his, "We will return as honored soldiers, or fill a soldier's grave."

We didn't know where we were going, but I knew by then a soldier isn't supposed to know any more than a mule. He just has to obey orders.

Once we got going, I knew without anyone telling me we were headed south. Exactly when we crossed over into Tennessee I wasn't sure, but I knew that's where we was headed.

*

The first dead man I ever saw was leaning back against a big tree as if'n asleep, but his guts were all over his legs, bloody and bloated. I looked away, but still felt deathly sick. Further on there were lots more dead men, scattered through the woods where they'd fallen the day before.

It wasn't long after that we had our first skirmish. We'd come upon a small group of Rebs, by accident I reckon. They opened fire on us and I saw a couple of men go down. Captain Lower led a charge into the brush and it was over almost before it began. I never even saw anyone to shoot at.

I learned later we were tracking a group of Johnny Rebs who'd caused some trouble in Kentucky and then crossed back into Tennessee. But these fellers weren't the ones. They was just some locals who didn't care for Yankees.

We kept moving south for the next three days, without incident. We rode long and hard. We'd wake each day to the sound of Sergeant Foley yelling, "Rise and shine!" Soon after that he was hollering "Mount up!" Before long we'd be covered in dust, caked by the early morning mist.

On the fourth day, we came upon a field where Sergeant Foley said he'd been part of a big battle a couple of years back. He called it Shiloh. Apparently, the rain from those years had uncovered a number of shallow graves. Awkward white leg bones and grinning skulls could be seen in all directions. I spotted a boot protruding from the ground, its sole warped open, leaving little skeleton toes pointing towards heaven. It wasn't my stomach that gave way on me that time, it was my head. I wasn't so much sick of the sight as I was horrified. It was a gruesome spectacle that incited all manner of bizarre thoughts.

I don't know exactly when it happened--weeks later, months later--but as time passed, such ghastly sights would no longer affect me as they once did. The time came when I wasn't even afraid of dying any more. I had no dread of it. What bothered me more than anything was the idea I would die alone, and that no one in my regiment would ever find me. That like the men in this Shiloh field, I'd be buried in a hole with a bunch of other nameless soldiers. It came about that my only wish, my only prayer, was that someone I knew would see me die, and do right by me.

*

Our company separated from the rest of the regiment when a group of the Rebels we were tracking splintered--part of 'em turning east, then north. Our company set off in pursuit, and our horses were almost played out when we finally caught up with 'em at a tobacco plantation near the town of Big Spring. They were loading up their wagons with the plantation's slaves when we got there--likely preparing to take 'em south and out of the hands of the Union.

Those Johnny Rebs were outnumbered and surrounded, but they put up quite a fight. I got my first chance to fire my carbine, though I don't think I hit anything of consequence. Despite their resistance, dying to the last man, I reckon the whole thing was over in less than 20 minutes. We whupped 'em good, losing only two of our own. General feeling was they were two good men, though I only knew 'em by name.

The slaves had scattered for cover during the fight, but the plantation's owner and his family had departed before we'd even arrived. Captain Lower ordered us to load all contraband onto the wagons--contraband being any weapons, foodstuffs, harvested tobacco, and the slaves themselves.

The first slave I found as we rounded 'em up had a sort of leather muzzle strapped on his face. He was an older feller, maybe 40, with flecks of gray in his hair. His clothes were typically threadbare, and the shirt on his back speckled with bloodstains. I helped him remove the muzzle, and asked him why he'd been bound so.

"It turned out, after all my years of service, the colonel, who be my master, had no ear for my words of wisdom."

"What did you say to provoke such cruelty?" I asked.

"When the Confederate soldiers showed up and told the old colonel he and his family needed to hightail it out of here 'cause the Yankees was coming, the colonel resisted. He proceeded to profane the Confederate officer something fearful. I simply suggested to the colonel it would be better for him to remain silent and seem ignorant, than for him to speak up and confirm it. He didn't really take my meaning until some of the soldiers started in on laughing. Then he had me whupped good and muzzled."

"Well, no one's ever gonna muzzle you again," I assured him. "President Lincoln has declared you a free man."

"I've heard tell of such, but it didn't seem likely, as I was still working in the fields of the same master I'd always had."

"You're your own master now. No one owns you anymore."

"The colonel's gonna be mighty upset when he finds his property gone. Not that I'll let it trouble *my* conscience."

It didn't occur to me at the time that this feller had no concept of what it meant to be a free man. He had no reference point to understand what exactly it would entail.

"What's your name?" I asked him.

"It's Jordan, sir, Jordan Anderson."

At that moment a negra woman ran up and threw her arms around him. She was followed by several children.

"My wife, Mandy, and my children, sir."

"You don't have to call me sir," I said. "My name's Martin . . . Private Martin Luther Deatherage."

"Pleased to make your acquaintance, Private Deatherage."

Other women and children began to come out of hiding, still fearful, but seeing our blue uniforms seem to calm 'em somewhat. One of 'em was a pretty young girl who had this distant stare and seemed almost like she was sleepwalking. Another woman had to help her along.

"What's wrong with her?" I asked.

"The young master had his way with her one too many times I suspect," replied Jordan. "And his way was rough. She hasn't been right for nigh a season now. Same thing happened to my two oldest daughters."

"Are they . . . ?"

"They was sold away some time back. Don't know where they be."

He shrugged as though the fate of his daughters was as common as the sun rising in the morning, but I saw the pain in his eyes. I couldn't begin to imagine what that pain must feel like.

I'd never seen such treatment at Horseshoe Estates. Slaves they may have been, but no one in our family ever treated Big Jim and his brethren with such cruelty. My father never would've countenanced such a thing. Still, a slave was a slave by my way of thinking, and the difference was only a matter of temperament.

"You must have hated your master," I said.

He shrugged again. "I don't reckon he was all bad," replied Jordan. "By all accounts he loved his children . . . and his dogs."

I wasn't positive if'n it was irony I heard in his voice, or just acceptance. Yet the more I listened to him, the more I came to realize it was the former.

"The colonel and the young master weren't nothing compared with the colonel's missus when she was riled. Of all the animals on the face of this earth, I'm most afraid of a raving mad slaveholding woman," he said. "I was lucky I had no white blood in me, 'cause it was those poor souls, fathered by the master when he'd lay with a slave woman, that were most abused by the

7

mistress. I reckon she could never hate 'em quite enough. Heck, I'd sooner lie down to sleep next to a bunch of mountain lions than risk the wrath of a white she-bear."

As we proceeded to gather the contraband, and load it onto the wagons, I saw one feller that looked too old to be a field hand. He was dressed somewhat different than the other slaves, with feathers hanging from his clothes, bones and beads in his hair. He didn't associate with any of the other negras, and they seemed to avoid him as well--almost as though they was fearful. When I first spotted him, he was stuffing something red in his pocket. I asked Jordan about him.

"That's Obi," he told me. "The colonel won him playing cards just last month, and only kept him 'cause he's so strange he made the colonel's children laugh. The young master told me he's fresh from some island somewheres, where he was a free man until recent. He also told me he's a hoodoo magic man, but I don't always believe what the young master tells me. He likes to play tricks on us darkies. But Obi's a strange one for sure."

"Strange how?"

Jordan shrugged. "I've seen him do some odd things. I saw him make a little doll out of an old piece of shirt that had belonged to the colonel, then poke it with a nail. For days after, the colonel was limping something fierce. Don't know if'n it was magic or just his rheumatism acting up. But I know if'n I had me some magic, I wouldn't have ever let 'em take me as a slave."

∫

When everything and everyone was loaded, Captain Lower ordered Sergeant Foley to pick a squad of men to take the contraband north, back behind Union lines. I was one of those he selected, though I would've rather stayed with the rest of the company, which was on their way to rejoin the regiment.

Even so, I didn't argue, and we set off with the wagons that afternoon. Come dusk, Sergeant Foley had us set up camp with our backs to a cliff face and the wagons forming a half circle out front of us. I was in charge of seeing our contraband negras were fed.

Though I was certain, by now, they all knew they was headed for freedom, their expressions were doubtful, their movements guarded and fearful. I guessed, though we'd freed their bodies, it might take some time for their minds to redefine life as they knew it.

Being among 'em gave me another opportunity to speak with Jordan. He was nothing like Big Jim, who was as quiet as they come. I found Jordan's conversation appealing, though, for the life of me, I couldn't figure out why his words struck me so. They was funny in a roundabout way. His manner, the way he spoke, left no doubt in my mind he'd been called uppity more than once, despite being a slave all his life.

He told me he was born as property of the colonel's father. "They say my mama labored for nine hours the night I was born, and that I just didn't wanna come out. You'd think they'd know why I was in no hurry to be a slave."

He told me he was torn from his family when the "young master," who wasn't a colonel yet, got his own plantation. Jordan had worked that plantation for the last 30 years, eventually becoming a kind of foreman. The way he put it was, "I've been fattening pigs for other people's bellies all my life."

You might think someone who was born a slave would see it as his natural condition, but I didn't get that sense from Jordan. He might not have had any idea what life as a free man would be like, but I'm sure he longed for it.

"A few times, when the master and the overseer didn't think we'd worked hard enough," he told me, "they'd punish us by not giving us any supper. Well, they learned quick that wouldn't work, 'cause the next day we'd be in worse shape, able to do even less work."

We got to talking about music, and 'cause I knew the slaves at home liked to dance, I asked Jordan about it.

"Oh yeah, we gots to dance all the time when the colonel played his fiddle," he said. "We danced right smartly too, or we got fitted for some leg irons we'd have to wear for days--usually 'til the overseer got tired of the noise."

As I listened to Jordan, I spotted Obi crouched over a pile of wood and tinder he'd built. I wasn't sure what he was doing, waving his hands about, but then, suddenly, without any matchsticks or flint, the tinder burst into flames.

I was staring, flabbergasted as you might think, when Obi turned and looked up at me. It was a strange look, and chills ran all through me. Jordan didn't see it. He just kept talking. He'd started in on a story about how one time he was chewing the fat with his fellow slaves, telling 'em how his mammy said his great grandfather had been an African chief.

"Well, the colonel overheard me talking, and something I said must have set him off. He started ranting and raving that no nigger was ever no chief of anything. He got so angry his face turned beet red." Jordan swiveled his head slowly side to side as though remembering the incident. "I guess it just shows the less a man knows, the more noise he has to make. Mostly, I reckon the colonel just liked to hear himself talk."

I smiled and replied, "I know a feller like that." Just as I said it, I heard a gunshot, followed by several more. I fell flat to the ground, as did most everyone. Some of the women started screaming, which set the children to crying. Meanwhile, I crawled to where I'd set my carbine.

Our pickets around the wagons had been fired upon, and were returning fire. I was about to join the rest of the squad at the wagons, when Sergeant Foley yelled at me, "Keep those people down, Deatherage!" So I hurried back to Jordan and his people. Some of 'em looked like they wanted to make a run for it.

"Y'all got to stay down," I said, motioning with my hands. "It's okay," I said to one little girl, "you don't need to cry. Y'all are gonna be okay."

I don't know if'n she believed me--I didn't believe myself--but she went quiet, as did most of the others. It weren't long before the gunshots stopped. Then it was real quiet.

Sergeant Foley came over and asked, "Everyone okay? Anyone wounded?"

"No, I don't think so," I replied. "What happened to the Rebs? Did they leave?"

The sergeant shook his head. "They ain't leaving. They got us pinned down good here, and outnumbered too. They was just testing us. Pretty sure they'll wait 'til daybreak to rush us."

He went back to the wagons and Jordan worked his way over to me.

"I heard what he said. We're in a heap of trouble, ain't we?"

I nodded, still clutching my carbine and staring out into the darkness.

"When they come I'm gonna fight 'em," said Jordan.

"We don't have any extra guns for y'all," I told him.

"I wouldn't know how to use one anyhow," he said. "But I'm gonna fight 'em just the same. I'll use my bare hands if'n I have to. I'm a free man now, and I ain't gonna make it easy for 'em to whup me again. I'm done being whupped."

I could see he meant what he said.

"Will the others fight?"

He looked at the other negras and shook his head skeptically. "I don't know. I got my doubts, but I'll talk to 'em."

I watched as he spoke with his people, and the fear on their faces was as plain as that which was tying knots in my own gut. I didn't reckon many had any fight in 'em. The only one who didn't look afraid was Obi. He listened to what Jordan was saying, but didn't react one way or the other.

/

There was no moon that night, but plenty of stars. Nobody slept much, which made the coming of morning seem to take forever. At the first hint of dawn, I saw Obi pull a Confederate flag out of his pocket. He must have taken it from one of the dead Rebs at the plantation. He began mumbling over it, using words I never heard of. He had some kind of bone in one hand, and a feathered rattle in the other. Sitting on the ground, his eyes closed, with the flag splayed before him, his body swayed to and fro as he spoke.

"What's he doing?" I asked Jordan.

Jordan shook his head. "I don't rightly know. Some kind of hoodoo magic I reckon."

"Why's he doing it?"

Jordan thought a moment. "Probably 'cause he don't wanna die."

The first shot rang out then, followed by several others and a Rebel yell that was a cross between a wolf howl and an Injun war cry. The Rebs were rushing us, just as Sergeant Foley said they would. Bullets began whizzing around our heads like a nest of riled hornets. In that instant, I witnessed men I knew, men I'd laughed and listened to music with, turned into bloody pulp. I saw right off there was too many Rebs for us. We were all gonna die.

I grabbed my carbine to do what I could. As I did, I saw Obi throw the Confederate flag into the fire he'd made. It caught right away, but I had no time to watch it burn.

There were so many Rebs, they'd swarmed past the pickets and were coming in. I aimed my carbine at one, then beheld a right peculiar thing. His eyes went all white and he stumbled before I could fire. At that same moment, all the Confederates began acting strange. Falling down, crying out, staggering into things. Some of 'em were still firing their guns, but the shots were aimed willy-nilly. They weren't hitting any of our boys--those few of us that were still standing. We all kind of stood and stared at the Rebs. Not just 'cause they was shooting strange, but 'cause all their eyes had turned white.

They'd gone blind.

Sergeant Foley began bashing the Rebs with the butt of his carbine, and the rest of us joined in. We didn't want 'em getting lucky and shooting one of us, but there was no right reason to kill 'em dead. Some of 'em weren't shooting at all. Several of 'em just wandered off, moaning and crying out. It was as strange and horrifying a sight as I ever hope to see. I felt the hair on my arms stand right up as a chill ran through me. For a moment, I actually felt sorry for them

Rebs.

Later on that day their sight came back to 'em, but nobody, neither Reb nor Yankee, really talked about what had happened. I guess it was just too strange to explain. In the end, it was like it never did happen.

After we'd secured the prisoners and retrieved the horses that had run off, Jordan came up to me.

"That was some real black magic, it was," he said. "I guess that Obi's got the hoodoo after all."

"I saw what I saw, but I still don't believe it," I told him. "How could he blind all those Johnny Rebs?"

Jordan shrugged. "I don't know how he did it, but it was a sight for these sore old eyes. I guess, in all the ruckus, he got confused and forgot who was the slave and who was the master."

Jordan Anderson, his wife, and children were amongst a group of slaves liberated from a Tennessee plantation by Union troops in 1864. When Colonel Patrick Henry Anderson somehow tracked him down in Ohio after the war, and asked Jordan to return to work on the plantation--which was deep in debt--Jordan responded with a letter that was published in a Cincinnati newspaper. That letter has since been anthologized many times, published all over the world, and praised as a masterpiece of satire. The colonel told Jordan he'd give him his freedom and do right by him. But, in the letter, Jordan informs the colonel he's already free, making a respectable wage in Dayton, and that his children are going to school. He tallies the monetary value of his services, and that of his wife, while on Anderson's plantation ($11,608) and tells the colonel, "We have concluded to test your sincerity by asking you to send us our wages for the time we served you."

As for Obi, many slaves from the West Indies practiced a religion of mysticism and folk magic that originated in West Africa, and was known by various names, including Santería, Voodoo, and Obeah.

Sixteen-year-old Martin Luther Deatherage lied about his age to enlist in the Union Army on New Year's Day in 1864, much to the displeasure of his slave-owning family. He served in Company C of the 2nd Kentucky Calvary, survived the war to father 18 children, and is my great, great grandfather.

Salem's Fall

'Twas a portentously gray day in April when disturbing rumors of pious, God-fearing folk being accused of witchcraft first assailed my ears. I was, at once, both astonished and skeptical of what I heard. News that traveled some 20 miles to reach me in Groton was often tainted along the coarse road with gossip and hyperbole. These recent reports, in particular, were beyond belief.

Tidings of young girls afflicted by all sorts of strange maladies, their bodies contorting, convulsing, their throats producing strange utterances. If true they were horrific events, but they had the gossamer fabric of puerile folk tales. There was nothing about what I'd heard that matched reality as I knew it.

Of course I knew Satan and his demons existed to tempt and torment mankind. That he was the source of all sin was a precept good men of faith accepted. To doubt demons existed was to doubt the existence of angels . . . of God Himself. But to believe, as many did, that all of a town's misfortunes were the work of the Devil--that every infant death, crop failure, and social conflict was caused by Satan . . . that belief I did not share. That his power had coalesced in Salem Village to such an extent to create a maelstrom of evil defied credulity.

I knew some men, some ministers of the gospel in particular, believed the Devil was everywhere. In the soil, in the water, in the air . . . . Even Indian attacks were blamed on the Prince of Darkness, though I doubted the savages had the slightest idea who Satan was. 'Twas more likely they thought of us as devils.

There were those of faith who touted the idea that men were either all good, perfectly devout in the eyes of the Lord, or they were dangerously evil. I was not trained in religious matters as was my brother, but I did not accept that postulation as truth. I'd always believed a good man could, given a set of circumstances, do a bad thing. Contrarily, a bad man, a truly evil person, might, at some moment in time, be capable of goodness. But I was merely a carpenter, a housewright. I knew nothing of holy doctrine and divine theorem.

When I heard the initial stories of the afflicted girls, I thought nothing of them. But now, it seemed, the accusations had spread like wildfire. The number of accused witches grew every week. Even John Proctor, whom I'd done some

13

work for, had been accused of witchcraft along with his wife. I knew them as good, church-going folk, and found it impossible to believe they'd succumbed to the Devil.

"What worries thee, Husband? I can see the furrow in thy brow from across the room."

Though my Sarah was a few years older and much wiser than I, I was loathe to trouble her with the hearsay from Salem.

"Nothing worries me when thee are about, Wife. Sunshine follows thee everywhere, even in the dark of night."

"I accept thy praise, even though I know thou jests," said Sarah with a little curtsey. "But watch thy words. Any hint of magic and I could be a witch accused."

"Do not say such a thing!" I knew she jested, but the thought alarmed me.

"Calm thyself, Husband." She came and put her hand on my shoulder. "Is it the news from Salem that weighs upon thee?"

"Then thou hast heard." I turned and took her hands in mine. "Yes, I'm troubled by the reports, though I believe less than half of what I hear."

"'Tis passing strange indeed. How could so many in one small town be witches? How could so many be afflicted?"

"If true, 'tis indeed worrisome. Yet if falsehoods are at the root of it all, the darkness of it is even more distressing."

"Why not seek out thy brother Samuel's counsel. He's a man of God--a man of rationality and logic. Mayhap he can soothe thy unease."

'Twas a sound idea. But then my Sarah was a sound thinker.

I'd visit Samuel and see what he knew of Salem's plight. From his Boston ministry he'd surely been consulted on the matter. He'd have insight I lacked.

/

My brother Samuel had been pastor of the Old South Church of Boston since I was but a lad. His mother had died when he was a toddler, and our father remarried. Though we were both raised by my birth mother, along with 14 other siblings, Samuel was a grown man before I was ever born. He had sons almost my age. And though he traveled in much higher circles than did a carpenter from Groton, we kept in touch and met for family gatherings. I'd even done work on his house. However, he was surprised when I appeared on his doorstep without invitation.

"Benjamin? What brings thee to Boston?"

"Come in, Benjamin, come in," said Samuel's wife Eunice from behind her husband. "Do not make thy brother stand out there like some beggar."

"Yes, please, come in, come in."

"Can I get thee some tea, or maybe some brandy?" she asked. "Hast thou eaten?"

'Twas a long, dusty ride to Boston, so I replied, "Just some water now, thank thee, Eunice."

A Boston minister lived well, and Samuel's house was a large one, richly furnished and comfortable. He led me to his study, bade me sit, then asked with concern, "Is Sarah well? What about little Sarah?"

"My wife and daughter are well, thank thee, Brother."

"Well something troubles thee," he said with the same stern face he used when preaching. "I can see it in thine eyes."

Eunice returned with my water and I held my tongue. She took meaning from the silence and said, "I will let thee talk, but later I will make thee something to eat while thou tellest me all about little Sarah."

She'd barely quit the room when Samuel prodded me.

"So, what is it?"

"I trust thou hast heard about the happenings in Salem Village?"

A frown creased his visage as though I'd cast aspersions on his honor. He chose a chair across from me and fell into it more than sat. A vibrant man, he suddenly looked all of his five decades.

"'Tis a sad condition indeed, this matter of witchcraft."

"But how can it be true? How can one small town be so afflicted?"

"I cannot say whether the Devil has been at work in Salem, but I have begun to have doubts about the extent of the accusations. They are not confined to that hamlet. The serpent's tongue has spread to other towns, and even reached Boston. A member of my own congregation, Captain John Alden, has been accused."

"Captain Alden?" I was dumbfounded. "He's one of most respected men in Boston--from one of the most important families. If he can be accused of witchcraft, then anyone can."

"I fear 'tis true. Amongst my theological brethren I have spoken out against these trials, but the prevailing opinion is they should be allowed to run their course. I think many such opinions rise from timidity. They fear if they speak out, they will be damned themselves. 'Tis true. A rational man would hold his tongue. A brave one might let it loose, only to lose it . . . and more."

"How did it happen? How began such incriminations?"

15

Bruce Edward Golden

"It began in the home of Salem's own minister, Samuel Parris." I knew by the intonation of my brother's voice that he cared little for Reverend Parris. An intuition he then confirmed. "The man is constantly preaching about sin and sinners and their punishments. To him there is only absolute good and absolute evil. No areas of gray--only black and white. He seems obsessed with Satan and the darkness within mankind. So 'twas no great surprise when I learned 'twas his own household that gave birth to these accusations.

"'Twas his 9-year-old daughter and 11-year-old niece who first began having fits described by a visiting minister as 'beyond the power of natural disease.' Soon after, the accusations began. First, against a family servant, then others who were of questionable character and thus easy targets. Before long, the number of afflicted girls grew like mold in a dank bin. So did the number and status of those accused."

"I'm glad to hear thou hast doubts concerning these accusations, Brother."

"At first," said Samuel, "when Reverend Lawson told me he'd seen, with his own eyes, girls screaming and throwing things about the room, uttering strange sounds, crawling under furniture, and contorting themselves into peculiar positions, I was sure they must be possessed. But now . . . ."

"If these girls are not afflicted, then surely they are lying," I said. "Why would they do such a thing?"

"I think, mayhap, they heard Reverend Parris speak of Elizabeth Knapp. 'Tis possible that tale planted the seed in their minds."

"Who is Elizabeth Knapp?"

Samuel rose from his seat and went to the table where his kept his brandy. He held up a glass and asked me, "Would thee care for some?"

I nodded.

He handed me a glass and resumed his seat. As if hesitant to begin his story, he took a long drink first.

"Elizabeth Knapp was a servant in my household long ago, when thee were still a lad. I was a minister in Groton at the time, and she'd only recently come to work for us. She was young, like the afflicted girls of Salem.

"One day she began having violent fits. She barked like a dog, wept, spoke in a sinister voice insulting myself and others, and even once attempted to throw herself in the fire.

"Of course I summoned the local doctor, who diagnosed her malady as 'diabolical distemper.' Though these fits continued for some time, I was skeptical. I became even more so when she began naming people who were

16

afflicting her--people I knew to be God-fearing church members. The outlandish nature and contradictions of her accusations fed my disbelief, and after five months her fits ended and she recanted, admitting 'twas all a fabrication."

"I can understand then," I said, "why thee would have doubts about the accusations of witchcraft in Salem."

"I do. Even if what these girls say is true," said Samuel, "that they are being tormented, 'tis not substantial proof to accuse people they see in visions. 'Tis wrong of the magistrates to accept it as so, for Satan can impersonate even an innocent person. This spectral evidence does not prove someone is in league with the Devil. At best the afflicted have been deceived by the Devil."

Samuel's words rang true to me, and I was struck by the grave injustice of what was occurring.

"What can be done about this? What can *we* do?"

Samuel shrugged. "I fear nothing. The tide has risen too far. The clamor is too great. No one voice could be heard above the din. It would drown in a sea of suspicion and madness."

That gave me pause. If a respected minister of Boston could do nothing, if important, wealthy personages were being accused, then what could I do?

"We must have faith," said Samuel, "that God, in His divine wisdom, will resolve this grievous state of affairs."

∫

Weeks passed as I busied myself with work and shunned rumors of witchcraft trials. Gossip was hard to avoid, yet I'd all but exorcised such scandalous tidings when Cousin John appeared at my back door.

He was anxious, bedraggled, tense to the point of near panic. When I ushered him in he looked round to see if anyone was witness. His wariness induced me to look for myself. I saw no one--nothing but a ragged old crow sitting on the fence, its head turned as if watching us.

Once inside he told me an improbable tale of vitriol and persecution. Or it would have been improbable had I not already heard worse coming from Salem.

He was a simple farmer, a landowner whom the chief constable of Salem Village had recruited as a deputy constable to aid in the arrest of those accused of witchcraft. At first he complied. Then he began to doubt the accusations of the afflicted children, as well as the validity of the trials. Before long his conscience intervened, and he refused to make any more arrests. He told me he spoke out at the proceedings, denouncing the so-called afflicted girls, saying "Hang *them*. They are all witches." Shortly after his public comments he found himself accused of witchcraft. Not only did the afflicted girls accuse him, but so did his wife's own relatives. He was accused of tormenting the girls as well as his wife's grandfather, and of having a hand in the deaths of 13 people, including a baby girl.

John told me his in-laws had disliked him since his marriage--which they disapproved of--because he was an outsider whose profits in land dealings they begrudged.

"On the basis of these pernicious lies I'm accused of sundry acts of witchcraft," said John, summing up his tale. "A warrant was sworn for my arrest. My properties to be seized to pay for my prosecution and incarceration. I tell thee 'tis a black nightmare from which I cannot wake." I thought he might break out in tears or collapse under the strain, but he took a deep breath instead. "What choice did I have? None but to flee Salem, leaving my wife and children behind."

I believed him, and his predicament touched me, but I'd no idea what he expected of me.

"By fleeing thou has marked thyself a guilty man," I told him.

"My guilt was already assumed," he replied. "Thou hast not been there. Thou hast not seen the court's gullibility, its complicity. Already nearly two score rot in prison, accused of witchcraft. I tell thee there will be more--many more."

"We must secure legal representation for thee. Thou must fight these charges."

"Thou dost not understand, Benjamin. There is no fighting. There is no denying. If thee are accused and thee dost not confess, thee are guilty and sentenced to death."

"What would thee have me do?" I asked him.

"Go see thy brother Samuel. He hath influence."

"He may have less than thee thinks in these matters, but I will tell him of thy plight. What will thee do?"

"I own a parcel of land outside Lancaster. I will go there and contact thee later. To return home is a death sentence."

/

'Twas three days later when I heard cousin John had been captured and returned to Salem. I'd been unable to travel to Boston in the interim, and felt no small blame for my neglect. So, immediately upon hearing the news, I saddled my horse and made all possible speed to my brother's house. I prayed Samuel might be able to intervene on behalf of Cousin John. Even so, I had grave doubts my prayers would be answered.

When I arrived I was greeted on the front porch by a crow sitting on the railing. It cackled and screeched at me in such a threatening manner as I approached that I stopped in my tracks. Samuel must have heard the noise. He opened his front door and the crow flew off, still squawking.

Samuel didn't look happy to see me, but invited me in. Apparently the topic of Salem had fostered heated conflict even in Boston, and he rightly guessed 'twas why I'd returned. However, when I told him of Cousin John's arrest, he agreed to do what he could to help. He suggested we go see Reverend Cotton Mather, the most influential minister in New England.

I'd never met Mather, and was surprised to learn he was not much older than I, despite his renown. Like most of Boston's prominent citizens, he wore a peruke. But his was more full of flowing white curls than I'd ever seen. Its prominence cascaded down either side of his head like tufts of his namesake.

I'd heard Mather had graduated from Harvard at the age of 15, so I expected he'd be a man of logic and intelligence. I was to be disappointed.

Samuel had warned me Reverend Mather suffered the self-delusion that he was always right, no matter the truth, and that he was obsessed with the topic of eternal damnation. More so, he told me Mather supported the witch trials. That did not bode well for Cousin John.

"'Tis an honor to meet thee, Captain Willard," said Mather in a tone of formality. Samuel had introduced me with my militia rank, which I hadn't used since the last skirmish with the Indians. "Thy father, may God rest his soul, and mine planted the seeds of this great city. Together they helped carve civilization out of a savage wilderness."

"The honor is mine, Reverend."

"To what do I owe the pleasure of thy visit?" he asked, looking at Samuel.

"I fear 'tis not pleasure but distress which brings us to thy door, Cotton. It concerns Salem Village and the trials being conducted there. These accusations of witchcraft have spread like a disease. Something must be done to quell the insanity."

"Yes, New England has become the front line in the battle against Satan," responded Mather, either ignoring or purposely misinterpreting Samuel's meaning. "I fear evil spirits summoned forth by the Prince of Darkness are all around us. For I have seen the afflicted children myself. 'Tis a sad thing to witness them suffer."

"What about the suffering of the accused?" asked Samuel. "Are they not due justice? Should they not receive legal representation?"

Reverend Mather turned, walked to his desk, and casually looked at some papers there. "Such representation in these cases is unnecessary. If a person is innocent, God will reveal it."

I was struck as if by a slap across the face with the flawed rationale of his statement, and the cavalier way in which he dispensed it.

"'Tis not better that **ten suspected witches should escape, than one innocent person should be condemned?**" asked Samuel.

Mather looked thoughtful, then replied with a certain hardness to his glare, "The flock must be cleansed, no matter the price." His voice took on a more genial tone as he added, "I'm confident justice will prevail, my friend. Governor Phips has ordered the establishment of a special Court of Oyer and Terminer for the three score now awaiting trial."

"What about those who have already died in prison?" I asked.

"May God have mercy on their souls."

"Is it true," I pressed, "that only those who refuse to confess sins of witchcraft are to be executed?"

"I'm not aware of such a decision. But they which lie must go to their father, the Devil, into everlasting burning. God will not forgive them."

The muddled logic of executing those who profess innocence and doling out lesser punishment to those who admit their crimes left my mind reeling. I intended to make just such a point when Samuel noticed my ire and placed his hand on my arm to silence me.

"My brother and I came here today, concerned that our cousin, John Willard, has been accused and arrested in Salem on charges of witchcraft," said Samuel. "We hoped thee might use thy influence to see through to the truth of the matter."

"I cannot, in good conscience, interfere with the court," said Mather. "But I will look into the charges against him, and see justice is carried out."

It sounded to me as if the Reverend Mather would do nothing of substance, and that cousin John's fate was already determined. But Samuel replied, "That is all we can ask."

*

As spring plodded towards summer, news from Salem continued to fall on my doorstep like ash from a distant blaze. Each day the reports were bleaker and more perversely capricious. The first hanging of an accused witch had taken place. The injustice was no longer simply a matter of theoretical concern. A poor woman's life had been taken, and I feared it wouldn't be the last.

Along with that news came a glimmer of rationality. Two days before the hanging, one of the seven trial judges, a Major Nathaniel Saltonstall, had publicly condemned the proceedings and resigned. I prayed his resignation would make a difference--that it would shine a light of reason on the arcane tribunal. But my faith in my fellow man would continue to be tested. I learned, not long after Saltonstall's resignation, the afflicted had begun to see his specter among the Devil's cohorts.

To any man of logic, the accusation was clearly retaliatory. Yet logic seemed in short supply. There were times when 'twas all too much to comprehend. I tried not to dwell on it, to keep busy with work, but Salem was seemingly on the lips of everyone in Groton.

It had been an especially long and trying day, and all I wanted to do was sleep. I was headed off to bed when I noticed a strange smell. 'Twas vaguely sulphurous. I doubted it could be rotten food. My Sarah was too fastidious for that. I worried a skunk might have gotten in, so I followed the odor to my workshop in the rear of the house.

I'd have lit a lantern, but moonlight poured through the open window. 'Twas bright enough to see 'twas no skunk but a crow, walking about my work bench as if inspecting it. I surmised it must have flown in and dropped a piece of carrion, causing the stink.

I ran at the bird waving my arms, hoping to send it back through the open window. It flapped its wings and shrieked at me as it took flight. But in the darkness I tripped and fell. When I got back to my feet the bird was gone. I hurried to the window and closed it.

When I turned I saw him, standing in a murky corner of the room. At first I thought 'twas only a trick of the shadows, for the figure was ill-defined, unsubstantial as a billow of smoke. But he was there. An apparition who'd appeared seemingly out of nowhere.

"Who are thee? How did thee get in here? Through the window?"

As my vision adjusted to the gloom I furtively searched for something I could use as a weapon. I spotted my hammer only a step away.

"That won't be necessary," he said, his voice resounding as if he were in a much larger room. "I'm not here to harm thee."

"Who are thee?"

21

"*Amicus curiae*--a friend of the court thou might say."

"The court?" I'd no clue to his meaning, but I could see him more clearly now. He wore a dark hat that nearly covered his face, and a billowing ebony cloak which enveloped his form. I made out a bit of a beard on his chin, but he wore no wig, nor did any hair show beneath the hat. "Dost thou mean the court in Salem?"

"Is there another exhibition as fascinating?"

"If that is thy idea of fascination, 'tis a morbid one."

The fellow laughed.

"I have always found the incongruous delusions and phobic fanaticism of mankind to be enticing theater. 'Tis such that it lies smoldering like insipient coals beneath the soles of humanity, concealed by the briars of theology. When their fleecy backs and jaundiced eyes are aflame with righteous obsession, I cannot resist."

"I ask again--who are thee?"

"I'm known by many names. *Cogito ergo sum.*"

I could not, at that moment, say this with any validation, but I began to suspect the intruder was no mortal man. His voice, his carriage, his words . . . .

"Are thou a demon, sent by the Devil to harangue me? Or are thou an angel of God, come to me with a message?"

He laughed again.

"Is there a difference?" he asked.

I thought his question absurd.

"Is there a difference if God's followers do such things in His name? 'Tis of no coincidence that Salem's hysteria began in a house of God--the residence of its own minister. 'Twas the man of God's infatuation with sin, his preoccupation with looking for evil in every corner, that infected the children of his household."

"Thou *art* a demon!" I shouted. "Or thou art Satan himself."

He did not answer right away, nor did he laugh again as I suspected he would. Instead, when he replied, I discerned a hint of anger in his voice.

"I'm whom everyone is looking for--looking at. I'm the one to be blamed . . . for everything. Am I not?"

"If thou art indeed him, then thou art the root of all evil," I said with conviction. "Thou hast fostered witchcraft in Salem."

He pointed a gnarly finger at me and replied indignantly, "*A contrario.* Thy rush to judgment mirrors the accusations thee claims to deplore. I'm not the cause here, but the effect. I'd never heard of Salem before these trials. I was drawn here by the frenzied contentiousness, the dread and anxiety, the intolerance, the wretched discontent, the euphoric retribution. I did not precipitate the darkness in this hamlet. I do not engender man's inhumanity . . . I feed off it.

"There is no witchcraft. 'Tis a myth of man. There is only ignorance and penury."

"If there is no witchcraft, then what of the afflicted girls?"

"'Tis not an affliction, but an affectation. Stagecraft not witchcraft. A portrayal so overwrought it becomes self-delusion. Mischief swollen to malice."

At that moment Sarah entered my workshop. I immediately feared for her safety and retrieved my hammer, knowing, as I did, it would prove no defense against the Prince of Darkness. Yet the part of me which grasped the hammer still refused to believe he was other than a man.

"Benjamin? Benjamin, what are thee doing out here? Who are thee talking to?"

"No one. Go to bed. I will join thee soon."

"What is that smell?"

"I think there's a dead animal outside," I lied. "I will dispose of it in the morning."

"Alright. Be not long."

Somehow she departed without seeing the intruder, though he was in her line of sight as she turned to leave.

"How is it she did not see thee?"

"People see what they want to see."

His platitude was no explanation at all. Neither was his presence.

"Why do I see thee? I have no part in this."

"But thou dost. Thou hast made thyself a part of it. Thou hast asked thy brother to intercede. Thy brother is a man of some influence. Thee are both men of reason. Reason does not feed me. Besides, carpenters can be troublesome. I know. I was thwarted by one once before." He aimed his bony finger at me again. "I'm here to warn thee, Benjamin Willard. Stop interfering. 'Tis useless. Let the nature of man run its course."

"I need not act," I said bravely. "God will intervene."

He laughed again, but there was no humor in his cackle.

"Thou believes so? Thou hast faith in the creator of all things? Did He not create man? Did He not mold the people of Salem to His liking? Is a blow struck or a single teardrop shed that is not of His making? Is a word spoken and heard that He did not sire? *A caelo usque ad centrum.* Is He not master of all from the heavens to the center of the Earth?"

"Thou dares blame God?"

"I do not blame." He held both hands up as if to reveal they were empty. "I did not plant the apple of discord. I simply take nourishment where 'tis cultivated."

I closed my eyes and balled my hands into fists. I wanted to pray but I was taken aback by his audacity, confused by his words. Confusion and deception--those were, indeed, the tools of the Devil.

When I opened my eyes with every intent to rebut his claims, he was gone.

His departure left my conscience troubled, for I could not shake the belief that many of his remarks rang true.

/

The excitement in Salem Village was palpable when I arrived on August 5th--the trial date for Cousin John and others among the accused. Sarah had wanted to come with me, but I forbade it. This was not something I wanted her to witness, especially not since she was with child again. I'd only come myself because of Cousin John.

Sarah implored me not to do anything foolish, but her concern was unnecessary. I knew there was nothing I could do, nothing I could say that would change the outcome of the day's events. I'd hold my tongue, for her sake and for the sake of my children, if for no other reason.

In the local meeting house, where the trials were conducted, people were squeezed into tall-sided pews, onto gallery benches, or pressed shoulder-to-shoulder along the aisles and in the back where I barely managed to find a place to stand. Apparently the Devil wasn't the only one who enjoyed such theater.

Most wore their Sunday-best, though 'twas only Tuesday. The men attired in their high-crowned black hats, cloaks, and fine breeches, the women with their layers of shifts, skirts, and bodices, their hooded cloaks and muffs to keep warm. Though with so many bodies packed together, warmth was not an issue. Sweat dampened my brow, though I cannot say whether from heat or apprehension.

I removed my hat to wipe the perspiration from my forehead, glancing up as I did. There, on one of the rafters, sat a crow. I should have known he'd be there somewhere.

24

I'd arrived late, but in time to witness the end of the morning's first trial. The accused, an ancient-looking fellow of some 80 years, stood defiant in front of the court and declared, "Well, burn me or hang me, I will stand in the truth of Christ." Despite his defiance, he was found guilty of witchcraft as charged, and marched out of the hall.

When Cousin John was led inside, bound by manacles, an entire group of girls fell into miserable fits and spasms the likes of which I'd never seen. The afflicted, as they were called, the alleged victims, were seated up front to the side of the magistrates' table. Not all of them were young girls. There were a few older women among them.

As the court officer read the warrant of charges against John, the afflicted, as if on cue, convulsed and made their awful sounds once more. Some within the audience reacted with terror, others smiled and shook their heads knowingly. They'd seen the same spectacle many times already. A few looked unsure, but most were smug with faith, certain they had a covenant with God. I believed their pact, unknowingly, was with someone else.

After the charges had been read, and they were lengthy, one of the magistrates, whom I recognized as Colonel John Hathorne, said, "Here is the warrant that thee fled from authority. That is an acknowledgement of guilt. But yet, notwithstanding this, we require thee to confess the truth in this matter."

John stood boldly in front of the court, without quaking or displaying any other signs of nervousness. I admired him for it, but pitied him all the same.

"I shall," responded John to the magistrate, "as I hope I shall be assisted by the Lord of Heaven.

"For my going away, I was afrighted. I thought by my withdrawing it might be better. Now I fear not, for the Lord, in His due time, will make me white as snow.

"I deny doing harm to any of the afflicted, either in person or by apparition. They are
mistaken . . . or they contrive falsehoods."

At this the afflicted began to contort and scream as if in pain once more.

"It has been found true that others they have accused were guilty persons," said magistrate Hathorne. "Why should it be false in thee? Why should the court believe him who fled from the law, and whose specter rages among the afflicted?

"If thou can find it in thy heart to repent, John Willard, 'tis possible thee may obtain mercy. Therefore bethink thyself."

25

Cousin John was steadfast.

"Sir, I cannot confess that I do not know."

At that moment I wanted to speak up--shout at the top of my lungs to impugn the accusations, to mock the magistrates and their cruel, spurious logic. As the urge struck me, a seductive whisper sounded in my ear. *"Qui tacet consentire videtur."* I turned to look, but no one was there.

I knew enough Latin to know it meant that by my silence I consented to the proceedings. Satan was goading me. He wanted me to speak out, to mark myself as a dissenter, to become one of the accused.

I looked to the rafters. The crow was gone. I looked round, knowing one of the gathered throng was likely him. But I'd not be incited. I'd not succumb to the prick of his pitchfork. I remained silent, wondering, as I did, if I'd damned myself.

"Thou art charged not only with this," said Hathorne, when the afflicted girls grew quiet, "but with dreadful murders. The evidence of the afflicted is overwhelming. If thee wants God's mercy, thou must confess."

"Sir," said John, "as for the sins I'm guilty of, if the minister should ask me, I'm ready to confess."

Another magistrate at the table spoke up. "If thou hast thus revolted from God, thee are a dreadful sinner, whose confession would fill with lies."

Showing his first sign of strain, John gnawed at his lip. Instantly two of the afflicted girls shouted, "Oh, he bites me! He bites me!"

"Open thy mouth!" ordered Hathorne. "Do not bite thy lips!"

"I will stand with my mouth open, or I will keep it shut," replied John. "I will stand any how, if thee tell me how."

Magistrate Hathorne began reading the depositions of John's in-laws, and all the crimes they accused him of. They were extensive, and when he finished, John said, "Only someone pledged to Hell from the cradle could be guilty of such things. If God were to--"

Hathorne cut him short.

"We do not send for thee to preach."

One of the afflicted girls tried to approach John, but collapsed into another fit, shouting, "Oh, John Willard, John Willard!"

"What was the reason thee could not come near him?" asked Hathorne when she became composed.

"A black man stood between us," she responded.

Had Satan blocked her, or was he, as he insisted, only a witness? It didn't

26

matter. At that moment, there was no doubt in my mind of the trial's outcome--had there ever been any. There was a reason not one of the accused had been found innocent, and that, from what I witnessed, was the *lack* of reason.

For one final test, magistrate Hathorne told John to recite the Lord's Prayer. I knew from religious lore that a person in league with the Devil should be unable to speak it.

John began, "Our Father, which art in Heaven, hallowed be Thy name. Thy kingdom come, maker of Heaven and Earth--"

"That is incorrect," interrupted Hathorne.

John quickly continued, but misspoke another phrase. I knew he'd sealed his fate then. He tried again, but again his tongue slipped.

"'Tis a strange thing," said John. "I can say it at another time. I think I'm bewitched as well as they." He laughed loudly, but no one else did.

Hathorne asked him one more time to confess.

Cousin John refused, saying, "If 'tis the last time I'm to speak, I say I'm as innocent as the child unborn."

He was found guilty as charged.

The next day I went to see Samuel. He was not at home, but his sons Simon and John were there, along with Captain Nathaniel Cary, his wife Elizabeth, and Philip and Mary English. I was introduced, then Simon escorted the two couples into another room.

"My father tells me thee are greatly concerned with the occurrences in Salem," said John.

"'Tis true," I said. "Only yesterday I witnessed the conviction of our cousin John. The trials are a travesty, an abomination of justice."

"Then I tell thee plainly," said John, his look of determination belying the fact he was two years my junior, "Simon and I intend to spirit our guests away, for they have been accused of witchcraft. One couple to Rhode Island, the other to New York, where they have family waiting and will be safe, God willing."

"'Tis a dangerous game thou plays, Nephew."

"Thy warning comes too late. I have already helped Mistress Cary escape from the prison in Middlesex. Before that, Simon aided in John Alden's flight to New York."

"I admire thy bravery. What does thy Father think of thine exploits?"

"He approves, yet, because of his position, he can take no active part. Did thou knowest one of the afflicted girls even accused our father of witchcraft?

Likely realizing the consequences of such an accusation, Magistrate Hathorne told those in attendance 'twas a case of mistaken identity. It seems those holding court understand the limits of their power.

"Even so, Father preached caution to us. But we could no longer stand by while such injustice was carried out."

That Salem's accusers had extended their talons to vilify my brother, one of Boston's most respected ministers, illustrated their hubris, but no longer surprised me. I'd seen conjecture conquer validation, distraught rumor surpass reason. Truth had given way to umbrage and angst. Surely Satan was enjoying his repast.

*

I returned to Salem on August 19th, the day of cousin John's scheduled execution. I do not know what drew me there, other than the idea that I *should* be there, that I *should* suffer in some way for my silence.

There was an enormous congregation of people gathered at the execution site. Several notable ministers from Boston had arrived for the occasion. My brother Samuel was not among them, but Cotton Mather was. He rode a pale horse onto the grounds and never dismounted. I assumed he wanted to be assured of witnessing all from a proper vantage point.

I looked but saw no crows, yet I knew he was there somewhere.

To my senses, those assembled bore the stench of collusion and anticipation. I felt the fascination, the allure of death all round me. Little did I suspect that would soon change.

The buzz of the gathering grew dim as the slow cart carrying the condemned rolled up the hill. I saw Cousin John, his face as stoic as a statue, along with John Proctor, George Jacobs, Martha Carrier, and old Reverend George Burroughs, the former minister of Salem Village. Their hands were bound, their visages solemn. When they were led from the cart, Mistress Carrier begged Reverend Mather to pray with them. He agreed, but looked unhappy when Burroughs asked that their sins and their accusers' sins all be forgiven, and wanted to pray that theirs would be the last innocent blood shed.

That was when I spotted him, standing far away, half hidden by the throng. But by his hat, his cloak, his posture, and the tuft of hair on his chin, I was certain 'twas him. His smirk alone would have marked him, except that it wasn't the only such expression in the crowd.

When their prayer ended, each of the condemned declared their innocence once more, and I sensed the multitude was affected by their words--especially by the sincerity of Burroughs and Cousin John.

As the former Reverend Burroughs was led up the ladder to his noose he spoke with such solemn eloquence of his innocence, prayed so movingly, it drew tears from many of the spectators. Then he began to recite the Lord's Prayer. He did so flawlessly. It seemed, for a moment, his audience might interfere with the executions, so moved were they. Some shouted, "No more hangings!"

I looked to the Prince of Darkness and recognized a hint of concern on his face. Then some of the afflicted girls began to shout and the Devil's stony apprehension thawed to a grin.

"The black man stands next to him!" they shouted to explain his ability to say the prayer. "The black man whispers the words in his ear!"

Someone, I know not who, gave the signal. The ladder was removed from beneath Reverend Burroughs, and he dangled 'til he was dead.

As soon as he fell limp, the crowd grew restive. Some amongst them even sounded angry. Shame and remorse colored many faces. 'Twas akin to the dishonor I felt in my own heart.

Reverend Mather, looking worried, spurred his horse into the mob and told them Burroughs had not been a properly ordained minister. He insisted they not be fooled. "The Devil has often been transformed into an angel of light," he said.

His words held sway enough that the executions continued, under the sometimes tearful gaze of an ambivalent crowd. John Willard and the others were hanged until dead.

The accusations, the trials, the executions would continue in the weeks that followed. The penurious zeal of the rampaging herd never slowed to examine who suffered under its stampede. The fevered quest to shine a light on the dark arts of witchcraft had, itself, become a righteously grim entity. Yet I refused to pay heed. My conscience was already burdened with the death of Cousin John. I decided if man was so determined to damn himself, I'd do nothing to impede him. Let the Devil feast.

More than 180 people were accused of witchcraft by the "afflicted" during the time of the Salem witch trials. Twenty were executed, including John Willard, who's remembered in most historical accounts as one of the few brave souls who spoke out against the trials, even though it cost him his life. Five more of the accused died while incarcerated, and more than 100 men, women, and even children languished in prisons for months, tortured, chained to walls without enough food or water, while losing their homes and all their worldly possessions.

The trials finally ended in 1693, more than a year after the first accusations, thanks in part to a handful of influential men like Reverend Samuel Willard, who would become the president of Harvard in 1701.

Reverend Willard's son, John, was ultimately prosecuted for helping accused witches escape custody, but was cleared of all charges. Willard's other son, Simon, would go on to marry Elizabeth Alden, whose father, John, was convicted of witchcraft, escaped to New York, and was later exonerated. Elizabeth Alden was the granddaughter of John and Priscilla Alden of Mayflower/Plymouth Rock *fame.*

Too late for the victims of the trials, Reverend Cotton Mather eventually retracted most of his statements concerning witchcraft and admitted errors were made. Magistrate John Hathorne is remembered as the only magistrate to never recant his actions. He's the great, great grandfather of Nathaniel Hawthorne, who wrote The Scarlet Letter.

The activities of Captain Benjamin Willard during the Salem witch trials were never documented. However, he was, indeed, the brother of Reverend Samuel Willard and cousin of John Willard, as well as my great (x7) grandfather.

The character of Satan is, of course, speculative, though there are those, even today, who persist in believing otherwise.

The Duke's Mistress

She felt as unwieldy as a pregnant sow whenever she tried to move about. That's because she *was* pregnant, and had been for many months now, much to her discomfort.

Herleva didn't know if it had been an easy pregnancy or not, because she had nothing to compare it to--being her first. All she knew was she didn't like the way it made her feel--the sickness, the mood swings, the constant peeing.

When she first began to feel ill, she called for Chamane to attend her. It was only right, she thought. For it was Chamane's potion that had led to her condition . . . or at least led to the thing that led to her condition.

Remembering what had precipitated her current state, Herleva couldn't deny she bore some responsibility herself. That day had begun like any other, working for her father, the tanner, trampling his leather in preparation for dyeing.

The dye pits were close to the river that ran through Falaise, just under the castle parapet. She knew Duke Robert liked to come to the parapet to watch the women, whether they were washing clothes in the river, bathing, or kneading leather. On that day, woe to her, she was feeling feisty--looking for a way to liven up her tedious morning of stomping leather into dung water to make it more supple.

When she looked up and saw the young duke above her, she decided to have a little fun and tease him a bit. As she stomped about, Herleva lifted her skirts a little higher than was necessary to keep them out of the putrid water. That was the start of it all. That was where providence decided to have a little fun of its own. For her actions had the desired effect . . . and much more.

She indeed caught Duke Robert's eye that day, but had no idea how smitten he'd become until later, after she'd cleaned herself in the river and was approached by two of the castle's men at arms. They told her the young duke, son of Duke Richard, had ordered her to be brought to him, and that they would escort her through the castle's rear entrance.

Herleva remembered how flustered she'd been at the time, not knowing what to do. So unsettled and confused was she, she took off running, ignoring the shouts of the men. She didn't even know where she was running to, but eventually decided to seek out the town's *chamane* . . . who also went by the

31

name "Chamane"--her calling morphing into her moniker at some point. She was a healer woman, known to possess mystic secrets--both dark and light. Some called her a witch--though even those who did used her services when needed.

Herleva was not a big believer in magic, but the old woman had once healed her sick mother, and often gave her advice about herbs. And that's what she needed--advice.

When she explained her predicament to Chamane, the old crone cackled until she was out of breath.

"You got yourself in fine fix now, don't you?" she said, pointing a gnarled finger at Herleva.

"What can I do?" asked Herleva, desperation coloring her face. "I can't refuse the duke."

"No, you can't do that," said Chamane, "but you don't have to make it easy for him either." She curled that gnarled finger under her chin as if thinking, then continued to wave it about as she spoke. "Both the young duke and his father are always sidling their amusements through the castle's back door. Tell him you'll see him, but only if you can come through the front. Then make a spectacle of it . . . that is, if you want to be more than just another amusement." Chamane stared at her with ancient green eyes. "Well, do you want the duke to take you through the back door, or do you want to be more?"

"I . . . uh . . . I guess so . . . I mean, I want to be more. It would be good to be the duke's wife."

Chamane snorted with derision. "A commoner the duke's wife? That's a day I'd like to live to see."

Herleva remembered feeling overcome with chagrin for thinking she could possibly be married to the next Duke of Normandy. She'd been a naive young girl back then to think such a thing. Even though she wasn't much older now, she was certainly wiser about the ways of the world.

"You may never be the duke's wife," said Chamane, "but if you want to capture his heart, to be more than just another *chatte* to him, you need a potion."

"A potion?"

"A love potion."

Herleva didn't know such a thing even existed.

"Let me see," said Chamane, beginning to rummage through all the pots and urns on her table, "I know I've got the ingredients here somewhere."

When she left the *chamane* that day, she hurried to her father and mother to explain her situation--not mentioning the potion of course. They agreed she had no choice but to answer the young duke's summons.

So Herleva sent word to the castle that she would see the duke, but only if she could do so not as a commoner, but through the front gates of the castle on horseback. No doubt ruled by his lust, Duke Robert agreed.

The next day Herleva, dressed in the finest clothes her poor father could afford, mounted on a white horse provided by the duke, rode proudly through the front gates, her head held high.

Even now, the duke's child within her, her place in his household secure, the memory evoked much pride in her, and made her giggle at the same time. For, unlike the women who'd been escorted through the back, that ride through the front gate had given Herleva semi-official status as the duke's mistress. It had been an exhilarating event for a lowly tanner's daughter, as had been her first encounter in Robert's bed.

Though the duke often professed his love for her in the months that followed, Herleva had doubts the strange brew Chamane had concocted really worked. Maybe it wasn't the potion that made Robert fall in love with her. Maybe it was just her company, her sweet disposition, her affection for him. Maybe it was the way she sometimes moaned in pleasure even when the duke's attentions weren't doing it for her. Her conceit wouldn't allow all the credit to go to some musty, sour-tasting concoction stirred up by a somewhat demented old hag.

After pouring the brew into the duke's wine that first night, she'd given it little thought--except on those occasions when Chamane reminded her how she was in the old healer's debt. Even doubtful of the potion's power, Herleva repaid the debt many times over.

Now, bloated and uncomfortable in her pregnancy, experiencing strange dreams, often queasy, short of breath, breasts leaking milk, and constantly being kicked from the inside, she felt Chamane was obligated to help *her*. Thus, temporary arrangements were made for Chamane to be nearby at all times, despite the withered old harridan's objections.

Herleva slept when she was able, though her sleep was never very restful. Her dreams were part of the problem, though she mostly dismissed them. Then one night a dream came to her that was so vivid, so overwhelming, she woke screaming.

Both Duke Robert and Chamane responded to her outburst.

"What is it, my love?" asked Robert, kneeling at her bedside. Though still a young man, he'd officially become the Duke of Normandy only days earlier when his father, Duke Richard II had died. "Are you in pain? Is there something wrong with the baby?"

"No, I'm in no pain," said Herleva. "I just had the strangest dream--a dream that was, at first, intriguing, then enveloped me in a frightening way."

"What was it?" he asked. "What did you dream?"

"I dreamt of a tree growing out from my belly. It grew and grew, so large, so tall, its branches covered all of Normandy. But it kept growing. And even when it grew to cover all of western Francia, it didn't stop. It kept growing, across the sea, covering the English isle."

Duke Robert stood and looked at the old *chamane*. "What does this dream mean?"

"A woman who's with child will often experience strange dreams," responded Chamane, shrugging. "It could mean the fruit of her womb will reach beyond these castle walls and reign over all the lands of the west . . . "

Herleva saw the vainglorious gleam in her duke's eyes at the thought his child might be a great conquering hero.

" . . . or," continued Chamane, "it could mean nothing more than she ate a bad piece of mutton."

Duke Robert scowled at the old woman for dousing his prideful notions, snorted in disgust, and exited the bedchamber.

Chamane stifled a laugh, but Herleva managed a chuckle before a kick to her innards reminded her being pregnant was neither funny nor fun.

f

The child of Herleva and Duke Robert would be named William. "William the Bastard," as he was called by his enemies, would survive several assassination attempts as a child, eventually take control of all Normandy, and launch the only successful invasion of England since 1066. During the siege of Alençon, the townspeople hung animal skins over their walls to taunt young Duke William about his mother's heritage. When he captured the town, he cut off the hands of his tormentors. Today he's known as William the Conqueror.

Without a time machine, there's no way of knowing whether the oft told story of Herleva's dream is fact or folklore, but the tale of how she first caught the duke's eye is still told by tour guides today.

Duke Robert was alternatively known by the epithets "The Devil" or "The Magnificent," depending upon whom was talking . . . and, I imagine, whom was listening. Herleva, whose name historians also list as Herleve, Arletta, Arlotte, Arlette, or Harlette, could never marry the duke because of her humble origins, and though etymology dictionaries will tell you the word "harlot" is of obscure origins, it grew into common use in France not long after her death.

Ancient though they may be, records of family lineages reveal that I'm the great (x28) grandson of Herleva and Duke Robert.

Micagor's Gold

L eaving my family again weren't easy. I'd done it too many times, and I was too long in the tooth for any more wild adventures. But I left them anyways, 'cause it was my last chance . . . my last chance to strike it rich. To take care of them the way I wanted--the way they deserved. So far, I hadn't done much to live up to the name I'd passed on to them. I was hoping to change that.

My Ann didn't say much when I told her I was going. I figured she was used to my "wild goose chases" as she called them. I didn't bother to tell her I was certain this time it would be different. That this time I'd come home with more than my hat in my hand. She wouldn't have believed me anyways.

Eliza and Richard were old enough to help with the little ones and keep our place going, such that it was. Still, I felt bad leaving, even though fate and happenstance were pushing me out the door. Part of me fought that push. Yet, in the end, I knew it was a chance I had to take.

My journey to the Arizona Territory was uneventful. The hours barely crawled by, and I was still tasting dust days after I arrived. I learned quickly that, after four decades in this world, my old body didn't respond well to the rigors of traveling. Though I expect nine days bouncing around in a stagecoach will do that to you no matter your age.

Once I reached Apache Junction, my first task was to recruit some men desperate enough, or foolish enough, to join me. By luck I ran into a bunch of young fellers at loose ends, ready for an adventure. You might say I had just what they was looking for.

I first met Wyatt when he offered to buy me a drink, even though I was a complete stranger. He'd come down to the territory with some other fellers who'd spent some time hunting buffalo up north. When the buffalo played out and they heard tell of gold and silver mines in Arizona, they came looking. I understand they were successful buffalo hunters, still flush from all the hides they'd sold, but they didn't know a wit about prospecting. They was talking about heading back East to see their respective families when I ran into them.

Though he had only 23 years under his belt, I was impressed with Wyatt. Not only was he experienced and confident for such a young man, he was obviously intelligent. But even more important to me, he seemed a trustworthy sort. The kind of man you could count on to keep his word. His companions, though younger than him, were cut from the same cloth. Not the kind to break and run at the first sign of trouble.

I'd learned Wyatt's pregnant wife had died of the typhoid the year before, and things had soured for him in the aftermath, including a couple of run-ins with the law. I reckoned his months of buffalo hunting had revived him. He was friendly, though his manner suggested a quiet reserve. Despite this, his younger friends looked to him as though he was their unspoken leader. He fit the bill, being broad-shouldered, long-armed, and as tall as me. And, though I hadn't actually seen him in action, word was he was good with a gun--very good.

I took all this into consideration before I decided to tell Wyatt and his friends about the gold, and offer them full partnerships. I didn't know how they'd react when I told them I aimed on going up into the Superstitions.

"That's Apache territory you're talking about," said Wyatt. "Those mountains are sacred to them injuns. They call it *Wikohsana,* 'The Devil's Playground.'"

"That's right," said Pat, a thin, angular fellow who was one of Wyatt's friends. "They believe there's a hole up there that leads straight down to Hell."

"I've heard plenty of tall tales about those mountains," said Wyatt, "but you don't strike me as a man who'd believe in such yarns. What makes you think there's really gold there, Mica?"

I knew this was the moment of truth. Either I'd hook them and they'd join up with me, or we'd go our separate ways.

We was all sitting at a corner table in what passed for the local saloon. There was Wyatt, Pat, and the three Masterson brothers, Ed, Jim, and Billy. The brothers were just teenagers, but good men according to Wyatt. Before I said anything, I looked each one of them in the face, as though to prepare them for something of import. Then I glanced around, not only to make sure no one could overhear, but to give an air of secrecy to what I was saying. When I figured I'd hesitated just enough to whet their appetites, I began.

"Me and some other men was working for this doctor feller, building a house for him. Word was he'd come into quite a bit of money--gold it was said. I didn't learn 'til later how he'd got his gold.

"Anyways, one day, after the house was mostly done and we was moving the doc's stuff, I saw this hand-drawn map with directions written on it. I didn't think much of it at the time, but I got a good memory. When I see something, I remember it, just as clear as one of those box camera tintypes. It wasn't 'til later on I heard the stories people told about Doc Thorne."

"Dr. Abraham Thorne?" asked Wyatt.

"That's the one." It hadn't occurred to me that any of those boys had heard the story of the doctor, but I was in luck.

"I've heard tell of this doctor," said Wyatt. "They say he treated the Apaches, took care of their ills, and they grew so fond of him they took him up into the Superstitions where they let no other white man go. He came down with as much gold as he could carry. That's what they say anyways."

"That's the truth of," I added. "It's the same story I heard."

"How do you know it's not just that--a story?" Ed Masterson's voice was ripe with skepticism. "Some tall tale he wove to explain ill-gotten gold."

"It could be just some yarn," said Pat, "but I've heard other tales about them mountains. There was some Mexican fellers a long time back that were supposed to have found a whole lot of gold up there. They called it the 'Sombrero Mines' 'cause they thought those mountains looked like a big hat."

"Mister, you telling me you got a picture of that map in your head?" It was the middle brother, Billy, who spoke up. "You know where the gold is?"

"I gotta be honest with you boys," I said, figuring it were the right thing to do. "I know where the map *says* the gold is. But I don't know any more than any of you about whether the stories are true. It's a gamble--no different than playing cards. Still, it's a gamble I'm willing to take. I left my wife and four youngins back in Missouri 'cause I think there's a good chance we'll find gold up in them hills."

I looked them over. A variety of expressions stared back at me. Pat looked intrigued, as did Billy, but his brothers not so much. I couldn't get a read on Wyatt.

"If any of you want to take that chance with me, I'll give each of you a full partnership. Whatever we find, we divide equally."

"I'm in!" said Billy enthusiastically.

"Hold it there just a minute, little brother," said Ed. "If you're so sure you know where the gold is, what do you need us for?"

"I'm just one man. As Wyatt said, we'll be going into Apache territory--dangerous country. You men are experienced buffalo hunters, good with your guns from what I hear. I figure it's safer to travel in a group than alone. If the stories are true, there's plenty of gold for all of us."

"Come on, Ed," said Billy. "What else you gotta do?"

"You know what we gotta do, *Bartholomew*," replied Ed. "We promised Ma we'd head back to Wichita once we sold our hides, and bring her some money."

I'd noticed, whenever he wasn't happy with his younger brother, Ed called him by what I guessed was his given name.

"Yeah, but just think how much money we can bring her if'an we find the gold," said Billy, his eyes bright with the fever I'd seen flash across many men's faces.

"And what happens if instead of finding gold we lose our scalps? Then what happens to Ma?"

Billy didn't have an answer for that. Ed Masterson stood and looked at me.

"Thanks for the offer, mister, but we gotta be getting back to Kansas. No hard feelings."

"I understand," I replied. "No hard feelings."

The Masterson boys got up and walked out, though I saw Billy did so reluctantly.

"What about you, boys?" I asked Wyatt and Pat.

I could see Pat was intrigued, but he looked to Wyatt.

"What do you think, Wyatt?"

Wyatt fingered his mustache, thought on it a moment, and said, "Well, we got nothing else to do. Let's go see if we can find that gold."

"Alright," said Pat. "I'm in too."

"Good enough," I said. "I'll fetch us some drinks to seal the deal."

When I reached the bar I saw a group of soldiers through the window. They was mounting up.

"What's going on?" I asked the barkeep.

"Injun trouble I imagine. Always is."

I nodded. "Three whiskeys."

When I sat back down I handed Wyatt and Pat their whiskeys, raised mine in the air, and said, "To Gold."

"To Gold," they repeated.

We finished our drinks just as Billy Masterson hurried back in.

"I'm going with you," said Billy.

"What about your brothers?"

"They're going back to Kansas to give Ma the money from the hides. I told them I'd meet up with them there after we got the gold."

"Not so loud," I said. "We don't want every down-on-his-luck prospector trying to follow us."

"Oh, yeah. Sorry," said Billy.

"Okay then. The four of us. We'll leave tomorrow--early."
Each of them nodded.

/

We set out at sunrise, me driving the wagon, my young companions on their horses. I'd bought a team of two for the wagon, hopeful we'd be coming back with a heavy load. Gold ain't like corn or cotton. It'll wear you down just moving it. But then I reckon if it were easy, it wouldn't be worth as much.

I was still sore from the trip west. My joints ached something fierce and my back felt like I'd been kicked by a mule. I envied the trio of young studs I'd joined up with. They were full of vim and vigor, so I wasn't about to let them see how the old man was hurting.

I'd been through the Arizona Territory before--before it was even a territory by name. But its harsh landscape of rocky prominences, scrub brush, towering cacti, and desert sands was still alien to me. There was something pure and clean about the desert, but also something sinister. It wasn't just the dry heat that made me feel as if I was a long way from the grassy plains of Missouri, and even longer from the green hills and meadows of Virginia where I grew up. I think it was the quiet desolation. Not a sound but the wind.

The sun was almost straight up when we spotted a troop of cavalry headed towards us. I stopped the wagon and they slowed to meet us. Calling a halt, their lieutenant and his scout rode up.

"Lieutenant Joseph Sladen at your service," said the cavalry officer. "Whereabouts you men headed?"

"Just doing a little prospecting," I replied.

"You know you're in Apache country don't you?"

"Yes, sir, I do."

"Well, if you had the sense God gave a horse, you'd turn around," said the lieutenant. "There ain't nothing but dust and death out here."

"Micagor? Micagor Golden?"

The cavalry scout was staring at me like he'd seen a ghost. I hadn't really looked at him, but when I did I recognized him right away, even behind a red beard that all but covered his face.

"Tom Jeffords, while I live and breathe."

"You know this man, Jeffords?" asked the lieutenant.

"Yes, sir. We worked together long ago, hauling mail from St. Jo to Sacramento for the Pony Express . . . before it was even called such."

"Well tell him he's an idiot if he keeps on the way he's headed," said the lieutenant, turning his horse around and motioning his troop forward.

"He's right, Mica," said Jeffords. "Cochise has jumped the reservation again, and the Apaches hereabouts are pretty riled up."

"With good reason I imagine," I replied, knowing how they was treated on reservations.

"You're right about that," said Jeffords. "Apaches, like most Indians, keep their word when they make a promise. White men . . . well that's a different story."

"I'm surprised to see you working with the Army."

"I ain't the only one. Remember Bill Cody? He's working as an Army scout now too."

"Skinny little Bill Cody?"

"He ain't so skinny any more, and they call him Buffalo Bill now."

I shook my head, remembering how Cody was one of our littlest Pony Express riders, but probably the best.

"Look, the only reason I'm working with the Army is 'cause I'm trying to patch things up with the Apache as best I can. General Howard hired me 'cause I know Cochise, but . . . ." Jeffords shrugged. "Things are so bad now, I don't know if it'll matter. The lieutenant's right. You should turn around and head back. If you keep on, well, I don't have to tell you. You know what the Apache are capable of."

"Sorry, Tom, I can't do that." As I said it, I looked at the men riding with me. There was no quit in their eyes. "We can't do that."

"Alright, it's your scalps. It was good to see you, Mica. If you find what you're looking for, maybe we'll have a drink some day and talk about old times."

"Sounds good, Tom."

With that he spurred his horse and rode off to catch up with the soldiers.

"You were a Pony Express rider with Buffalo Bill?" asked Billy in disbelief. Apparently Cody had made a name for his self, even if I hadn't heard about him back in Missouri.

"No, I was too old to be a rider. At the time Cody was even younger than you. Just 14 or 15 as I recall. Tom and I managed the relay stations and such."

"That Jeffords feller says he knows Cochise. Do you know him too?" Billy was wide-eyed and brimful of curiosity.

"I didn't know him, but I saw him once. In those days the Apache would chase our riders, sometimes catching and killing them. So Tom, he decides we needed to pow-wow with the Apache chief. I wasn't so sure that was such a good notion, but I went with him anyhow. We rode right into Cochise's camp, pretty as you please. I think the Apaches were so surprised, they let us come instead of killing us outright. I stayed with the horses while Tom strolled right up to Cochise. I saw him alright. He was less than a stone's throw from me, already an old man, but as fierce-looking as you can imagine. Tall for an injun, muscles everywhere--you know his name means strong as an oak.

"Anyways, he invited Tom into his *wickiup,* and by the time they'd come out, Cochise had agreed not to attack our riders. No Apache ever harmed them after that. Fact is, the great Cochise was so impressed with Tom's bravery, he made them blood brothers."

"I bet you wish you'd gone into that *wickiup* too," said Billy. "Then you could tell everyone you were Cochise's blood brother."

I looked Billy square in the eyes and told him, "That's not something you brag about, at least not in these parts. Tom did what he thought he had to do, and I admired him for it. But he's gotten a lot of grief for being a so-called 'injun lover,' even though all he's ever been is a fair man.

"Let's go. We're losing daylight."

/

The Superstitions were quite a sight with the sun setting behind us. The orange-gold light reflecting off the sheer rocky cliffs seemed to advertise the wealth we hoped waited for us within. But above them was an ominous thundercloud hanging so low it appeared to graze the mountaintops. I didn't like what it foreshadowed, for the Apache believed their thunder god lived there.

It was the setting sun that pointed the way. The doctor's map had a rough sketch of a mountain with a circular black hole drawn on the face of it. As we approached and the sun fell to the horizon, I saw the shadow created by one of the mountain's outcroppings. For a time, the shadow was nearly a perfect circle. That was where we were headed. That was where we'd find the cave that would lead us inside . . . if the doctor was as good a mapmaker as he was a humanitarian.

"Everyone mark that shadow on the cliff face. Remember it. That's where we'll be going tomorrow."

We found a place to camp for the night at the base of the mountain, and built a small fire where it couldn't be seen. After we'd eaten, young Billy was after me with more questions than a lawyer. Apparently he'd heard all kinds of stories about Buffalo Bill Cody, and the Pony Express--which didn't exist anymore thanks to stagecoach lines and railroads, and Wild Bill Hickok--who he'd seen once in Kansas. I'd made the mistake of telling him I'd replaced Hickok at the Russell, Waddell & Majors Freight Company after he'd been attacked and sorely wounded by a bear. After that, he wanted to know about Hickok.

"Is it true he wore two pistols and used a cross-draw?"

"Well, I never actually seen him draw, but, yeah he had two guns tucked into a belt at his waist."

"Was he really a cold-blooded killer like some say?"

"I can't rightly say, Billy. He seemed a good enough sort to me. He had a wicked sense of humor, liked the ladies, and I once heard him say he'd never killed a man that didn't need killin'. I imagine famous men like him get all kinds of stories told about them. Some true, some not. Maybe someday you'll be famous and they'll be telling stories about you, Bartholomew Masterson."

He laughed at that like he couldn't ever believe such a thing.

"Did you ever--"

I wanted to get some sleep, so I stopped him right there.

"Did anyone ever tell you that you ask too many questions, Billy?"

"My brothers."

"Well you remind me of this writer feller who used to follow me and Tom around asking us all kinds of fool questions. Wanted to know all about the Pony Express and other things. Clemens was his name. He was a funny feller from back East, but he was always pestering us about what it was like to rough it out on the plains."

"I got a question for you," said Pat. "That Jeffords feller called you Micagor Golden. Is that your name?"

"It is."

"Your family name is Golden?" He asked again as if he didn't believe it.

I nodded.

"You're telling me I'm out here in the middle of Apache country, looking for gold, with a man who says he has a map in his head to lead us to it, and his name is Golden?"

Pat looked at me serious-like, then started laughing. Wyatt and Billy joined in, and I chuckled a bit myself.

"Okay--alright. That's enough. I been made fun of my whole life, so you jokers are nothing new. Sure I always had a little fascination with gold 'cause of my name, but I never had much of it at any one time. That don't mean there ain't no gold up there. Now get to sleep. We got a long hard climb tomorrow."

We had to leave the wagon at the end of the first gorge we rode up. I unhitched the horses, saddled one and used the other as a pack mule to carry what I could. Even without the wagon it was slow going, finding just the right paths for the horses. It was no straight line up to the shadow mark I'd seen, and it was all I could do to keep us going in the right direction. Fortunately, once we passed a craggy lower ravine we came upon a clearer path.

"Horses have been up here recently," said Wyatt.

He was right. I saw the signs the trail had been used not long ago.

"They ain't shod," I said. "Must be Apache. Keep your eyes open."

We moved on, not seeing anything for quite some time. Not a bird, not a snake . . . 'cept for the clomp of our horses, it was as quiet as a church.

It took us a good two hours to reach the cliff where we'd seen the shadow. Sure enough, there was a cave there, large enough for us to ride through without even ducking, for the most part. There was a slight curve to it, but we could see the light at the end.

We came out the other side looking down into a canyon spotted with boulders and thick scrub. And there was something else. Something we couldn't rightly believe.

"Is that a train car?" asked Pat, shading his eyes to see better.

"Damned if it isn't," replied Wyatt. "How in the blazes did that get there?"

At first I couldn't believe what they was saying, but then I saw it myself. A train car, lying on its side amongst the scrub, half buried by some landside, looking like it had been there for some time.

"There aren't even any trains in the territory yet," said Pat.

"Even if there were," I said, "how would you get a train car in these mountains? It ain't possible."

"I don't know if that's the strangest thing I've ever seen," added Wyatt, running his thumb and forefinger down each side of his mustache as he pondered it, "but it might be."

We all sat there on our horses, staring at it 'til I said, "Well, it's a mystery we ain't gonna solve now. Let's go."

The map I'd seen wasn't real clear from here, but I wasn't about to tell the boys that. I knew we had to go down, and there was a small horse trail from the cave that did just that.

"This way."

The way down was easy, but once there we discovered several possible paths along the arroyo.

"Which way?" asked Wyatt.

"I don't know," I replied, searching the canyon walls for the sign I remembered.

"You don't know," said Pat in disbelief. "What do you mean you don't know? I thought you had a map in your head."

"I do. We need to wait."

"Wait for what?" asked Billy.

"For the sun to come up over the rim," I said, hoping I was right. "It'll show us which way to go."

"Another shadow?" Wyatt was understandably skeptical.

"I ain't sure. The map showed the sun above the cliffs and an arrow pointing to another cave."

"I don't see no arrow," said Billy.

"Like I said, we wait."

Fortunately we didn't have to wait long before the sun peeked over the rocky rim. I looked around. Nothing--no arrow, no direction. It rose a little higher. Still nothing. Just when I was about to give up, there was a blinding flash of light, forcing us to shade our eyes. It was like the sunlight had hit a giant mirror high above us. It was so bright it was hard to see. Yet as the sun continued to rise, the brightness eased and we made out the vague shape of an arrow, pointing us in a new direction.

"What's that? What's causing it?" wondered Billy.

"Diamonds maybe," said Pat.

"More likely quartz," I said.

"Look where it's pointing," said Wyatt. "Another cave, up there."

We all saw it.

"I expect that doctor's map was the real thing after all," said Wyatt.

"I reckon it was," I replied, relieved it was true.

"Well then what are waiting for?" Billy was already turning his horse. "Let's go, boys."

*

The cave we found at the top of the path was dark as pitch. After just a short distance it narrowed and shrank so our horses could go no further. Pat tethered them while I made us a torch. We proceeded on foot and it was a long walk--

longer than I would have guessed. Gradually the tunnel began sloping downward. We were headed into the bowels of the mountain.

"How much further?" asked Pat.

"I don't rightly know," I said. "But this cave should take us right to the gold."

But it wasn't gold we found first. It was something else. Something strange.

"What is it?" wondered Wyatt.

I held my torch closer to the cave wall to get a good look. It was some kind of writing. At least that's what I reckoned it was. But it weren't no alphabet. They was symbols I'd never seen before.

"Is that Apache writing?" asked Pat.

"Apaches don't write . . . as far as I know," I said, though I wasn't positive about it.

"I wonder what it says." Billy traced the symbols with his fingertips. "Is it paint or blood?"

"Blood wouldn't likely stay so red after it dried," said Wyatt.

"Well, we can't read it, so let's keep moving," I said.

We hadn't gone far when Billy asked, "You fellers hear something?"

We stopped and listened. I didn't hear a thing. I turned around and the light of the torch illuminated my companions. When it did, I noticed something on top of Billy's hat. So did Wyatt.

"Billy, looks like you found a friend," said Wyatt.

"What do you mean?"

"Tarnation, Billy!" exclaimed Pat. "You got a bat on your head."

"What are you talking about?" Billy reached up and took off his hat. When he saw the varmint he was so took with fright he tossed his hat, danced a little jig, and pulled his gun.

"Don't shoot it," I said. "A gunshot could cause a cave-in."

Wyatt walked calmly over to the bat and used the walking stick he'd picked up to nudge it off the hat. It flew off into the darkness. He picked up the hat and handed it to Billy.

"Here you go, bat man," he said, smiling at Billy. "Try not to make any more friends 'til we get back to town."

Billy looked the hat over carefully before he took it.

"That's a good name for you, Billy," joked Pat. "I think I'll call you Bat from now on."

"You do and I'll shoot you."

Wyatt, Pat, and I laughed. Billy dusted his hat off and put it back on.

We continued down the slope of the cave, wondering where it would end, when the torchlight caught a gleam up ahead. A couple of more steps was all it took for us to see it.

Gold.

It was a vein of gold in the side of the cave the likes of which I'd never seen or even heard tell of. It was larger than a coffin--which came to mind 'cause it was pretty much shaped like one. The boys were speechless . . . for about five long seconds.

"Yeehah!" shouted Billy.

"I didn't really believe it, Mica," said Pat, "but you were right. The map was real."

"There's a fortune right there in front of us," calculated Wyatt.

"Look," I said, moving the torch to the end of the vein. "Someone's been mining this gold. They've dug in here."

I bent down and hefted a small chunk of pure ore just lying there, feeling the weight of it in my hand.

"Why'd they stop?" wondered Wyatt. "And where'd they go?"

Wyatt kept moving down the cave. When I looked to see where he was going, I noticed a soft blue glow in the dark. I had no notion what kind of mineral would give off such a light.

"There's something down here," called Wyatt.

We followed him to where it looked like the cave ended. I couldn't tell where the blue light was coming from, but it cast an eerie pall over Wyatt. He looked like he saw the source of the light and reached out to touch it. I thought that was a poor idea, but before I could call out a warning, Wyatt's body convulsed like he'd been shot. Blue lightning flickered all around him. He collapsed and we ran to him.

"Don't touch him," I warned, seeing his body still had a blue glow about it.

"Is he dead?"

"I don't know."

As I speculated Wyatt may indeed have been killed, the cave wall in front of us opened. I don't mean like a door. I mean it was a cave wall and then it weren't. All at once there was an opening with light shining from it.

Wyatt stirred, moaned, and rolled himself over.

"Wyatt, you okay?" asked Pat.

The glimmer of blue light around him faded as he sat up.

"What happened?" asked Wyatt.

"You got struck by some kind of lightning . . . I think," said Pat.

"We thought you was dead," added Billy. "You turned all blue."

"What color am I now?"

"You're alright now--normal color I mean," said Pat.

As they helped Wyatt to his feet, I ventured a look through the hole in the cave wall. It was a wonder to behold. There was lights everywhere, but I saw no candles, no lanterns, no flame of any kind. The room was immense, and there was gadgets all around, many of them made of gold and other shiny metals. I'd never seen anything like it.

"Where'd this all come from?" Wyatt still appeared dazed, but then, seeing what there was to see, we all were a bit addled.

"After that blue lightning hit you, the cave just opened up," I said.

"What is it?" asked Billy.

"I don't rightly know," I said. "It kind of reminds me of a paddlewheeler I once took up the Mississippi, but it was nothing like this."

"This ain't no steamboat," said Wyatt. "Whatever it is, it's buried inside the mountain."

"Let's see how big it is--how far it goes," said Pat.

"I don't know . . . ." Before I could voice my doubts about exploring the bizarre room we'd walked into, something came at us. I say *something*, 'cause I still don't know to this day what it was. 'Cept that it must have been ten feet tall. It was shaped like a man alright, but it had six fingers on each hand, scraggly red fur on its head, and its skin, if indeed it was skin, was as white as bleached bones. Yet the strangest thing about it was its face, which was no human face at all, but one that looked like a snake or a lizard.

It charged us so quickly I stood frozen by the sight of it. But Wyatt drew and shot it several times before Pat and Billy had even cleared their holsters.

"What in the name of God is that?" said Pat, staring down at the beast.

"Nothing godly I'm sure," said Wyatt.

Looking at it, I realized I hadn't even noticed the thing was wearing clothes. It had on some kind of vest, and trousers that ended just below its knees. I didn't look too close, 'cause its smell was awful pungent. Something akin to a mixture of mildew and onions.

"You said the Apache believe there's a hole that goes straight to Hell in these mountains," said Billy. "Maybe that's the Devil you just killed, Wyatt."

"It's some kind of devil," said Pat.

"We should get out of here," I suggested with some urgency.

48

"Not so fast," said Wyatt. "Let's have a look-see. Look at all the gold in this place. Maybe they got some already mined we can take with us."

"It's the *they* part of that which worries me," I countered.

Wyatt shrugged. I figured he wasn't feeling too threatened after taking care of the creature so easily.

We followed Wyatt from the chamber we'd entered to another. This one wasn't so lit, so bright, and not so full of strange gadgets. But it had something else just as strange, and we all saw it.

"Look," said Billy. "An injun."

Standing like a statue in some kind of glass box was an old Indian. He had long black hair streaked with silver, high cheekbones, and clear eyes that were open but lifeless. He was thickly muscled and tall compared to most of the Indians I'd seen. I realized he looked familiar.

"It's Cochise," I said, flabbergasted by my own words.

"Cochise? You sure?" asked Wyatt.

"He's older, but I'm sure," I said. "You don't forget someone like him."

"Is he dead?" wondered Pat.

"He looks it," said Billy.

"Look closer," said Wyatt. "You can see he's breathing--barely."

"Let's get him out of there," I said, running my hands over the glass box, trying to find a way in.

"You sure we should?" asked Pat.

"I ain't leaving no man to these creatures," I said. "Injun or not."

Wyatt hit the glass with the butt of his revolver trying to break it, but it didn't so much as crack.

"What about this?" asked Billy, pushing on some kind of lever. It did the trick. The glass box opened pretty as you please, and me and Wyatt pulled the Apache chief out and laid him on the metal floor.

He woke right away, though he appeared too weak to move. He looked up at us and said something in Apache.

"Any of you speak injun?" asked Billy.

"No, but I speak a little Spanish," I said.

"*¿Está bien?*" I asked him.

He nodded, tried to sit up, but didn't have the strength.

"*¿Qué pasó?*"

He struggled to respond, but the more he spoke the easier it was for him. He told me he'd gone off alone to listen to the spirits of the mountain--the *Ga'an* he called them. When a strange creature approached him he thought he was having a vision.

"What's he saying?" asked Billy.

"He says he thought that thing Wyatt killed was a mountain spirit, but he was wrong. He thinks the thing was what the Paiutes used to call *Si-Te-Cah*—a beast that eats both animals and people. Either that or some kind of devil come up from Hell."

"I told you," said Billy.

"It shot him with something that froze him like ice, and he didn't wake 'til now."

Somewhat recovered, Cochise sat up and looked us over with distrust. He asked how we came to be there. I knew he'd been lied to before in his dealings with white men, so I understood his suspicion.

"Estábamos buscando el oro." I told him we were there looking for gold.

He nodded. He knew about white men's fascination with gold. He stared at me and nodded again.

"Lo visto a usted antes. Usted estaba con Tom Jeffords hace muchos años."

I was surprised he remembered me, being as how I never even conversed with him, but I nodded and said, *"Jeffords y yo trabajábamos juntos. Lo vi ayer. Él lo buscaba a usted."*

Cochise smiled.

"Well, what'd he say?" wondered Billy. "Why'd he smile like that?"

"He just says he remembers seeing me with Tom Jeffords. He smiled 'cause I told him Jeffords is looking for him. He knows Jeffords could never find him up here."

"Let's help him up and get out of here," said Pat.

Cochise was able to stand, though he was a bit wobbly. We headed back the way we came, but the opening to the cave was gone, and no matter how we pushed or prodded, it wouldn't open. There was nothing we could do but turn around and try to find another way out.

We passed through the room where Cochise had been held and eventually reached a much larger space that looked like a warehouse for storage. They was waiting for us there. They must have known what happened to their companion, 'cause they didn't charge at us. Instead they ambushed us, firing some kind of light. The first shot hit me in the leg. It was as hot as a smithy's coals. I felt the burn on my skin even before my pants caught fire. I dropped to the ground and smothered the flames with my hat as everyone took cover.

50

I think when we hid the snake creatures became overconfident. There was at least seven of them, and they advanced on us, out in the open, firing their strange light weapons. That's when I saw I'd chosen my companions well. They drew their guns and fired. The sound inside that chamber was deafening. When the gun smoke cleared seconds later, each and every giant monster lay dead.

My leg was hurting something awful. I felt like a branded steer. Cochise helped me to my feet and, with his support, I limped after the others as they continued to search for a way out.

Wyatt led the way, and soon I spotted daylight . . . or what was left of it. There was an opening ahead, a way out of the snake creatures' lair, and by the orange glow I knew the sun was setting. But before we could escape, the mountain began shaking. Pat and Billy got knocked off their feet. Cochise kept his footing while holding me from going down.

I'd felt earthquakes before, and I was sure that's what it was. It lasted only a few seconds, but I heard a rumble that made me think another quake was coming.

"Come on!" yelled Wyatt as he ran outside.

We followed, but as we did I heard several gunshots, and saw some ricochet near the opening. Wyatt dropped and I was sure he was dead.

We rushed out and I saw he wasn't dead after all. He'd just ducked for cover 'cause someone was still shooting at him. It was a group of Apaches on a nearby rock outcropping.

Cochise saw them too, and ordered them to stop. As we scrambled outside, another quake shook us, even harder this time. We hurried up the slope to where the Apache waited for their chief. He shouted another command, and they took off. We followed.

We made it to a table of cliffs, but all the while the ground shook and there was a sound like a thousand cattle stampeding. We stood watching, white man and injun alike, as something grew out of the side of the mountain. The hillside, its boulders and brush, gave way--opened up as a great metallic shell forced its way out and up. I say up 'cause it didn't fall into the canyon like it should have. Instead it hovered there, like a hummingbird. Indeed there was a humming sound to it, and the air around us seemed to vibrate. There was a blue glow about it too, just like the one around Wyatt when he was struck down.

It didn't hover long. Once clear of the debris, the egg-shaped monstrosity rose up above the mountain tops and flew off like a bullet.

51

I think we all stood and stared at the empty sky for some time, as if we expected, maybe feared, it would return. The Apache were mumbling uneasily, and I saw Billy cross himself in that way some religious folks do. I figured I was right in calling it a ship, though like Wyatt had said, it was no steamboat. But it didn't return. Devils or man-eating demons, mountain spirits or Apache thunder gods, they were gone.

We hightailed it out of there as fast as we could. Fortunately, the Apache had found our horses and led us out of the mountains by a different trail. The way we'd come was gone--gone with half the mountainside, as was the gold we'd found. But we weren't thinking much about gold. Every man, white and red, was pretty quiet as we rode out. Each to his own thoughts about the strangeness we'd seen.

When we reached the plain, we parted ways with the Apache. Cochise didn't say much. I think the experience affected him as much as the rest of us. He simply told me to tell Jeffords he was ready to talk. Then he rode off.

My leg still hurt like hell. It looked like a bad burn, but it would heal up with time.

"Well I reckon it'll be easy enough for us to divide up our treasure," joked Pat, "seeing as how we got none."

"That's not exactly true," I said, pulling out of my pocket a gold nugget the size of a small plum. "I picked this up inside the cave. I expect we should get it assayed and split it four ways."

"Hell, Mica, there's not much there anyways," said Wyatt. "Why don't you take it home to your wife and youngins. That way you don't have to go home empty-handed. What do you say, boys?"

"You just buy us a drink when we get to town and we'll call it even," said Pat.

"Sounds fair to me," agreed Billy.

"That's awful nice of you fellers."

Before I could say anything else, Pat exclaimed, "Tarnation! Look at you, Wyatt."

"What do you mean?" asked Wyatt.

With the sun setting behind him, and the evening wind blowing open his black range coat I saw it clear.

"There's bullet holes in your duster," said Pat. "At least three I can see."

"There's one in your hat too," I added.

Wyatt took off his hat and fingered the hole there. The bullet couldn't have missed his head by more than an inch.

"When those injuns shot at you, Wyatt, I was sure you was headed for the bone orchard," said Billy.

"You're one lucky son of a gun," said Pat. "You sure you weren't hit at all?"

Wyatt felt his head and appeared to take a mental inventory of his body. "Not a scratch," he said.

Apaches are pretty good shots, so I figured Pat was right. Wyatt must have had a strange kind of luck working for him. But it weren't near as strange as what else we'd seen that day.

Not much is known about my great, great grandfather Micagor Golden and what he was doing in 1871, when this tale takes place. What is known is that he was accidently shot while hunting deer in the winter of 1875. He and his fellow hunters had just laid their rifles on their sled when Micagor reportedly said to the rest, "Let's secure these rifles before someone gets hurt." Those were his last words. One of the rifles discharged, killing him instantly.

Wyatt Earp and the Masterson brothers met while hunting buffalo around 1870. William Bartholomew "Bat" Masterson and Earp would work together again in Dodge City, where they were both deputy sheriffs. Their friendship would continue years later, when Earp hired Bat to run his gambling house in Tombstone, Arizona. Pat Garrett, most famous for shooting Billy the Kid, was also hunting buffalo around this time. It's not known if he ever ran into Earp or Masterson, but it's certainly possible. All three men had trouble with the law at various times, but all three would be remembered for being famous lawmen. Like Micagor, little is known and less is documented about what Earp, Masterson, and Garrett were doing in 1871. There's nothing to say they didn't join up and search for gold in the Superstition Mountains.

Legends of gold in the Superstitions go back as far as the 16th century, when Spanish Conquistadors, led by Francisco Vasquez de Coronado, were looking for the Seven Golden Cities of Cibola. They're also the legendary location of the Lost Dutchman's Mine.

Tom Jeffords, whose first meeting with Cochise is reported to have happened just as detailed here, was able to track down the 67-year-old Apache chief and convince him to return to the reservation in 1872, ending a decades-long war.

The mysterious ship, its technology, and the creatures who inhabited it are speculative. However, one of the legends to grow around Wyatt Earp, was that he couldn't be touched by bullets. Indeed, though he lived for more than 50 years in the Wild West and took part in numerous gunfights, he was never so much as nicked by a bullet, though several times he discovered bullet holes in his clothing and hats.

Puck and the Virgin Queen

O f all the queen's palaces, I always enjoyed Hampton Court the most. Its gardens, its tapestries, its sumptuous furnishings were among the finest I'd seen. And I'd visited countless castles and noble homes. As head of the royal household, I'd traveled the breadth of England with the queen.

Of course, just as I thought of the grandeur of Hampton, the wind reminded me of the single thing about the palace I did not care for--the foul smell wafting in from the Thames. I would have to remember to have the maidservants renew the pomanders in the royal residence.

That was just one of my countless duties, which kept me on the go all the day, and often well into the night. Nonetheless, I can't say my life was ever dull. The queen had her ups and downs, and I had been there for most of them. I was on my way, now, from the kitchen,--where I'd passed on Her Majesty's complaints--to her bedchamber, to see that all was as it should be. Normally, by that time of night, she'd be preparing for bed instead of dressing in her finest. This night, however, she was expecting a visitor--one she'd summoned.

On my way to her bedchamber I came upon the royal footman and asked, "Is the queen dressed?"

He shrugged and replied, "A ship is sooner rigged than Good Queen Bess is made ready."

I barely stifled a laugh. The image of a ship's ropes and sails did indeed remind me of the queen's bodice and petticoats and stomacher with all their corresponding laces and hooks.

"William Head," I scolded the footman with a smile, "I can't believe you would say such a thing."

He shrugged again and continued down the gallery hall.

When I reached the bedchamber the queen was fully attired, and shooing her dressers from the room. She struggled beneath the restraint of her gown to take a deep breath and sighed.

"Sometimes, Dorothy, I wish I had never become queen."

"Your Highness, how could you say such?" I wasn't as surprised as I sounded. The queen had become more melancholy with age.

"'Tis true. If not for a battle here, a marriage there, the fates might have

55

conspired differently, the Tudors never would have come to power, and I would never have had to bear the burden."

"Your Majesty, that's like saying if the sun never set, the moon would never rise. Life turns upon the whims of fate and happenstance. Why would you wish not to be queen?"

She adjusted her russet wig and replied, "'Tis not really a wish, just a musing. I often wonder what it would have been like to have had a simple life, with a loving husband and children and . . . .

"You've been with me for my entire reign, Dorothy--more than 40 years now. You know what it has been like for me, balancing my stewardship of England, duty to my people, with my . . . personal desires."

"I know, at times, it has not been serene for Your Majesty."

"You know, Dorothy, it could have easily been thee. You could have been queen instead of me. Do you ever think upon that?"

"Me, queen? Whatever do you mean, Your Majesty?"

"Come, come. I know the lineages of everyone in court. I know thee are only a few generations removed from Edward IV and Richard III on thy mother's side, and on thy father's you descend from the line of Edward III. You are a noblewoman, the direct descendant of kings, Dorothy Stafford. Your blood is as royal as mine. Had providence woven a different tapestry, thee could easily have been queen instead of me."

"I've never considered such a thing, Your Majesty. 'Tis a preposterous idea."

Her Highness laughed with gusto.

"Royalty is an incestuous business. Consider that the first wife of thy late husband was my own aunt, who, if rumors are true, had dalliances with my father before he even knew my mother."

"Your Majesty," said the royal footman, announcing his presence.

"Yes, what is it, William?"

"Master Shakespeare has arrived in response to your summons."

"Good--good," said the queen. "Light the candles in Wolsey's old office and show Master Shakespeare in. I'll speak with him there."

The footman turned to do as commanded and the queen asked me, "How do I look?"

There were no mirrors in any of the queen's palaces. She had forbidden them for many years.

"You look radiant, Your Majesty," I said, though her skin seemed more pale with the passing of each day.

"Master Shakespeare and I are not to be disturbed, Dorothy, but stay close by that I may summon thee if need be."

I understood her meaning, and hurried straight to the alcove next to what had been Cardinal Wolsey's office when he was master of Hampton Court. From there I could both hear and, if necessary, observe the queen and her guests.

I was not an admirer of Shakespeare as was the queen. I thought his comedies to be crude and his tragedies often seditious and sacrilegious. But Her Majesty liked anyone who could make her laugh.

"Master Shakespeare," she said upon entering the room, "how good of you to visit me."

He doffed his cap and bowed as the queen chose her favorite chair, one resplendent with red velvet and gold satin.

"I wish only my steed had the wings of Pegasus to convey me into your presence with even more alacrity," he replied, rising to his feet as the queen directed him.

Though he was still a relatively young man, the master playwright had begun to bald. His forehead was a dome of flesh not unlike a melon, and his hair lay to either side like a beagle's ears. He was not a particularly handsome fellow, but that wasn't why the queen valued him.

"I never got the chance to tell thee how much I enjoyed your most recent play, *The Merry Wives of Windsor*. I found its humor most appealing."

"Gracious praise indeed, Your Majesty. It was your command for me to reprise the character of Falstaff which served as inspiration. You are my muse-- always. I'm grateful it was to your liking."

"Indeed it was, and now I have a new task for thee."

The playwright looked askance at the queen as if her words were unexpected.

"I want thee to write a play for the Feast of Epiphany. Something light, joyful--a comedy."

By the expression on his face, Master Shakespeare was not only caught off guard, but unenthusiastic about the prospect. Nevertheless, he responded affably.

"As you command, Your Majesty. I will be honored to create such for the noble Queen Elizabeth. I beg only one favor."

"What is that?" queried the queen, suspicion in her voice.

"Could you speak with your master of revels, Sir Edmund Tilney, and command him to cease censoring my plays? I only ask so I may be allowed to write my finest creation for Your Majesty without outside influence."

"Of course, of course," said the queen, waving her hand as if it were a trifle. "I'll command Sir Edmund to leave thee be."

"Your Majesty is most generous." He cleared his throat. "Speaking of your celebrated generosity, I understand Edmund Spenser has been granted a royal pension for his poem *The Faerie Queene*. May I suppose--"

"Yes, yes," said the queen waving her hand again, but more dismissively this time. "You will be adequately compensated."

"Your Majesty is as generous as she is beauteous, as wise as she is tolerant, as righteous as--"

"Master Shakespeare, don't you think I know when I'm being flattered? No one in history, methinks, has likely been blandished more." The queen smiled slyly. "But I interrupted. Do go on."

Shakespeare returned her smile--rather impudently I thought, though it could have just been the candlelight.

"Shall I compare you to a summer's day? You are more lovely and more temperate." He stopped unexpectedly then, looked thoughtful, and reached into his doublet for a scroll of paper. He searched his costume elsewhere, but didn't find what he was looking for.

"A pen! A pen! A king's ransom for a pen!"

He looked as desperate as he sounded. The queen pointed at the desk and the playwright hurried to it. Once he'd secured the pen and dipped it in the ink pot, he wrote furiously.

"Forgive me, Your Majesty, but I must make note when an idea strikes."

"I understand. I myself can no longer trust importance to memory." She waited a moment while he wrote, then asked, "Tell me, what kind of play do you think thee will write for the Epiphany?"

The playwright thought for a moment, then replied, "In my mind's eye I see a shipwreck . . . a love story complicated by a case of mistaken identity . . . yes, that could work. But I need inspiration. Would Your Majesty grant me the honor of being my muse once again? Tell me of your loves. Inspire me."

Her Highness rose from her chair looking very serious. Her temper was legendary, and I thought, for a moment, she was about to reprimand the playwright for his brash familiarity. I was wrong.

"Oft times, Master Shakespeare, I think love is merely a form of madness. I may be queen, but in that respect I am no different than any common washerwoman. I, too, have suffered from this malady of the heart. Do you know I have received more than a score of marriage proposals in my time?"

"I doubt it not, Your Majesty."

"Yet most had nothing to do with love. Love is a much rarer beast," she said wistfully. "My first and greatest love was the Earl of Leicester, Robert Dudley, my sweet Robin, whom I'd known since childhood. Though he had no royal blood, he might have become my king, except . . . except he was already married. When his wife was found dead there were scandalous whispers of murder--murder that would free him to marry me and become king. They were untrue, of course, but I was forced to banish him from court, as well as from my thoughts of marriage."

"A tragedy itself worthy of dramatization."

"Then there was François, my frog, the Duke of Alençon, brother to the king of France. He was so young, so short, and so ugly, but he made me laugh. He was so very charming that when he wooed me I behaved like a moonstruck girl, though I was nearly twice his age."

"Love is indeed blind," said Shakespeare.

"That it is. But the Duke was Catholic, and my advisors, my people, didn't like the idea of a Catholic king, not after my sister Mary's bloody reign."

I knew all about the queen's romantic heartbreaks. I'd been there for each and every one. Yet I could not believe she was being so indiscreet as to relay them for the master playwright. I'm not certain she cared he was in the room. She was caught up in her reminiscences.

"Then there was Sir Christopher Hatton, my dancing captain of the guard, and Sir Walter Raleigh who wooed me while secretly marrying another. I threw him in prison for that."

"But you released him later," said Shakespeare.

"Yes, after he'd learned a lesson."

"What of the Earl of Essex?"

The queen frowned at the mention of the name. I knew her wounds on that account were still raw.

"Robert Devereaux is a disrespectful, vain young boy who titillated an old woman's heart. I spoiled him, always forgiving his trespasses, his disobedience, until he tried to foment rebellion. That I could not forgive."

"He's in prison, is he not?"

"Yes. And there he'll rot until I decide to part him from his head."

I could tell Master Shakespeare now regretted his query about the queen's love life, for the mood had turned morose. The queen, her ire sparked, turned on the playwright.

"What about thee, Master Shakespeare? Have you ever known true love?"

"What is true love, Your Majesty? Can love be false if 'tis truly love? If it be false, then it never was. But if thy heart says thou art in love, then it must be true."

"Your argument has merit, yet I'm assured I will never know true love," said the queen.

"Say not never, Your Majesty. Not while your heart still pounds."

"You don't understand, Master Shakespeare. I was cursed as a young girl."

"Cursed? By whom? By what?"

"By whom or what indeed." The queen resumed her seat and said to her guest, "You have my permission to sit as well."

The playwright chose the chair behind the desk, feathered pen still in hand, paper at the ready. He sporadically made notes as the queen spoke.

"I spent much time alone as a young girl. But one night I was visited by what I thought was a spirit. At first he just blew out my candles and laughed. And oh what a laugh it was--like ice crystals breaking off a fairy's bell. But it was no spirit, no ghost that came to my room. I learned later he was an imp, a magical sprite.

"When I first heard the laugh, I called out, 'Who's there? Who is it that invades my bedchamber?' A sweet but mocking voice replied, 'I am that merry wanderer of the night called Robin Goodfellow.' That's what he called himself at first."

Though I was the queen's closest confidant, she'd never told me the story of this Robin Goodfellow. I was at once both curious to hear more, and jealous she'd chosen to reveal such to a lowly playwright.

"When next he visited, and it was always at night, he not only blew out my candles, he made my bedclothes vanish. I berated him for it, but he only laughed that impish laugh of his. Over time, other things vanished. Sometimes I would hear the laugh, sometimes not. Sometimes, after the lights blew out, he would steal a kiss--only a peck upon my cheek, yet an affront all the same.

"Then, one night, after the candles blew out, I saw him. The light of the full moon poured through the window next to which he stood. He was quite a sight--more gnome than sprite to my mind. No taller than a child of six, with the hindquarters of a goat, cloven hooves, and two tiny horns protruding above a baby face. 'I see thee,' I told him. He only smiled a wicked smile and said,

'Because you've seen me, I must reveal my true name. 'Tis Puck who is thy knavish lad, thy midnight love.'

"I was angry, annoyed with his mischief, so I said, 'What do you know of love little hobgoblin? No one could ever love such as thee. You're too funny looking.'

"He looked at me with such hatred I pulled my bed covers up so that my eyes could barely see over them. He pointed a stubby little finger at me and said, 'Thou thinks thee knows beauty? That thy vision sees with the clarity of nature in all its pulchritudinous? What fools mortals be. I curse thee, Elizabeth Tudor, for all time. Thou will never know true love--only the cold comfort of a scepter shall be thine.'"

The queen finished her story and sighed longingly.

"So you see, Master Shakespeare, while I did not always believe it, I've known for some time that true love would never be mine. My sun will soon be setting, and the curse will be fulfilled."

I watched for Shakespeare's reaction. He put down the pen, placed his scroll back inside his doublet, and rose from his chair.

"Think upon the truth of it, Your Majesty. You did find true love. You have sacrificed much for it over the years. Your true love was for England, the bright country of your birth, the nation that was left in your care. Your country, your people, that is what you have treasured most, and to your own self you have been true."

"You are a wise man, master playwright. I would hear more of thy wisdom, but the hour grows late."

"Then I will bid you adieu, Your Majesty, though parting is such sweet sorrow."

The playwright bowed, doffed his cap, and backed out of the room, even though Her Highness hadn't given him leave. Well quit of him I thought. He'd only served to stir the coals of unpleasant memories for the queen.

I was about to hurry to her side, to console her as best I might, when I saw from my alcove peep each and every candle in the room go dark as if a sudden gust had extinguished them. I moved to the hall outside the office and saw that even the lights there had gone out.

Before I could rush to her side and re-light the candles, I heard the queen say, "Puck, is that thee?"

Then I heard something I will never forget. A laugh that reverberated through the room and out into the hall where I stood. It was more giggle than belly laugh, but it sounded, indeed, like crystals of ice breaking from a fairy's bell.

Shakespeare would write the romantic comedy Twelfth Night *for Queen Elizabeth's Feast of Epiphany, and the mythical woodland sprite known as Puck would become a key character in one of his more popular plays,* A Midsummer Night's Dream. *Long before entering the service of the queen, Dorothy Stafford married Sir William Stafford, the widower of Mary Boleyn, once Henry VIII's mistress. After her husband died, she and her children fled to Geneva to escape the persecution of Protestants by Elizabeth's half-sister Queen Mary I. There, she met Protestant reformer John Calvin, who'd fled religious persecution in France. He would become godfather to her youngest son. After Queen Mary's death, Dorothy returned to England, where she served Queen Elizabeth and exercised much influence at the royal court.*
Both Dorothy Stafford and the royal footman, William Head, are my direct ancestors. Their family lines would intersect more than a hundred years later in 18th-century Virginia, the state named by Sir Walter Raleigh for Queen Elizabeth I ("The Virgin Queen").

Robin Hood, Inamorato

"Yea ... yea ... doest it, Robin, doest it."

Despite her rousing cries, Robin wasn't certain the lady was so aroused. More likely she'd had plenty of his goodly length and was praying for an end to it. He would comply, but not without one last attempt to carry her with him.

With her countenance down, her arse up, and the sleight of his hands on her breasts, he thrust and stabbed until his lust was quenched.

"Yea ... yea, Robin ... I bid thee doest it, doest it!"

He came hither and she cried out--more, he thought, from the force of his manhood than her own pleasure.

She rolled over and he collapsed next her, breathing heavily from his exertions.

He looked at her lying next to him. She was indeed beauteous, but she made love like the proper lady she was. Certainly he'd had better--maids more enthusiastic--but none with Marian's royal bloodlines. She could trace her ancestors all the way back to the emperor Charlemagne--a name she would drop at the slightest provocation.

"'Tis time we considered marriage," said Marian, shattering his postcoital reverie.

Robin laughed. He couldn't help himself. "Thy father would love that," he said with a full quiver of sarcasm. "His Norman daughter, the lady Marian, descendant of kings and emperors, married to a Saxon outlaw."

She rolled over and draped her arms round him. "Verily I don't careth what my father says. I'll run thither and yon with thee if I must."

"And live in Sherwood Forest?"

"Whither thou goest, I goest, my love."

A timely knock on the door rescued Robin from further conversation. The hushed voice that followed from the other side was Marian's maidservant.

"My lady, the sheriff's men are about. Someone hath told them they witnessed the outlaw Robin Hood in the vicinity. We must go."

Marian was on her feet as quick as a deer, dressing herself. For all her bluster about caring naught what her father thought, she cared indeed.

"Don't worry, my lady," said Robin. "I'll go out the back and distract the

63

sheriff's men forthwith."

"Nay," she begged. "'Tis too dangerous, my love."

He laughed. "I doubt it, my lady. "Forsooth, the sheriff's men are a collection of halfwits, ne'er-do-wells, and buffoons. They'll never catch me." Robin grabbed her, gave her a kiss and swatted her on the arse. She let out a little shriek. "Fair thee well, my lady."

With that, Robin made his way out the back of the inn, generating plenty of noise as he went. Sure to his plan, the sheriff's men, four in all, came round and saw him. At first they froze, as if unsure how to proceed, having the most notorious outlaw in all the land standing before them.

"Come, come," said Robin, encouraging them. "I haven't all day. There's poaching and thievery to be done."

One of the men took affront to his comments and charged, sword held high. Robin stepped aside, parried, and, with the flat of his own blade, whacked the man's buttocks.

The idea of marrying Marian had never occurred to him. He knew 'twas just the fanciful idea of a silly young girl. Her father, Baron Roger Bigod, had likely already arranged for a husband of nobility. They were Normans all, and as a loyal Saxon he despised them. Of course that didn't stop him from seeing Marian as oft as possible.

Another soldier came at him and Robin was forced to cut the man's wrist to disarm him. He didn't think the fellow would lose his hand.

Despite her shortcomings in bed, Robin was hopeful he might soon be able to teach Marian to let loose of her prudery and enjoy herself. Her education would be his pleasure. But marriage? He thought not.

Parry . . . lunge . . . parry . . . feint . . . thrust . . . parry . . . riposte--another of his pursuers fell with a minor wound to the chest.

Marian would soon forget about marriage. He knew she was a flighty sort of girl, ruled by whim and fancy, and her fancy of the moment was one none-too-respectable rogue named Robin. That would change. He was certain.

The two remaining lackeys had cornered him between an ox cart and a hovel, so he leapt onto the cart, pushed off and landed behind them. Without further ado, he pressed his advantage and disarmed them both without injury. He wasn't interested in harming the poor fellows. With the pommel of his sword he dispatched them and fled for the sanctuary of the forest. It occurred to him, with all the lovemaking and fighting, he'd worked up quite an appetite.

*

King John worried at his nails as he sat looking at the ancient tome. He had paid a high price in silver to the self-styled wizard who'd brought the book to him. Now that he'd found the proper passage, he was afraid to speak it. Instead, dressed in his finest opulence, with the crown of England resting upon his short-cropped, dark red hair, he kept discovering another fingernail in need of trimming.

Like his favored pastime of rolling dice, calling forth a demon was a gamble. It could give him ultimate power--everything he desired . . . or he could lose what he already had. He'd been John "Lackland" once, but now that his brother Richard was dead he was king. That reminder bolstered his courage.

He stood, picking up the enchanted dagger the traveling magician had thrown in to consummate the deal. Holding it with both hands, he raised it high above his head.

"*Lirach tasa vefa wehlic, Caim,*" he said, hoping he'd not mangled the pronunciation too badly. That was just to get the demon's attention. Now for the summoning spell.

"Magic forces dark and light, reach out both day and night. Be he far or be he near, summon the demon Caim right here!"

John waited . . . and waited. Naught happened. He was about to call forth his guard and order them to hunt down the swindling charlatan who sold him the book, when a voice behind him uttered the phrase, "King John, I presume."

Always wary of assassins, John spun round, still clutching the dagger. Before him, dressed as elegantly as a king himself, was a tall, raven-haired fellow who appeared to be standing on a bed of hot coals. Smoke swirled about his boots and the rich ebony mantle covering his shoulders looked more like wings than a cloak.

"For what purpose hath thou uttered the evocation, mortal? What dost thou want?"

"Everything," said John.

The demon Caim laughed and the torches illuminating the room quivered as if a foul wind had passed.

"Is that all?" sneered Caim. "Thou art sure thee wants naught else?"

John tried to swallow, but found his throat dry. Mayhap he shouldn't be so bold--ask for so much.

"And what would thee like first?" inquired Caim.

"I want Isabella of Angoulême," stated John forthrightly, trying to disguise his fear. "I want to make her my queen."

65

The demon paused, stroking his dusky chin-beard as if his mind were searching the cosmos. "The one thou speaks of is betrothed to marry Hugh le Brun, Count of Lusignan."

"I know," said John. "But I must have her for my own."

Caim paused again, then responded as if he'd just happened across new information. "This Isabella is but 12 years." The demon smiled slyly. "Thou likes them young, Your Majesty, doesn't thou?"

"She may be young, but methinks she's the most beautiful thing I've ever laid eyes upon. She's my sunshine, my starlight, my Helen of Troy."

"Thou knowest what happened to Troy--right?"

"I must have her."

"Then take her," bellowed Caim. "Thou art the king. Who's going to stop thee?"

"Well, I thought thee might use a little magic to foster the transition more smoothly."

"Magic? Anybody can use magic. Thou art the king." His voice grew more thunderous as he spoke, echoing through the chamber. "Thou must think like a king, act like a king, with ruthless certainty, by the infinite power of thy commands."

"But I want the people to love me."

"*Love* thee," sputtered Caim derisively, the brittle timbre of his annoyance mounting with each word. "*Love* thee? Thou doesn't need love. Thou needs swift obedience. Whither be thy royal fortitude? Stand tall and present those regal bollocks with the authority of thy throne. Slaughter any who stand in thy way. Thou art the king!"

John thought about what Caim was saying. He was right of course. He, John, *was* king of England. But . . . .

"Can't the people just like me a little?"

The demon groaned as though stabbed by a hundredfold blazing hot knives.

*

Robin and his men watched as the king's tax collectors engaged in a contest of knife-throwing. Already embedded in their target tree were a half dozen blades. The soldiers had stopped on the outskirts of Sherwood to roast one of the chickens they'd taken in payment, before moving on to gather more royal revenue. But they wouldn't be collecting any more taxes this day.

Robin gave the signal and a score of arrows flew into the encampment, landing all round the soldiers . . . except for one misguided shaft which now protruded from the foot of a soldier. He fell, crying in pain, while the others froze in place.

"Damn thee, Little John. 'Twas only supposed to be a warning."

John Little shrugged his massive shoulders. "Sorry, Robin."

"Well, go down and help the poor fellow."

Robin's men swooped down out of the trees and from behind the thickets. The king's men dropped their weapons and surrendered without a fight. The gold, the silver, the livestock and produce they'd collected, their weapons, even their clothes, were all forfeit. In addition, the outlaws engaged in a volley of insults as they forced the men to disrobe.

Robin watched with amusement from above, but reached for his sword when he heard a voice.

"Thou hath protected me and mine."

Robin looked up. There, in the branches above him, was an exquisite creature--a stunningly lovely forest nymph--nature's embodiment of beauty and grace. Of course, he'd never actually seen such a nymph, but he'd heard stories. Looking at her, he was certain she could be naught else.

She was naked, and yet she was not. Though she wore no clothes made of human hands, she was thinly draped with a veil of vines and leaves. Golden flowers sprouted from her emerald hair and round her pointed ears. Her fingernails were like bark, her skin as lustrous as the moon. Her flaxen eyes, shadowed by a verdant tint, were those of an old soul, yet her body was young and so well-formed Robin could doest naught but stare.

"We're ready, Robin," called Little John from below.

Robin was mesmerized. He didn't hear a thing.

"Robin!"

Roused from his stupor, Robin responded with annoyance. "What?"

"We're done here."

"Splendid, splendid. See them on their way. I'll join thee anon."

"Thou art going to stay in that tree?" wondered Little John.

"Aye," said Robin, still perturbed. "I might stay here all night if it pleases me. Now off with thee."

"Alright. No need to get thy ire up. We're going."

When Robin turned back, the nymph was gone. He searched the tree without success. Finally he gave up and made his way to the ground.

"What be thy name?"

She'd appeared out of the misty air. Robin held tight to his wits and responded.

"My name is Robin. What's thine?"

"Daphne," she said, circling him, examining him.

Robin stood still for her inspection.

"Whence thou came? Are thee a nymph--a creature of the forest?"

She didn't respond, but continued round and round him.

"What did thou mean when thee said 'Thou hath protected me and mine'?"

She ceased her circling and replied, "Yonder tree those foul ugly wight were cutting is mine. 'Tis where I live--whither the force of my life is rooted. Thou stopped them."

"'Twas my pleasure, my lady," responded Robin with a slight bow.

She moved close to him and touched his face, feeling his skin as though it were a novel sensation. She smelled of lavender and mint.

"Thou art not ugly."

"Well . . . uh, thanks."

"Thou art not like those others. There is no malevolence in thy soul."

Until that moment, Robin had thought the lady Marian to be the most beauteous woman in the land, but the nymph made her look plain. Whether she'd bewitched him or he was acting solely on instinct, Robin suddenly kissed her. He half expected her to turn him into a toad, or, at the very least, disappear. Instead, she returned the kiss in-kind. In the next instant they were in each other's arms.

Her kisses left him reeling, but her touch braced him. Robin steadied himself, feeling a growing need to delve deeper into the quintessence of this mythical entity. Out of reflex, his hand found its way between her legs, and what he discovered there was indeed strange. 'Twas not unlike the damp moss one would find next to a running river. Yet she responded to his touch like any woman--any woman as lusty as a troop of mercenaries.

ʃ

"Robin, there thou art."

Robin found John Little and the rest of his men finishing up with their good deeds, and a merry bunch they were.

"Have all the taxes been returned to their rightful owners?"

"Aye, Robin, minus our usual tithe."

"Good. Then they'll have payment next time the king's tax collectors come round."

"And then we'll take it again," chortled John. He glanced at Robin in dismay.

"Look at thee, Robin. Thou looks like thee hast been rolling round on the forest floor." He brushed dirt and leaves from Robin's vest.

"Aye," replied Robin. "I took a fall. Whither be the goodly Friar Tuck? Hast thou seen him about?"

"Aye. He ventured into yonder inn, no doubt to fortify himself for a night of prayer and penance."

Robin found the friar at a table heavy with venison and wine--his two favorite things, next to the Almighty of course.

"Good Friar, a word with thee if I might."

"Of course, Robin. Will thou join me in a small repast?"

"Small? Nay, thank thee. I have a question of moral concern for thee."

"Ask away. I am nothing if not concerned for the morals of the good men of Sherwood."

"Thou knowest I follow not the teachings of the church, but is it wrong for a man to give sway to his lustful appetites?"

"In this, dear Robin, I also part ways with the teachings of the church--though I would not admit such under penalty of pain. Verily I believe 'tis part of God's plan for a man and woman to engage in the act of love whenever the whim strikes them. There is no evil in such an undertaking."

"What if 'tis not a woman the man lusts for?"

The friar sputtered and spit out a bit of venison he was chewing. When he'd composed himself, he replied, "Dear Robin, are we speaking of a man lusting for another man, or mayhap a sheep?"

"Nay, nay, I was speaking more of something unnatural, like a banshee or a fairy or a wood nymph."

"Well, I . . . I don't know," said the friar looking perplexed. "Would this act of lust be consensual?"

"Of course," replied Robin with umbrage, "what kind of man dost thou take me for?"

"I meant no insult of course, dear Robin. I know thee to be a man of fine character. I just . . . well, I've never advised anyone about such fantastical creatures. Hast thou seen such?"

"Nay. Of course not. 'Twas just a philosophical query for a man of the cloth."

"I see. Well, Robin, my philosophy hath always been . . . be careful whither thou puts it."

King John followed his soldiers into the room. Once there, he could hardly

69

take his eyes off the object of his desire. Isabella de Angoulême sat in a chair in the corner, looking not at all frightened of the soldiers. Indeed, she looked at them with contempt. Her shimmering blonde hair, the hauteur of her blue eyes, pushed Cupid's arrow even further into John's heart.

"Leave us!" commanded John.

As the last of the soldiers left the room, a blackbird landed on the window ledge. John knew 'twas the demon Caim, there to oversee his moment of triumph.

"How dare thee enter my chambers?" fumed Isabella. "I'll have thee flogged."

John advanced on the young girl, but she showed no fear.

"Dost thou knowest who I be?"

"Aye, thou art King John. But I'll still have thee flogged."

John laughed. "And who will thee get to doest the flogging?"

She stood and put her hands on boyish hips. "I'll doest it myself."

"Thou will, will thee? That might be fun . . . some other time. But for now, thou will be coming with me. I'll summon thy maidservant to pack thy things."

"I don't want to go with thee," she said, crossing her arms and turning from him.

"Sometimes little girls don't always get what they want."

"I'm not a little girl," she pouted, stamping her foot. "I'm Isabella de Angoulême, daughter of the Count of Angoulême, betrothed of Hugh le Brun, Count of Lusignan, great granddaughter of King Louis VI of France."

"Well, my mother was once married to King Louis VII," said John, "so I guess that makes us cousins by marriage."

"I don't care," she shrieked. "I'm not going with thee."

In tandem with her tantrum, the blackbird at the window screeched.

John moved closer and she turned her back on him. He whispered in her ear, "What if I were to make thee Queen of England? Would thee come with me then?"

"Queen?" she said, her tone softened and her interest piqued. "Verily?"

"Aye. We'll get married and thou will become the Queen of all England. Anything thou wants shall be thine."

"Anything? Can I have a pony?"

"Thou can have a stable full of the finest ponies in the land."

"Can I have a masked ball?"

"Thou can have a hundred masked balls, and all the ladies and gentlemen of the realm will attend."

70

"Can I have France?"

"We'll see."

/

'Twas a noble party of less than 20 travelers on the only road to London, which, by happenstance, passed through a corner of Sherwood forest. When Robin had been made aware of the party's approach, he'd set his trap forthwith. His men hid in wait until he gave the signal. At once they all appeared, surrounding the wayfarers, bows drawn.

The knights and house guards among them pulled their swords and prepared to defend themselves and their ladies, despite their untenable position. They were outnumbered, and 'twas obvious the first volley of arrows would end their defense.

Robin dropped from the tree whither he'd directed the ambush. He walked straight to the lead horse, fell to one knee, bowed, and doffed his cap.

When he rose and fit his cap back on his head he said, "Sheath thy swords, noble sirs. No blood must be shed this day."

The lead knight reined in his horse and replied, "Who art thou, and how dare thee threaten travelers on the road to London?"

"I be Robin Hood. Who be thee?"

The knight straightened in his saddle. "I am Sir William Marshal, Earl of Pembroke, defender of the realm."

Robin bowed his head slightly, and with a courteous wave of his arm said, "I've heard of thee, Sir Marshal. They say thou art the greatest knight who ever lived. I'm honored by thy presence."

"I've heard of thee as well," said Sir Marshal. "They say thou art a thief, a vagabond, a ruffian, an uncouth outlaw extraordinaire."

"'Tis true I'm afraid, though I'd hardly describe myself as a ruffian." Robin's men laughed at this. "And whom, may I ask, be the other members of thy party?"

"Sir Roger Bigod, his wife, the lady Ida de Tosny, and his son, Hugh. My wife, the lady Isabel de Clare, and my daughter, Maud. We're on our way to Westminster Abbey to attend the wedding of the king."

Robin hadn't recognized him, but he knew Sir Bigod to be Marian's father. That would mean altering his intent. However, though his plan be thwarted, he could still poke the lion and have a bit of fun.

"Tell me, Sir Marshal, why dost such a stalwart, gentilesse knight of thy stature serve a softsword like John? Dost thou knowest many believe thee to be a snollygoster for the king?"

Robin could tell the man took umbrage at the term. There was fire in his response.

"I serve England, sir. I served the realm for Henry, I served it for Richard, and now for John."

Sir Bigod prodded his horse forward and added, "We all serve the crown. All good men doest."

"Until it suits their purposes otherwise," said Robin. "I may be an uncouth outlaw, but I'm not ignorant of the ways of the world. As I recall, Sir Bigod, thy own father rebelled against King Henry II--yet now thee serves his son. The ebb and flow of history and politics makes strange bedfellows, dost it not?"

Sir Bigod made a sound of derision and then asked, "So, dost thou intend to rob us now?"

"Such a noble party? I would not endeavor to even consider such an act . . . on one condition."

"What is thy demand?" asked Sir Marshal.

"Why only that thee extend my congratulations to King John, and I prithee not to besmirch my name to any who ask of me."

Sir Marshal hesitated, then replied, "I will convey thy message to the king. May we pass now?"

To the astonishment of his men, who believed he was simply toying with the knight, Robin stepped aside and motioned the way clear. Robin's men lowered their bows and moved aside as well. The party spurred their horses and galloped past.

"We've come a long way to go home empty-handed," groused Little John. By the sounds the others were making, Robin knew the dispositions of all his men were none too merry.

"Come, come, dear fellows. All will be well. Methinks they'll be plenty more pigeons on this road, bound for the king's nuptials. Let's be off and find ourselves a fat merchant or a wealthy lord to rob. Who knoweth, we might even come across a wealthy fat bishop ripe to be plucked."

He wouldn't tell his men, but he didn't want to offend Marian's father, even if he was certain the fellow would never approve of him. Who knew how fate's hand might move her pieces on the morrow.

*

"Is my bride ready, Mother?"

Eleanor, the queen dowager, folded her arms and gave her son a disapproving look.

"Methinks she's too young to be anyone's queen," she said. "She's just a girl. Thou needs a strong woman by thy side to rule."

"She'll be a woman soon enough," replied King John. "She's already a little hellion."

Eleanor sighed. "Why aren't thou more like thy brother was?"

"Thou meanest ol' Richard the Lionheart? Richard, who rebelled against our father and took up arms against him? Richard, who ran off to play knight in the crusades? Richard, who lived in France and actually spent little time in England? Richard, who used the kingdom's treasury to finance his adventures, leaving the realm bankrupt? That brother?"

Eleanor turned away with a contentious grunt. "He was a good boy . . . and a great leader of men--a warrior."

"A warmonger be more like it," hissed John.

Without looking at him she asked, "Then I assume thou art determined to proceed with this wedding?"

"Aye, Mother. Isabella shall be the queen, and that's that."

"Verily, thou be the king. I guess thou gets what thee wants. Never say I didn't warn thee, when some cold night thy puerile queen uses a kitchen knife to chop off thy royal member."

John shuddered at the thought. He was about to chastise his mother for such a foul and distasteful image, but she was already quitting his chamber.

In her stead, materializing from a smoky mist, was the demon Caim. Standing on his bed of coals, he watched the queen dowager storm out.

"Methinks I wouldn't care to meet her in a dark alley," declared the demon. "No wonder thy father locked her in the tower."

"That's not exactly what . . . oh, it doesn't matter. Thou art not here to discuss my family's foibles."

"Nay, that would take an epoch. Why *hath* thou summoned me hither, Your Majesty?"

John didn't care for the inference about his family, nor the tone in which the demon said "Your Majesty." There was something impertinent about it. Yet he didn't want to be sidetracked.

"I want to give my betrothed a wedding present."

"Oh? Was thou thinking of a lovely little doll, or mayhap a miniature tea set?"

"I want to give her France," said John flatly. "And I want thee to get it for me forthwith."

Caim laughed. "And what be the size of thy army?"

"I don't want thee to use an army. I want thee to use magic."

A devious grin formed on the demon's countenance. "As thou commands, my liege." Caim waved his arms over his head and bellowed so loud it reverberated off the stone walls of the chamber. "*Ic agifan ou Galia!*

"Alright, France is thine," said the demon matter-of-factly.

"Just like that?"

"Just like that."

"But how will I hold it? How will I tax it? How will I take my beloved on leisurely trips through Aquitaine and Gascony?"

Caim tugged at the hair on his chin, pretending to mull it over for a moment. "Methinks thou will need--"

"An army," groaned the king.

"Verily thou art wise, sire."

The king whined like a wounded animal.

*

Robin would never have chanced sneaking into Bigod Manor if he didn't knoweth the baron was away at the king's wedding. However, he found his way to Marian's bedchamber without being seen. She was looking out her window. He imagined she was wistfully thinking of him, so he crept up from behind, grabbed her and covered her mouth to mute her scream.

"Oh, Robin. Thou frightened me to the bone."

They embraced and kissed. The fright surely boosted Marian's cupidity, because her kisses were fevered--more passionate than usual.

"I came cross thy family on the road to London," said Robin. "How is it thou art not with them, attending the king's wedding?"

"I feigned sickness so I wouldn't have to go."

"I would think the pomp and pageantry of such an occasion would delight thee."

"Aye, but I despise King John. When I was much younger and went to court, he made lewd advances toward me. I was only a little girl--'twas repugnant. Here, help me with my dress."

Readily Robin complied.

"Thou witnessed my family on the road? Did thou rob them?"

"I assure thee I did no such thing."

"Well 'tis thy trade," she said, pulling off her outer garment and continuing

74

to disrobe. "Is it true what they say about thee, Robin--that thou steals from the rich and gives to the poor?"

"Aye . . . of course there be expenses . . . but yea, to the heart of the matter 'tis true."

"Thou art a good man, Robin Hood. A kind and gentle man who'd be a goodly father for any child."

He wondered straightaway if she were trying to tell him something. But soon she was naked and helping him off with his clothes.

She was certainly being more aggressive than usual, but Robin didn't dwell on that aspect, as more than his suspicions had been raised. She pulled him onto her bed and guided him inside her.

"Oh, Robin. Take me . . . take me away from here. Marry me and I'll go anywhere with thee."

"'Tis not the time to speak of such," said Robin, distracted.

"If thou doesn't marry me, I'll have to marry Baron St. John."

"Verily?" Robin tried to concentrate on the matter at hand, but she wasn't making it easy. "I hear he's a goodly fellow."

"He's ugly and old," she protested. "He must be 30 years."

Robin deemed it best not to mention he was almost of that age himself. Another time mayhap.

"Oh, Robin, I love thee."

Robin appreciated the sentiment, but he would have preferred silence . . . or perchance just a moan or two.

"Dost thou love me?"

"Of course I doest," he responded, though his love, at that moment, was beginning to wilt.

Robin knew he must find another occupation for her mouth or all would be lost.

He pressed his lips against hers, kissing and thrusting, hoping to revive his yearning. Just as he was afraid he might lose the battle, he thought of Daphne. The memory of the wood nymph's wanton innocence stiffened his resolve and he forged onward.

∫

"The penalty for poaching the king's deer is death," said the sheriff.

The man kneeling before him, next to the dead animal pleaded, "Have mercy, my lord. I only ventured into the forest because my children are starving."

"Knave, there can be no mercy for one who defies the king's law."

Robin had watched the scene play out from his treetop perch. But he dared not wait a moment longer. He grabbed hold of a thick vine and swung down, toppling the sheriff with his booted feet. He disarmed him, cut the vine and tied the semi-conscious man with it.

"Take the deer and go feed thy children," said Robin. "I'll make proper recompense with the sheriff."

"Bless thee, goodly sir, bless thee."

"I'm no knight, so no 'sir' for me. If thou art asked who came to thy rescue, speak of Robin Hood."

The man's look of recognition confirmed he'd heard the name. He slung the deer over his shoulders and was off.

Robin stood over the sheriff. The fellow had a dueling scar above his left brow and Robin considered returning his sword to him to see what he was made of. But the prince of thieves had other things on his mind at the moment.

"So thy law says the lives of animals are more worthy than the lives of men?"

Groggy as he was, the sheriff growled, "Thou will pay for this affront, Robin Hood."

Robin unsheathed his sword and placed the tip at the sheriff's throat.

"Would thou agree thy life is proper payment for both the affront and the deer?"

Without much hesitation, the sheriff replied, "Aye."

Robin helped the fellow to his feet and swatted his arse with the flat of his sword. "Then be off with thee."

The sheriff hobbled down the path as fast as he could go with his arms still tied behind him.

Robin would have laughed at the sight, but he was in no mood for merriment. Though he had no interest in marriage, Marian's plight concerned him. He could let her marry Baron St. John and live the rest of his days as an outlaw and vagabond. Or he could use the treasure he'd hidden away and make a change in his life. Alas, he wasn't sure he wanted to change. He liked being an outlaw. He liked the occasional romp with a willing maid. He even liked living in the forest, though his back could use a proper bed.

Entwined by his thoughts, and the choices facing him, Robin found he could think of naught but Marian, and saving her from the fate she dreaded so much.

"What weighs upon thee, fair Robin?"

He looked up to see his winsome wood nymph high in the tree above. The mere sight of her comely form stirred his manhood. Before he could speak she dove towards the ground head-first, flipping in mid-air, and landing on her feet as softly as a fallen leaf.

Her aerial ballet astounded but did not slow him. He didn't wait for an invitation to take her in his arms.

"Daphne, I've thought of naught but thee since we last departed."

She looked at him quizzically. "Verily? Was it I that furrowed thy brow this moment? If so, I shall be gone and worry thee no more."

"Nay, nay. Forsooth, there art other travails which plague me."

"Tell me of thy woes."

"I must decide whether or not to marry. It would mean leaving the forest I love so dearly."

"All things in nature should have a mate with which they produce offspring."

"Then let thou be my mate, lovely Daphne. Together we would create the most exquisite children."

"Nay, for thou and I can give no life to progeny. We are not the same."

"Yet I can love thee . . . drive thee to passionate frenzy."

"But there can be no issue from our love, no matter the fervor."

Robin released her and turned away, lowering his head.

"Be not sorrowful, my Robin. Whether thou choosest to marry, whether or not thee fathers children, thy legend will live for a thousand years. All manner of tales will be told, and over time, many men will take thy name, though not all so selfless as thee."

Robin wasn't feeling so selfless at the moment. He wanted Daphne, but he also wanted Marian and the forest and a comfortable bed and the kind of life his hidden riches could buy.

"Dost thou knowest what thee wants?"

Robin shook off the doldrums of his worries and took the wood nymph in his arms again.

"I want thee."

Without another word they proceeded to make love there in the forest. Robin found his nymph to be every bit as ardent and withy as in their previous encounter. If he was enchanted, he didn't ever want the spell to end.

He buried his face in her bountiful breasts, lost himself in the sight of her ample posterior, let his fingers dance across her satiny thighs, and found refuge in her mossy cavern.

Soon enough to marry ol' what's-her-name.

15 Years Later

The selling of lands and titles by the monarchy was common practice, but after the turn of the century, King John became desperate for coin to finance his continuing war with France. Desperate enough to deal with the famous outlaw Robin Hood. Robin had decided to use his ill-gotten gains to become respectable and settle down with Marian. Shortly after the king's marriage to Isabella, Robin and John came to an agreement. Robin would forswear his outlaw activities and King John would receive the treasure Robin had hidden away in Sherwood Forest--no questions asked as to its origin. Thus Robin became Sir Robert, otherwise known as Ralph fitz Robert, Lord of Middleham.

Now, more than a decade after this compromise, Robin and Marian were married, with the grudging consent of her father . . . facilitated by a bit of royal prodding. They still had no children, but that didn't dissuade Robin from continuing to try. Alas, Robin found married life tedious and uneventful. Marian, or Lady Mary as she liked to be called these days, was rarely enthusiastic about joining him in the bedchamber, let alone the forest. It seemed, even though he'd given up everything for her, it would never be enough. She seemed determined to find fault with him, no matter what divine leap of logic it required. Her days were filled with bedighting their manor with all forms of trumpery--a touchstone of nobility he assumed.

Robin oft longed for the simple days of yore, and would, at times, call forth his retainers, John Little, Will Scarlok, and Alan Adale to venture back to Sherwood Forest. There they would regale each other with stories of deeds and debauchery from a time bygone. Still, sometimes Robin's mood turned dark.

"'Tis time all of thee returned to the manor," said Robin abruptly. "I want to be alone for the nonce."

"Alright, Sir Robert," responded Little John.

"What did I tell thee?" said Robin gruffly. "In this forest I'm just Robin, not Sir Robert."

"Sorry, Robin. Force of habit."

"Well go on now. Get thee back to the manor and see to thy duties. I'll be along presently."

When they were gone, Robin wandered into the woods, searching the trees as he'd done oft times over the years. But never, since he'd become betrothed to Marian, had he found his nymph. Despite his failure, he kept trying.

78

"Daphne . . . oh, Daphne . . . 'tis I, thy Robin Hood. Whither art thou, dearest Daphne?"

He kept expecting her to appear, wishing to hear the lyrical timbre of her words, longing to feel the softness of her touch.

"The hair of my head may have thinned and my stomach swelled, but 'tis I, thy Robin. Come to me, fair Daphne. Show thyself."

Alas, only the hollow sound of his own voice retreating through the trees greeted him. Until . . . .

"Don't reach for thy sword, my lord. If thou doest, thee will find a shaft or two sprouting from thy body."

'Twas a trio of very young men, two with bows drawn and aimed at him. The one who spoke had a dagger in his hand and a cocky smile on his face.

"Give us thy purse, thy boots, and that jewel-hilted blade of thine, and I'll set thee free to live another day."

"Who, may I inquire, be thee?" asked Robin, holding his ground.

The lad sheathed his dagger, put his hands jauntily on his hips, and replied, "I am Robin Hood, prince of thieves, Lord of Sherwood Forest."

Robin curtailed the smile longing to grace his visage. "So thou art the famous Robin Hood, are thee. I would have thought thee to be much older."

His namesake didn't care for such a comment, and a scowl took the place of his smirk.

"If thou art wise, thee won't trifle with us," blustered the lad, adding, "I'm older than I look."

Robin raised his hands in mock surrender. "I would never trifle with the great Robin Hood. Tell me, is it true thou robs only the rich, in order to give to the poor?"

"Yea . . . sure . . . that be what I doest. Now, hand it over--sword first."

Robin unsheathed his sword so quickly, the three would-be robbers took a step back. Robin granted himself a chuckle, then offered the sword, hilt first, to their leader.

"Sorry to say, but the gem on the hilt is not exactly a jewel. Only a bit of quartz I had the smithee work into it."

Before the lad could reach for the sword, John Little and his compatriots rode into the clearing, their horses' hooves pounding in warning.

The trio of bandits quit the field in a sprint.

"What art thou doing back here?" asked Robin.

"We came across a messenger from the lady Mary," said Little John. "She's in a boil for certain. Says if thou doesn't make haste, she and thou will be tardy for the signing ceremony."

Robin thought for a moment. "Yea, the great charter the barons are forcing on King John."

"Come, Robin. We'll take thee back to thy horse," said Little John. "I don't want to be the knave upon which Lady Mary focuses her wrath."

"Thou and I both."

*

King John worried at his fingernails as he paced the parapet's length atop Windsor Castle. He stopped his pacing and looked southward. He couldn't see past the trees, but he knew the barons were gathering on the field at Runnymeade, waiting for his capitulation. Some of his staunchest supporters had joined the rebels. Even the loyal Sir William Marshal, who'd remained true to the crown, had advised him to give in to the rebel demands and make peace . . . for the good of England.

"For the good of England." John spit the words from his mouth and continued pacing. "I *am* England. Is this great charter good for me? Nay, 'tis not."

There was only one thing he might try--a last resort to avoid signing this document--black magic. He'd brought the book with him to the castle's highest vantage, hoping the demon would fly directly to him.

"*Lirach tasa vefa wehlic, Caim.*" It had been many years since he'd last summoned the demon, but he was desperate. "Magic forces dark and light, reach out both day and night. Be he far or be he near, summon the demon Caim right here!"

He waited . . . and waited . . . and waited, yet the demon did not appear.

"That damn demon was never any good anyway," mumbled John. "He never wanted to use his magic. He always had some excuse. All he ever did was give me scitte for not being ruthless enough, regal enough. I know naught why I bothered . . . ."

The king's tirade ended when a profusion of fowl excrement splattered across his royal robe. He looked up and spied a blackbird overhead, squawking and screeching as it passed.

*

Robin and Marian (Sir Robert and Lady Mary) stood on the outskirts of the field with the other nobles who'd gathered to witness the signing of the great charter. More than a score of barons stood round a table set in the center of the

80

field. Among them were Marian's father, Sir Roger Bigod, and her brother Hugh (who'd married Maud Marshal), as well as Baron William St. John, who found salve for his wounded pride over losing Marian by marrying one Godechild de Paganel, a buxom blonde whom Robin had the occasion to bed long before he met Marian.

At the table, surrounded by the barons, was King John. He looked none too happy. Robin had gotten the chance to meet the king at several royal gatherings, and found he wasn't a bad fellow . . . for a king. He wondered how history would portray him. Not well he guessed.

The proclamation King John was about to sign was refuted to set forth a new set of laws that would dispense justice more forthrightly for the people of England. Alas, Robin had read the document, and, in truth, it protected the barons, the earls, the landowners, the clergy . . . but not so much the common man. It promised limits on taxation, protection of church rights, and swift justice for so-called "free men," yet naught for the serfs and bondsmen.

'Twas just one more piece of parchment as far as Robin was concerned. Yet another treaty, another covenant, to be broken when divine direction or Norman convenience intervened. Until then, he would place his trust in gold and silver, keep counsel with sword and bow, and plow the mossy fields of willing maids . . . whenever Marian wasn't looking.

f

By all accounts, the legend of Robin is just that. While there are many stories, from different eras, of a Robert Hood, a Robert de Locksley, a Robyn Hode, and many varying tales of his exploits, there is no definitive proof that Robin Hood, the taker from the rich/giver to the poor, ever existed. However, all of the "noble" characters portrayed here (except Marian) were historical figures that I'm a direct descendant of, including King John and Sir Roger Bigod, whose family lines would intersect more than 300 years after the signing of the Magna Carta, under the family name Conyers. Roger Bigod did have a daughter named Mary, who wed a lord named Ralph fitz Robert, but who can say if she was ever called Marian.

Red Indian

His interest in the New World was more than just financial. As of yet, his investment in the Virginia Company's Jamestown colony had not yielded a penny of profit, unlike his more lucrative investment in the East India Company. But this unexplored continent to the west was full of promise and mystery, and that intrigued Calvert more than coin--though he was certain, in time, there was plenty to be gained monetarily.

As part of his duties as secretary of state, he'd read all the reports sent to the king from John Guy, governor of the first English settlement of what they called "Newfoundland"--a very unimaginative name he thought. There were hardships, as there were with any new colony, but Calvert never let that deter him. He was more interested in long-term potential.

He'd invited William Vaughan to Whitehall, having heard he was looking to sell his investment in this new land. He knew Vaughan from his days at Oxford, where they were fellow students. Vaughan had been a year ahead of him, and a chance meeting had led to the Welshman shepherding Calvert around the school his first few weeks.

Vaughan had been very scholarly, but a bit of a dreamer whose dreams were not always practical. He often complained bitterly about the poverty in his homeland, and Calvert got the sense from his writings that he felt it was his duty to, one day, do something about it. Being from Wales was not something most students bragged about. But, despite the penury of his countrymen, Vaughan had always been a proud Welshman, and Calvert admired him for it. He'd even named his colony in Newfoundland "New Cambriol," from the ancient name for Wales. From what he knew of the man, Calvert speculated Vaughan saw himself as the Welsh Moses, who would lead his people from poverty and oppression to the promised land of the New World.

Vaughan had always had a literary bent as well--a good writer who'd helped Calvert with his papers. Two decades earlier, not long after he'd left Oxford, he'd published a book that Calvert had made a point to read. *The Golden Grove* was a general guide to the morals, politics, and literature of the time, being highly critical of each. It praised poetry, but denounced current plays, even those of master Shakespeare, as folly and wickedness.

Despite his success as a scholar, a lawyer, a writer, and investor, Vaughan had known much tragedy. In tracking the man down, Calvert had learned Vaughan's son had died as a toddler, and soon after that his wife was struck and killed by a bolt of lightning. Yet he'd persevered. That's the way Calvert remembered him from their days at Oxford. As a fellow who always persevered, no matter the obstacles.

That's why he wondered what had influenced the man to part with his interests in the New World. Calvert was as curious as he was anxious to purchase a piece of Newfoundland for himself.

"Your lordship, William Vaughan Esquire awaits an audience," announced Calvert's secretary.

"Show him in, show him in."

The William Vaughan who walked apprehensively into his office was not the one he remembered from Oxford. He was not only decades older, he'd grown paper-thin, his clothes rumpled and threadbare for a man of his station. A doleful look clouded his eyes, and his posture spoke of apathy, as if there were no fight left in him. The tenacious Welshman Calvert had known was gone.

"Thou summoned me, your lordship?"

"Come, come, my good man. Call me George as thee used to. None of this *lordship* nonsense," said Calvert, coming forward to grasp Vaughan's hand. "And I did not 'summon' thee. I requested thy presence on a matter of business."

"What business could I have with the king's secretary of state?" asked Vaughan, concern coloring his voice.

"Come--sit down and we will discuss it. Would thee like a glass of sherry?"

"I beg pardon?"

"I say sherry--would thee like a glass of sherry?"

"My apologies. I hear not as well as I used to. Yes, yes, sherry would be nice."

Calvert wondered why his old acquaintance seemed so ill at ease. Possibly he'd had problems with government officials in the past. Or he was simply suspicious of the motives behind this belated reunion. Calvert intended to promptly alleviate any misconceptions he might have.

He handed the sherry to Vaughan.

"I'll get right to it. I understand thou art looking to sell thy interests in Newfoundland. Is that true?"

"'Tis true, though, to be honest, I cannot, in good conscience, recommend it as promising investment."

"Not a very strong stance for a negotiation, my friend," said Calvert. "Why would thee say such?"

Vaughan cleared his throat and took a sip of the sherry. "Because we are old friends and I want to be honest with thee."

"I appreciate that, William. But, pray tell, why would thee discourage such an investment. I believe the New World to be full of auspicious opportunities."

"I believed the same . . . until I actually visited my colony of New Cambriol."

"Oh? I was not aware thee had actually set foot there."

"Yes, I have been there . . . much to my regret," replied Vaughan. His eyes darkened as if haunted by the memory. "That is why I speak naught of it, and few know of my journey . . . my ordeal."

"I know establishing a new settlement can be fraught with hazards, but surely it could not have been all that bad."

Vaughan let out a laugh that was part cackle, part cough. "I thought the same thing when I got the initial reports from Captain Richard Whitbourne, whom I sent there to take charge after the first settlers reported problems. Then, ere I left for the colony myself, I went to visit John Guy, whom the London and Bristol Company had lead their first attempts at colonization."

"Yes, I know of him."

"Well, his wife would not let me in to see him, because he had taken ill. But as I was leaving she ventured out her door, and in a curious whisper told me that for many years after his return to England, Guy would wake up screaming in the middle of the night. And each time she would have to convince him he was no longer in Newfoundland.

"Of course I dismissed her words as the prattling of an old woman, but now I know different. I know what incites the nightmares of John Guy. I experience them myself, from time to time."

Calvert was more intrigued than ever to learn what had happened to the man. He didn't remember his old school chum being so dramatic, but time had a way of changing people.

"Come, come. Enough preamble. Tell me why I should not invest in Newfoundland."

"Well, first, there are the pirate raids. Spanish pirates, French pirates, even deserters from Sir Walter Raleigh's Guiana fleet. Mongrels all, they harry our coasts, steal our livestock, raid our fishing vessels."

"I am aware of these brigands and have spoken to King James about dealing with them," said Calvert.

"The weather is also a major problem. The winters are longer and more harsh than thee can believe. What crops will grow in the rocky soil are stunted by the late spring and short summer. Fishing is the only industry which could thrive there, but . . . ."

Vaughan shrugged and took another sip of his sherry.

"Tell me about the natives," said Calvert, encouraging him to continue. "What about these 'red Indians' I have heard of. Is it true their skin is the color of blood?"

Vaughan hesitated, then shook his head. "No, but it might as well be."

Calvert wondered what he meant by that remark.

"'Tis not their skin which is red," continued Vaughan, "but a combination of a powdered red ochre mixed with fish oil or animal grease they cover themselves with. I believe the coloring began as an insect repellant, but among the Beothuk the red color hath become sacred, with much cultural significance. They paint their canoes with it, their weapons, even their newborn children as a way of welcoming them to the tribe."

"How are relations with these Beothuk?"

"Not cordial. The language barrier is a problem. There have been attacks . . . thefts."

"Jamestown hath dealt with similar issues," said Calvert. "But they have been able to establish friendly relations with their natives, and even trade."

"In the beginning there was a bit of trade, but relations soured when one of the settlers occupied himself with a native girl. Whether 'twas consensual or forced mattered not to the Beothuk. They attacked the settlement. They were rebuffed, but since that incident relations were all but severed."

Calvert stood and paced behind his desk. Vaughan took another drink and Calvert refilled his glass.

"I understand why thee would warn me, and I appreciate thy candor, William. But all that thou hath relayed to me is simply the cost of doing business. The normal hazards of exploration and colonization. I see no reason why thee and I should not be able to agree upon a fair price, and--"

"There's something else," said Vaughan, then looked as if he regretted his words.

"Well, what is it, man?"

"Thou will not believe me. Thou will think I am mad." He laughed. "Indeed I would be mad if I expected thy belief. At first I rejected the evidence of my own senses. Then I doubted my sanity, as thee will. I even considered that I had been dreaming. But I was awake, my senses were sharp, and I am as sane as the next man, if now more wary."

"Tell me," said Calvert, intrigued more than ever. "I'll believe thee."

Vaughan hesitated, took another sip of sherry, and began his tale.

"'Twas my third night in New Cambriol. I was staying in the settlement I had named Vaughan's Cove. 'Twas only late autumn, but the weather had already turned bitterly cold. The wind upon that hill was like shards of ice cutting into our skin, and the stone structures in which we slept were as dank as tombs.

"We were settling for the night when we heard a scream so awful from outside it sent even greater chills through us. We looked at each other, then heard another, more muddled shriek. The men grabbed their muskets, I clutched a torch, and we rushed outside in search of the poor soul whose cry we had heard. We did not have to go far.

"One of the men, who had likely gone outside to relieve himself, lay across a hillock, his torso in bloody shreds. At first I could not see it, but I sensed the darkness around him was alive. Then the torchlight struck it and we all caught a glimmer of what would beset our nightmares from then on.

"Crouched over the fellow, who was surely dead, was this . . . this thing. Vaguely human in shape, emaciated but larger than any man I had ever seen. I watched as it tore the flesh from its victim and devoured it.

"Transfixed by the sight, each of us stood as frozen as the ground beneath our feet. Until it turned and saw us. With an ear-shattering roar it stood, growing larger as it did. It must have been at least ten feet tall, with enormous fangs. Mangy strands of silver-gray hair sprouted here and there from its body, but the rest of its skin was lathered with ice crystals."

Vaughan paused, glancing at his host.

"I see the look on thy face, George. I recognize the expression of disbelief. But I swear to thee we all witnessed this monster."

Incredulous though he might have been, Calvert was entranced by the tale.

"Go on. What happened next?"

"The men opened fire with their muskets. Having been struck by at least a half dozen balls, the thing fell to the earth. The men began to reload, but ere they could, this demon from hell stood as if fully resurrected and gave voice to a wail so potent we fell to our knees, covering our ears. Even dulled by our hands, the sound created such pain as thee cannot imagine.

"Though we were at its mercy, it did not attack. Instead it scooped up the remains of its victim and vanished into the night. Reloaded, we gave pursuit, but found no sign of the creature. We climbed a ridge and came upon a large pond where a group of Beothuk had gathered. By their fearful expressions, I knew they had seen the demon as well. Using hand signs we tried to ask them about the creature, but their replies were beyond our grasp. They were so agitated I knew not whether they were warning us about the monster, or threatening us with its return. The one word they kept repeating was *Chenoo--Chenoo*. I gathered that was what they called the thing.

"We returned to our shelter, shaken from the experience as thee might guess. Most of the men, including myself, were still plagued by a ringing in our ears. We posted guards, but I doubt anyone slept very well that night. The next day I went directly to see Oubee, the Beothuk girl who had been staying with the settlers. After her assignation with one of the men, she had become an outcast from her tribe. She had learned a few words of English, so I was able to question her to some degree. She told me that, indeed, the monster was called *Chenoo*. Her people believed it had once been a human being--someone who had committed a terrible act and become possessed by evil spirits. Its heart had turned to ice, and 'twas cursed to forever roam the land as the behemoth we had seen. What she could not tell me, was why it had appeared now, at this time. She did not say the words, but I think she believed 'twas because of my own arrival in New Cambriol."

Calvert's first thought, as Vaughan paused his story to take another drink, was his memory of how good a writer his old friend always was. A yarn such as this was certainly within his capacity. And yet the way he told it was so authentic. Calvert heard the dread in his voice, the trepidation with which he relayed it.

"The next night it came again. This time neither musket nor arquebus slowed it. It howled until our ears felt as if they would burst. Men scattered to reload despite their weapons' ineffectiveness. Then, for some reason, the *Chenoo* focused on me. I saw the malevolent hunger in its eyes, but was immobile with fear. It came at me. In that moment I resigned myself to a gruesome death.

"From my left, someone doused the monster with whale oil. A torch was tossed and flames erupted from its back. The *Chenoo* screeched as though 'twas dying. It was not. It turned hence from me and fled into the night. Yet on its way it seized another man who tried to brain it with his musket.

"We never found the fellow, nor any remnants of his existence."

87

Vaughan looked at Calvert, gauging his reaction. The king's secretary was both terrified and enthralled. He spoke not, only waited for Vaughan to continue.

"It took not long afterwards for me to realize 'twas the end of New Cambriol. Even if the ice creature had burned to ash--and many amongst us doubted it--I knew no one who had seen it would ever rest easy anywhere in Newfoundland. If I had not declared we were returning to England, I am certain Captain Whitbourne and his men would have marooned me there.

"We spent the next day making preparations to leave. As night began to fall, I sensed the fear amongst us growing. 'Twas a tangible thing, oppressive in its weight. Come dark we gathered inside the largest shelter, barricading the door as well we might. 'Twas for naught. The *Chenoo* came once more.

"It pounded and clawed at the door, soon ripping it from its posts, sending stones from the wall flying like round shot. There was not a burn mark upon it. If indeed it had ever burned, it had healed all but its anger, for it came with a vengeance. Ignoring the musket shots which must have stung it, it waded through us like a scythe through wheat. Men were flung like dolls. Those who could escape through the portal that had been the door ran for their lives. Others tried to hide or play dead. The *Chenoo* roared and I fell to the ground in pain, covering my ears. When I looked up I saw the monster had grabbed hold of Oubee. She screamed but I heard it not. I had gone deaf."

Vaughan paused, looked down at the floor, then up into the eyes of his old friend. "I swear to thee, George, if thee doth not already think me mad, what happened next was even more preposterous than the monster itself. Whether 'twas the *Chenoo*'s abduction of the girl Oubee or God's own hand I cannot say. But there appeared before the *Chenoo*, blocking its path, a scarlet specter. I say specter because this apparition, this ghost, though it seemed substantial in every way, drifted more than walked as it moved. It revealed itself, in every aspect of its features, to be a native of the land. Its face, its costume, its hair, even its red coloring rendered it one of the Beothuk tribe. Yet the red tint was not simply ochre grease spread along its skin. The crimson hue was complete, coloring everything from its bare feet to its clothing to its eyes. I knew immediately 'twas no mortal man.

"When it blocked the *Chenoo's* way, the monster tossed aside its captive. The girl fell, stunned but alive. She stared up in horror as the new player on this otherworldly stage grappled with the much larger *Chenoo*. Their strength seemed evenly matched until the red man, in the blink of an eye, swung round, attached itself to the monster's back, wrapping its forearm under the Chenoo's neck. The ice creature's wail was cut short as the apparition jerked its head, apparently breaking its neck. The *Chenoo* fell to ground. Its slayer floated back to the earth.

"I stood there, as thee might imagine, unable to reconcile what I had seen, let alone speak. The apparition looked at me, and the gaze was not a welcoming one. Then it vanished. Dissipated like red smoke in the wind.

"We left the next day. Oubee came with us, though she was silent for days. When the terror lifted from her soul I was finally able to question her about the scarlet ghost. She told me he was *Kluskap*, the legendary hero of her people, sworn to protect them, even in death.

"I doubt not 'twas Oubee this *Kluskap* was protecting--not I nor my men. Just as I am certain the *Chenoo* would have returned, despite its apparent demise, had we not departed New Cambriol in all haste."

Vaughan paused, took a breath that was part sigh, sipped his sherry and set down his glass. He stood to leave.

"So thee can see, my old friend, why neither thee nor anyone should want to purchase New Cambriol from me. Thou hath already done well for thyself. Thou hath been knighted, made secretary of state to the king, and 'tis said thou art one of the most powerful men in England. Is that not enough? If thou must, seek fortune and adventure at Jamestown. For I have heard of no monsters there."

It was a harrowing tale, and Calvert had no doubt Vaughan believed every word of it. The dispirited gloom in his eyes was no literary fabrication. The horror which had touched his soul was no lie.

Nonetheless, the essence of it had to be a figment of the man's imagination-- a dark figment to be sure. Whether it was the death of his child, or that of his wife, or something even more grievous that had befallen him, Calvert knew not. But he knew the man's psyche had been damaged by something. He also knew Vaughan's finances were in dire straits. He needed to sell at least a portion of his Newfoundland investment in order to return to Wales with some modicum of stability.

"Old friend, I understand and appreciate thy reluctance to sell me thy interests in Newfoundland, but I am determined to gain a foothold in the New World, *Chenoo* or *Kluskap* be damned. Now I need not acquire thy entire holdings, but surely we can come to some arrangement regarding a portion of it."

Vaughan did not reply. He simply shook his head slowly side to side as if he'd done all he could. Then he sat back down, waiting for Sir Calvert to begin the negotiations.

/

In that year, 1621, Sir George Calvert did purchase a portion of William Vaughan's interests in Newfoundland, and gave the peninsula its current name--Avalon. Yet his two attempts to colonize Newfoundland also failed, due to what he described as "a winter which lasts from October to May," as well as pirates, a war with France, and his policy of religious tolerance for all colonists--which did not sit well with the protestant majority. Eventually giving up on Newfoundland, Calvert did as Vaughan suggested in this tale, turning his attention to Jamestown, and later to colonizing the territory that would become known as Maryland.

Sir William Vaughan (knighted in 1628) retained possession of one small portion of Avalon, but made no further attempts at colonization. Yet he wrote about Newfoundland in a fanciful book he titled The Golden Fleece. *Vaughan spent the rest of his life in Wales, where he remarried and fathered six children.*

Word of the Beothuk tribe's use of red ochre to color their bodies spread to Europe, where they began to call all Native Americans "Red Indians," a designation which would last for centuries.

While the preponderance of this story is based upon historical fact, there is a speculative element. There is no official record of a Kluskap *or* Chenoo. *They are folk legends of the native peoples of Newfoundland. However, there is a ridge with a pond near Vaughan's failed colony which still, today, carries the name of Hell Hill.*

In a case of truth being stranger than fiction, a direct descendant of William Vaughan, one Stephen Gregory Vaughn, would encounter the author of this tale, a direct descendant of George Calvert, more than 300 years later, more than 3,000 miles west of Newfoundland, at Horace Mann Junior High School, in San Diego, California, beginning a friendship that would last a lifetime.

Crossroads

1908

"Come on, kiddo," urged Johnny, "come into town with us. Joe rented this little flivver, and we're gonna raise some hell in Galveston--maybe meet us some real peacherinos."

"I don't know, guys. We got a game tomorrow, and I gotta--"

"There's always a game tomorrow. You gotta live a little, Eddie."

That was easy for him to say, thought Ed. He and Joe were established ballplayers--confident and carefree. They'd played in the last two World Series. They weren't taking one last shot to make the big club like he was. He'd either make the Cubs roster or return home to Missouri. He'd promised himself that already. He didn't exactly know what he'd do when he got there, but he was 26--too old to be playing a kid's game for peanuts in the minors. If he didn't make the major league club this spring, he'd hang up his spikes and find a real job so he could start a family.

"There's this wiz of a fortune teller you gotta see too," added Joe. "I saw her last spring training and she was a real humdinger. Predicted what kind of season I would have."

"Was she right?"

"She was dead-on," said Joe with an unusually serious look. "She told me I was gonna miss the first part of the season and I laughed at her. Then *bam*, two days later I got appendicitis."

"She didn't even know we were ballplayers, and she predicted we were gonna win the World Series," said Johnny. "Hell if she wasn't right."

Ed's future was so uncertain, he couldn't deny his curiosity, even though he didn't believe in such superstitious nonsense. Besides, he'd only been in a horseless carriage once before and wanted to try it again.

"Alright," said Ed, "I'll go."

"Let's skiddoo then!"

/

They passed through Galveston proper to a seedy-looking neighborhood on the edge of town. After Joe parked the flivver and turned off the engine, Ed heard a mutt barking. He looked around, ignoring the foul odor blowing in from somewhere.

A faded sign read, *Madam Rekourda Fortunes Told*. It hung over the entrance to a little shop squeezed in between a sleazy-looking tavern and a giant warehouse.

"This is the place," said Johnny. "Come on, kiddo, don't be afraid."

Ed wasn't afraid, not really. But he didn't care for the way Johnny always called him *kiddo*. After all, he was the same age as both of them, and they were little guys, almost a head shorter than him. But they were established major leaguers, big city boys, and he was just a rube from the minors.

He followed them across the dusty sidewalk and inside the shop. A bell hanging over the door chimed when they opened it. It wasn't what Ed expected. There wasn't much there. A couple of old worn chairs and a sign saying, *Readings 50 Cents*.

They didn't have to wait long before a woman pushed aside the heavy burgundy curtains separating the front of the shop from the back and stepped out.

"May I help you?" she asked. "Read your palms, divine your fortunes?"

She was an older woman, though Ed couldn't pinpoint her age. She wore no lipstick, but her eyes were lined in black, matching her hair. A purple scarf wound about her head, along with some copper bangles shaped like coins. In her ears were matching copper hoops bigger than a baseball that shimmered like shiny new pennies. She wore a colorful peasant dress, but her feet were bare.

"Yeah, Madam Rekourda," said Joe enthusiastically. "We were here last year, and you knew I was gonna get sick and miss the opener, but that we'd win the series."

"I do my best," she said, bowing her head ever-so-slightly. "I trust you are recovered from your illness."

"Oh yeah, I'm great," said Joe. "We wanted to see what you got to say about this season."

"Let's let Eddie go first," said Johnny.

Ed balked. "That's okay, guys, I don't . . . ." He tried to decline, but his teammates were already pushing him forward.

"Follow me," said the fortune teller, turning and parting the curtains.

Ed followed.

The back room stood in contrast to the front of the shop. The light was dim, but a vibrant rug covered the floor and bright tapestries the walls. In the center was an ornate table that looked to be carved from a giant emerald, though Ed knew that wasn't possible. On the table was a glass ball the size of a cantaloupe, situated in a brass setting with four legs cast like eagle talons. The air smelled vaguely of sage and stale perfume.

"Sit," she said, gesturing to one of the two simple wooden chairs on opposite sides of the table.

Sitting across from him, she took his left hand, studied it earnestly, and ran her fingers over the lines that mapped it.

"A crossroads, a life-changing decision is forthcoming," she said. "I cannot say what you will choose, but I see it will be the correct choice. I see you carrying a message to someone . . . no, I see hundreds of messages, thousands. You will marry and have many children. Your lifeline is fair, it's . . . ."

Abruptly she stopped. Ed saw the concern on her face, the surprise, like she was fooled by a curveball.

"What is it?"

"I am not certain. It's . . . I must look into the crystal."

She held fast to his one hand and placed her other on the crystal ball. She peered into it like she was looking through a peephole. Ed looked too.

Despite the dimness of the room, he saw flecks of luminosity in the glass, distorted movement, but no shapes he recognized. As he stared into it, he heard a steam whistle he figured must have sounded from somewhere outside. He looked up at Madam Rekourda and saw her concern grow to apprehension.

"What is it? What do you see?"

"I see danger. I see . . . you must be wary of railroads. Trains will be your undoing. A train will be the end of you."

"What does that mean--the end of me? Will I make the team? Will I play for the Cubs?"

"I can say no more." She released his hand and collapsed back in her seat as if she'd expended great energy. "That is all. You must go."

It was more mysterious than enlightening, and Ed suspected his teammates might be playing an elaborate trick on him. He reached into his pocket, pulled out two quarters, and started to set them on the table.

"No, I don't want your money," she said almost fearfully, waving him away. "Madam Rekourda does not take payment for ill fortunes. It is bad luck."

"Uh, alright." Ed didn't understand why, if this was part of a prank, she wouldn't take his money. He guessed Joe and Johnny must have already paid her when they set it up.

"How did it go?" asked Johnny when he came out.

"What'd she say?" wondered Joe.

"You know what she said," replied Ed. "Very funny, using the thing about trains."

"What are you talking about?" They both looked befuddled. Ed had to give them credit for the great acting job.

"You wisenheimers told her about the time back in oh-one when I busted my ankle getting off the train," said Ed sourly. It was the bitter memory more than the dirty trick that made him angry.

He had the big club made back in 1901, when he hopped off the train coming back from spring training and broke his ankle. By the time he healed, the Cubs already had other players, and in the years to follow they found even better ones, like Joe Tinker and Johnny Evers, making it that much harder to make the team. For the rest of his career, it seemed like he was always behind in the count. He'd never come close to playing in Chicago again.

"We didn't tell her anything," said Joe. "We don't know anything about you busting your ankle. Johnny and I weren't even on the team in oh-one."

"Well, somebody told you then," responded Ed. "And I don't think it's very funny."

He pushed open the door, heard the little bell chime, and walked outside.

*

On his way to the dugout, the Cubs manager and first baseman, Big Frank Chance, stopped him.

"Golden, I'm starting you at third today. Steinfeldt's down in the locker room puking his guts out. Got food poisoning or something."

That was good news for him. He didn't care where he played these days, as long as he got a chance to be in the lineup. It was the only way to get noticed. Hopefully he could get a couple of big base knocks and make the team as a utility man.

In the dugout Joe, Johnny, and Mordecai, the Cubs' ace, were up on the top steps, watching something. One of them whistled.

"The kid's got some serious heat," said Joe.

"If I could throw that hard, nobody would ever touch me," said Mordecai.

Mordecai Brown was quite a story. Whenever Ed was feeling sorry for himself, or thinking about how his bum ankle had cost him his shot, the thought of Mordecai brought him back to reality.

When he was just a boy, Mordecai lost parts of two fingers on his throwing hand in some farm machinery. Yet he turned what could have been a handicap into an advantage. Somehow, with those mutilated fingers, he threw the most hellacious curveball in baseball, and "Three Finger Brown" had become one of the best hurlers in the game.

Ed walked over to see what they were gawking at, and Big Frank joined them.

"Check out this rook, Skipper," said Mordecai. "He's bringing it. The catcher can barely handle his stuff."

Ed looked at the pitcher warming up. He was an angular mountain of a man, except he still had this fresh-off-the-farm baby face--a boy in a tall, broad-shouldered man's body. He had the longest arms Ed had ever seen. It looked like they'd hang past his knees even if he stood straight up.

Big Frank watched a couple of throws, then stated matter-of-factly, "Kid's name is Walter Johnson. They brought him up late last year. Word is he doesn't throw a curve or a changeup, just the fastball."

"With that kind of gas, he doesn't need anything else," said Mordecai. "It's coming in there like an express train."

"He had seven straight shutouts and a couple of no-hitters in the Idaho State League," said Big Frank.

"That was the Idaho State League," said Johnny. "He's got a live arm, I'll give him that. But this is the bigs. He's a green rookie. I can hit him."

"We'll see," responded Big Frank. "You're gonna have to be quick to catch up with that big train."

That got Ed to thinking about the fortune teller. Joe and Johnny had insisted all night long that they'd had nothing to do with what she'd said. Joke or not, it was kind of eerie hearing this new pitcher called a "train."

Joe saw the frown on Ed's face and nudged him with his elbow. "Don't worry, kiddo. We'll get on base and you knock us in."

Ed smiled confidently, but inside he was anything but.

*

"Tinker to Evers to Chance--a double play!" exclaimed the public address announcer. *"That's the end of the inning."*

Ed hustled in and got his bat. He was due to lead-off the third, and was anxious to get up there. It was a hot day and his palms were sweaty, so he added a little pine tar to the bat's handle. If he was going to catch up with the big righty's fastball, he was going to need a good grip.

After the warm-ups, the umpire motioned him into the batter's box. Ed stepped in, took a couple of swings, and got set--gripping the bat like his life depended on it. He knew his baseball life did.

The tall young pitcher went into his windup and . . . .

So sudden it was like a lightning bolt, the spheroid hummed through the zone and the catcher's glove popped. The ball was by him before he knew it. He wasn't sure he'd even seen it.

"Strike one!" called the umpire.

Ed stepped out of the box and composed himself. Okay, he thought, he's throwing nothing but fastballs, so be ready, sit on the heat, move to the back of the box. He stepped back in, moved as far back in the batter's box as he could, and got into his stance.

The windup . . . the throw . . . he swung and missed.

"Strike two!"

Way late he thought, stepping out of the box. I gotta be quicker.

"Come on, kiddo," called Johnny from the dugout. "You can hit this guy."

"Climb aboard that big train," yelled Mordecai.

"He's nothing but an Idaho farm boy," ranted Johnny, one of the league's best bench jockeys. "He's just a rag-armed cow-kisser. A sheep-lover. He's got nothing."

Ed looked out at the tall rookie pitcher. He didn't seem bothered by Johnny's ragging. His only expression was one of quiet confidence.

Ed got back in the box. He knew he had to cut down on his swing. He choked-up. No practice swings this time. He was ready to go. Ready to pull the trigger. The ball came flying--a bullet shot out of Johnson's hand.

f

Ed struck out all three times against the rookie that day, as Johnson pounded the strike zone for seven shutout innings before being pulled. Despite some *attaboys* for a couple of nice plays in the field, Ed could read the writing on the dugout wall. He was finishing dressing when he got called into the manager's office.

"Sit down, Ed," said Big Frank, taking a seat behind his desk. "I'm sorry to tell you we're gonna have to let you go. It's getting near the end of spring and I've gotta make my final cuts."

Ed nodded. He'd heard the spiel before.

"You're a gamer and you've got a great glove. I know I could play you anywhere, but I don't have a spot for you."

"I understand."

"I know the Sioux City manager," said Big Frank. "I could put in a good word for you there."

Ed shook his head. "I can't go back to A ball, Skipper. I've been doing this too long. I had my shot. It's time I headed home. Maybe marry this gal I met when I played in Colorado. We've been writing letters back and forth."

"What kind of work you thinkin' of doing? Factory work?"

"I don't think so, but I don't rightly know what I'm gonna do. I'm used to working outside after all these years playing ball."

"Maybe farming?"

"My parents were farmers," said Ed. "I don't think that's the life for me. But I'll find something. Something that'll keep me outdoors."

1948

It was a beautiful day outside. A few lazy clouds gave the perfect blue sky some texture, while the sun dried the previous night's rain. The air was clear and clean, and even the old mail truck was running smooth. It seemed to run better when there was a little moisture in the air.

Ed pulled the truck up to the next mailbox. He opened it and put in a pair of letters before driving on to the next one. That was pretty much how his day went--every day--one box after another. But he liked it. He was outdoors, with no one to boss him, smiles greeting him almost everywhere he went. It was the job he chose, the life he chose, and he never regretted it.

It wasn't long before he saw the local ball field up ahead. It was full of kids. Like he often did, he pulled over to take a look. A boy of about ten hit a two-bagger, though Ed grimaced as the youngster slid awkwardly into second. Sliding was an art the kid obviously hadn't perfected yet.

He still loved to watch the game, even though he gave up playing it decades ago. It didn't matter if the players were pros or tiny tots, he loved to spectate, to keep his eyes peeled for young talent. Once in a while, when he had the time, he'd suggest ways the boys could improve their game. Being boys, sometimes they listened and sometimes they didn't.

Of course whenever he watched he couldn't help but remember his own short-lived baseball career. Full of ups and downs it might have been, but it had been a big part of him for many years. He missed the camaraderie of his teammates, the smell of pine tar and chewing tobacco, the droning patter of the vendors, and even the catcalls of the bleacher bums. He'd heard some pretty hilarious barbs in his time. But his time was long gone.

If nothing else, he could say he took his last at bats against Hall of Famer

97

Walter "The Big Train" Johnson. When that tall skinny kid filled out and became baseball's best pitcher, Ed was always proud that if he had to leave the game, finishing against the best was the way to do it.

He checked his watch. He knew he couldn't dawdle for long. He took his responsibilities as a postman seriously, and was proud of it. Delivering the mail was a public trust he'd accepted a long time ago, and neither snow nor rain nor heat nor gloom of night would stop him from doing his job. But today there was no snow, no rain, and it wasn't even that hot. It was a perfect day to be outdoors, driving through the countryside.

He started up the truck and eased away from the field. Before he got going, the engine died. He'd had trouble with it a few days earlier, but it had been fine since.

"Damn!"

It took three tries before it started up again. He'd need to have it looked over by someone who knew more about engines than he did.

The thought reminded him of his son, Bobbie, who was always working on cars, always mechanically inclined. Of his eight children, Bobbie was the only one he hadn't seen in years. He'd joined the Army Air Corps during the war, and was still overseas. According to his last letter, he'd be getting out soon and coming home. Ed figured when he got here it'd be a good occasion for a big family get-together.

He knew he was blessed to have such a large family, a good family, a good wife. He already had a couple of grandkids, and figured more were on the way. He had a good life, but much more to live for . . . much more to come. It didn't matter if he never played a day in the majors. He'd found his place in the world, and that was all that mattered.

He pulled his truck over to the next mailbox, made his delivery and drove on. The engine hesitated as if it might die, but didn't. He turned it back onto the road and headed towards the center of Heyworth. He liked to take care of all the outlying houses and farms first, so he could finish his route closer to home.

He hadn't gone too far when the engine began to sputter again. He pumped the gas pedal, but it didn't do any good. The engine died and he coasted the truck to a bumpy stop. Exasperated, he tried several times to start it again. It wouldn't take. He heard a steam whistle and looked out the passenger window. It was the Illinois Central, coming down the tracks on schedule as usual.

Ed knew its schedule, because he timed his route to avoid having to wait for the long train to pass. He must have dallied watching the kids play ball longer than usual. He'd better get the truck going if he was going to . . . .

Ed looked down and realized the truck had come to rest on the train tracks. He tried starting it again. It coughed and spit like an old man, but it wouldn't start. He threw it into neutral and jumped out. He tried to push it, but the front tires were wedged in the groove of the train tracks. He pushed until his bad knee started to give out. It was just too damn heavy for him. He couldn't budge it. He had to save the mail. He rushed back, desperately trying to start the engine. He kept trying. If only it would start. Just for a few seconds. Long enough to move it a few feet. The train's whistle got louder. They were warning him away. Instead of a whistle, in his head he heard the chime of a little bell. Something he hadn't thought of in 40 years came to him. *A train will be the end of you.* He had to save the mail. He had to get it started. He had to--

Family lore says Edward Lee Golden played professional baseball in the Chicago Cubs organization, and though minor league records for that era are sketchy, there were several professional players in the organization at that time with the last name Golden, whose first names went unrecorded. Whether he ever faced Walter Johnson, or met a fortune teller in Galveston, is pure speculation.

The Chicago Cubs would go on to win the World Series in 1908--their last one to date. "Tinker to Evers to Chance" would become a popular refrain about double-play combinations after a poem about the players was written in 1910. All three, along with Mordecai "Three Finger" Brown and Walter "The Big Train" Johnson, would be inducted into the Baseball Hall of Fame.

Edward Lee Golden died while stubbornly trying to save the mail when his truck got stuck on the tracks, years before his grandson, the author of this tale, was born.

Running in Place

It was an average-looking house on an average-looking block of houses . . . at least from what I knew of homes in this part of the world. It wasn't a large house, or in any way lavish. Grass covered the front yard, which was divided into three sections, separated by a driveway where an automobile was parked and a walkway leading to the front door.

The address was designated by four metallic numbers near the door. I checked them to be certain I had the right location and proceeded up the walkway. I pressed the button next to the door to announce my presence.

The door behind the outer metallic screen opened. Through the screen I could see a woman, looking out at me cautiously, but not with fear. There was nothing particularly remarkable about her. She was of average height, with light brown hair and a slim build. Her eyes, however, attracted me for some reason. They were a striking green color, with a shape and spark of intelligence I immediately found appealing.

"Are you Mary?"

"Yes," she replied, her caution morphing to wariness.

"I called about your room for rent."

Her expression, her manner, changed immediately. She smiled. "Oh yes, Mr. Matheson." She pushed open the screen door. "Come in, come in."

The inside of the home, much as the outside, was in no way ostentatious. It was clean, functional, with a dash of color that was welcoming.

"Let me show you the room," she said, motioning me to follow her. "It was an addition that my . . . well you don't need to know all that."

She'd been about to explain something. I was curious, but said nothing.

She led me through a hall that was more the intersection of four other rooms than a room itself. "Here's where we keep the phone, and that's our only bathroom, so you'd use that. I can give you towels if you need." She proceeded through one of the connecting rooms. "This is my son's room, and back here would be your room. As you can see, it has its own entrance, so you can come in through the side of the house."

It was a fairly large room--larger than I needed for my purposes--with a bed, a dresser, a small desk, and a chair. A window at the rear of the room looked out onto the home's backyard. I walked over to see. Outside was a patchwork of grass and bare earth. Where the yard ended, there was a fence, and behind that a dirt hill rose up to where there was another fence, and, presumably, another home.

"What do you do?"

I'd been looking out the window, not paying attention. "Excuse me?"

"What do you do?" she asked. "What kind of work?"

"I'm a writer."

"Oh." She sounded intrigued. "What do you write?"

"Books, short stories."

"That must be interesting."

I shrugged. "It can be, but most of the time it's work, like any other work."

She didn't look like she believed me. It was a common reaction. I'd learned most people thought writing for a living was somehow glamorous. I'd been the person I was now long enough to know it wasn't.

"What about you? Do you work?" I asked, knowing many women stayed at home while their husbands generated the necessary income.

"Right now just part-time at H&R Block." She shrugged. "Sometimes I babysit or take in ironing. You know--whatever I need to do."

"What kind of work does your husband--"

"Oh, I'm not married," she said, cutting off my question. "I'm divorced." She went on quickly. "I know the room's not much . . . ."

She paused and I quickly said, "I don't need much. Just peace and quiet so I can write."

"Then you'll take it, Mr. Matheson?"

"You can call me Richard. Yes, it'll be fine. The rent is the amount we discussed on the phone?"

She nodded, looking relieved. I suspected she really needed the extra income a renter would provide.

"You can use the kitchen whenever you want--put stuff in the refrigerator."

"Thanks, but I mostly eat out."

"My son's at school during the day, but I'll tell him not to bother you when he comes home. When would you like to move in?"

"Now, if it's okay."

"Sure," she said, a bit surprised.

"I'll go get my things out of my car."

The street was quiet, not a main thoroughfare at all. The neighborhood was void of activity for the moment, and it seemed the perfect little place for me to work and wait. Though waiting was likely the wrong word, since that implied hope. Hope was something I had in short supply. I'd traveled from place to place, person to person, while austere hope had been recast as futility. Yet part of me wouldn't surrender that last vestige of longing, that yearning to return home. It was still there, somewhere deep in my soul, no matter what superficial shell I wore.

⨍

I was busy working on a story, one not unlike my own tale, when Mary's son came home from school. I'd forgotten to close the door separating my room from the rest of the house, and I heard him quite clearly. I was certain he could hear the clattering of my typewriter as well.

He wasn't bothering me, so I continued until I reached a good stopping point. I was reading over what I'd written when I glanced to my right and saw a mop of blond hair, followed by a pair of eyes peeking around the doorway.

I'd stayed pretty much to myself during my first week living in the home, and hadn't spoken with the boy. It was the nature of my itinerant existence not to open any unnecessary dialogue. For his part, I assumed his mother told him to leave me be.

"Hello," I finally said.

He accepted this as permission to enter and took one brave step into my room.

"What'cha typing?"

"A story."

"What kind of story?"

"This one's about a spaceship. Do you know what a spaceship is?"

"Sure," he said as if I'd insulted him. "That's what astronauts use. John Glenn flew around the Earth in a spaceship."

"That's right. My story's kind of like that, only the astronaut in my story travels a very long distance and is stranded on another planet."

"Do you write any other kinds of stories?"

"I write all different kinds. I write westerns, I write about aliens, monsters, ghosts . . . that kind of thing."

"You mean like comic books?"

"A little like that. Have you ever seen the television show *The Twilight Zone?*"

"Sure."

"That's the kind of thing I write."

"I like *The Twilight Zone.*"

"What kind of comic books do you like?"

"Mostly I like the superhero kind." He thought about it and added, "I just read this comic about a Connecticut Yankee who goes back in time to King Arthur's court and changes everything."

"That's a book by Mark Twain."

"Well I read it in a comic book called a *Classic*."

"What do you like besides comic books?"

"I like the *Flintstones*. They're pretty funny."

"Bruce? What are you doing in there?"

His mother appeared at the door.

"Are you bothering Mr. Matheson?" She looked at me for confirmation.

"No, it's okay, Mary. We were just talking about comic books and TV shows."

"Alright, but you'd better leave him to his work now," she said to her son. "You need to go feed Pudgie."

"Okay, bye," he said and was gone in a flash.

I noticed Mary's eye makeup had run a little, and her cheeks were damp.

"Is there something wrong?" I asked.

It took her a second to realize why I'd posed the question. She wiped her face.

"No, no. I just heard on the TV that Marilyn Monroe died."

"Oh? How did she die?"

"They're not sure yet. They found her in her bed."

"Were you a big fan of hers?"

"No, not really. It's just so sad, I couldn't help myself. Well, I'll leave to your work."

I found it intriguing that the death of someone she didn't know, that she wasn't particularly enamored with, would cause such a reaction. Whether it was raw emotion or empathy, I couldn't be sure, but I regarded her tears as strangely admirable. Either it was the trait of a single individual, or humanity had come even further than I'd thought. I surmised it was more likely the former.

*

The days, the weeks, passed as slowly as all those preceding them, but my time in Mary's house was agreeable, if uneventful. I'd overheard a phone conversation in which she told a friend she was "so grateful" I'd rented her room and stayed for as long as I had, because she needed the money to "make

103

ends meet." It gave me a pleasant feeling to help her make her ends meet, though my longing to return home was ever-present.

I knew that longing was a double-edged sword. What would await me if I ever did return was an unknown. It had been so long. Would my transgressions have been forgiven by now, or was I still a pariah?

The idea, the probability I'd never go home--that I'd never be found--I buried deep in my subconscious. All I could do was carry on. My continued existence, my protean nature, by necessity, infringed upon the existence of others. Yet all I'd ever done was what was required to survive. I was no different than any man who takes the life of an animal for food, or strips its fur to endure a deadly winter.

I'd never taken a life, never trespassed too long in one place--against one individual. I kept moving, ghostlike, from incarnation to incarnation. Impermanence was more than my lifestyle--it was my mantra. I tried to select those whose lives would be least disrupted . . . though that wasn't always possible. I convinced myself it was all in the name of self-preservation. I was only doing what any being would do. Still, the guilt, the echoes of so many ids, never completely deserted me.

I got up from my chair to stretch and walked outside. The sky had turned gray, and the wind carried the promise of rain. I could smell the imminent precipitation.

I heard the boy in the backyard, so I thought I'd see what he was doing. Before I rounded the corner of the house to look for him, his voice called out in surprise.

"Spooky? Spooky, it *is* you!"

I saw him crouched over a cat, stroking it lovingly. I knew he had a dog and a couple of other cats, but this one's fur was entirely black. Distinctive as it was, its body was scrawny, its fur ragged in patches. I knew I'd never seen it before, but there was something about it . . . something familiar. Not in a visual sense, but the sensation was there . . . a vague notion I couldn't define.

"Where've you been?" said Bruce to the cat.

"I take it this is a reunion."

He looked up at me and nodded. "Spooky's been gone a long time--more than a year. I thought he was . . . well I thought I'd never see him again."

I was not that familiar with the species, but it certainly seemed to know the boy and was enjoying the affection it was receiving.

"How do you know it's him?" I wondered. "I've seen many black cats."

104

"It's him alright," said Bruce. "Look at the tear in his ear. He got that fighting another cat a long time ago."

Indeed a piece of the cat's left ear was torn and folded outward.

"He looks pretty old."

He thought about it and said, "I think he's only about four or five now. I don't know his exact birthday, because he showed up at our door on Halloween one year when he was still a kitten. We couldn't ever find out where he came from, so Mom let me keep him. I was going to name him Halloween, but Mom said Spooky was a better kind of Halloween name."

Mary walked out into the backyard at that moment with their dog, Pudgie.

"Is that Spooky?" She was as surprised as her son had been.

"Yeah, Mom. Look at his ear."

As if in confirmation, the chubby old dog waddled over to the cat, wagging its tail. The cat hesitated, looked like it might bolt from the canine, but its manner suddenly modified, and it rubbed against the dog in greeting.

"I'll be darned," she said. "I can't believe he's back after all this time. He looks all skin and bones. You'd better take him and give him some food and water."

"Alright," said Bruce, picking up the cat and taking him away. The dog followed.

"I was sure that cat had been run over by a car somewhere," said Mary once her son was out of earshot. "I was just glad Bruce didn't find him dead. I wonder where he's been."

I didn't think domesticated cats could provide for themselves, so I said, "Someone must have been feeding him."

"Yes, but why did he leave in the first place? Maybe someone picked him up and took him somewhere, and it took this much time for him to find his way home."

I shrugged. I didn't know if felines had such a homing instinct.

"Black cats are supposed to be bad luck," said Mary, "but I'd say he's pretty lucky to have found his way back."

Bruce came running. "Mom, we're almost out of cat food."

"Don't worry, I'll get some more." She turned to me and said, "I came out to ask you if you'd heard about all those missiles in Cuba. It's scary isn't it?"

I'd heard about the situation, but I hadn't found it any more frightening than most of mankind's other militant actions. Still, I responded, "Yes, it is."

"At school we had a drill where we had to hide under our desks in case of an attack," said Bruce. "They called it 'duck and cover.'"

I didn't want to tell them such precautions would be useless in the event of a nuclear attack. There was no reason to frighten them any further.

*

I'd been living in Mary's home a few months when she convinced me to join her and a friend in a night out. It wasn't the first time she'd asked, and, as I had before, I declined the invitation. However, she said she "wouldn't take no for an answer." She said I needed to go out--that I never went anywhere or had any fun that she could see.

She was right. I rarely went anywhere, and having "fun," as she put it, was not something I had much experience with. I finally agreed to go, because I liked Mary and didn't want to keep declining every time she suggested it. It was, in part, because I liked her that I'd rejected her previous invitations. Emotional attachments were something I avoided, and with Mary I felt the need for avoidance more than ever.

For her part, I thought she was just "mothering" me. She'd once mentioned how she was the eldest of ten children, and that she'd spent much of her youth raising her younger siblings. I assumed it was simply her maternal instincts that spurred her concern for my well-being.

"Will Bruce be going with us?" I asked.

"No, we're going to a nightclub, silly. Besides, he's going to stay with his dad this weekend."

I was not acquainted with the boy's father, though I knew he saw him from time to time, and always looked forward to the visits.

That night, when Mary's friend, Cathy, came to pick us up, and I saw the splendid nature of their attire, I knew immediately my clothing was inadequate. They didn't say anything, so neither did I. As we left the house I saw the black cat, Spooky, sitting on the porch, watching us go. That same strange feeling came over me. There was something about the creature, something disconcertingly familiar. I sensed it, though not through any of the five physical senses my body employed. Since there was no justification for my feeling, I dismissed it.

We drove to a place called *The Catamaran*. It was located near the ocean, and sitting outside the front entrance was an actual construct of its namesake.

Though I normally avoided alcoholic beverages, I let Mary order one for me and found it pleasant enough. When the band started, both Mary and Cathy tried to get me to dance with them, but I insisted I didn't dance, so they stopped asking. My lack of interest was, apparently, a signal to other men.

They kept coming over and asking my companions to dance--which they did.

When they returned from the dance floor, they both sipped their drinks and Cathy asked," So, Richard, where are you from?"

"I've lived in many different places. I've moved around quite a bit. Most recently I lived in Los Angeles."

"Have you ever been married? Do you have any kids?"

"Cathy!" exclaimed Mary, looking embarrassed. "Quit interrogating the man."

"I was just curious."

I suspected Cathy was only looking out for the welfare of her friend, and I took no offense. However, I wasn't prepared to elaborate on my background, and was glad Mary put an end to the inquisition.

"I assume this band plays your favorite kind of music," I said in an attempt to change the subject.

"They play all kinds of things," said Mary. "Most of it I like. My favorite singer is Nat King Cole, but I don't think they play any of his originals."

It wasn't long before they were both asked to dance again, and no sooner had they returned to their seats, than the band leader, speaking to his audience, said, "I see we've got one of San Diego's finest singers in the house tonight. Maybe if we give her a hand, she'll come up and sing a little for us. Come on up, Mary."

The audience began to applaud and I joined in, even though I didn't realize whom he was talking about until I saw Cathy urging Mary on.

"Go on, go on," she said.

Without much hesitation, Mary rose from her seat and joined the band.

I'm sure it was my look of surprise that prompted Cathy to explain.

"It happens all the time," said Cathy. "All the local bands know Mary. Sometimes they even hire her to sing with them, but most of the time she just sings in talent contests. She almost always wins."

"I had no idea she was a singer."

"She could probably make a career of it," added Cathy, "but that's not easy with a son to take care of. I know, I've got three kids of my own."

I nodded and sat back to listen. The first song she sang, I guessed by the lyrics, was called "That Old Black Magic." I enjoyed it, amazed by her talent, by an aspect of her I never imagined. If the resulting applause was any sign, the song was a crowd-pleaser as well.

"She likes you, you know."

I was listening to Mary as she began another song about putting on a happy face, and not paying attention to what Cathy had said.

"What?"

"I said Mary likes you. You like her too, don't you?"

"Why do you say that?" I thought it was a strange comment.

"I can tell by the way you look at her."

I didn't respond. I continued to listen to the song, but wondered what she meant. Of course I liked Mary, but at first I didn't understand how the way I looked at her meant anything. Then it occurred to me she was speaking of liking Mary in a romantic or sexual way. That worried me. I wondered if Mary had reached the same conclusion about how I looked at her.

"Mary thinks you're very mysterious. That you're on the run from the law or from your wife, or something like that."

I forced a laugh to deflect suspicion. "No, I'm just running in place. There's nothing that mysterious about me."

Cathy looked as if she didn't believe me.

I wasn't bereft of emotions, of desires, but mutability had its drawbacks. I'd learned long ago that all lives were transitory--mine more than most.

Mary sang several songs that night, and everyone appeared to enjoy themselves, myself included. However, my concern about emotional attachments left me subdued. When Cathy took us home at the end of the night, I quickly said good night and went to my room.

Though I knew it could still be many years away, if ever, I would not surrender my expectation to one day return home. Whether that day arrived tomorrow or in another decade, I couldn't become entangled in any interaction that might have to be severed without notice. No matter my desires, I knew my isolation must remain firm. I'd long ago given up the conceit that I could walk between raindrops without getting wet.

*

It was less than a week later that my resolve, my patience, was rewarded. Mary came to my room and told me, "There's someone here to see you. He says he's an old friend. His name's Roland."

I knew no one by that name, and I had no old friends.

She saw the blank look on my face and said, "I told him you were here. I hope that was alright."

"Of course. I'm just surprised Roland found me here."

"I have to run to work, so you and Roland can use the living room if you want," said Mary. "Gotta go--bye"

I went to the front door and, without any exchange of words, I knew immediately who the "old friend" was. I let him in.

"You found me," I said plainly.

"Your identifier is sporadic, barely active. I was not certain at first. I have been observing . . . until I was positive."

"You were the feline . . . the long-lost cat."

"I acquired the image from the child's mind, then found the missing animal. I knew, if it was still alive, it had a limited range of travel. Using it allowed me to be present without detection."

"And the body you inhabit now?"

"Not one that will be missed for the short time I will need it. Yours?"

"I've been using it for some time. I told pertinent family members I was going on a writing retreat, which I knew from a previous host was something he did from time to time."

"Practical."

I nodded.

"You seem neither surprised nor agitated that I have located you."

"It's been so long. I wasn't certain anyone would ever come. But I will not resist. I want to go home. I would have before now, but my craft was disabled."

"Are you prepared to leave? What disruptions will your departure cause?"

"Not many. I've kept it that way. I must restore my host and return him to his previous locale. First, I must announce my departure from this residence."

"Is all that necessary?"

"Yes. A sudden disappearance would result in endless questions. I want to leave with as little disturbance, as little evidence of my incursion as is possible."

"That would be best." He nodded as if he understood, but I knew he couldn't possibly. He offered me a time limit to complete my tasks, and warned, "I will remain in close proximity."

I didn't know if he believed I wanted to go home, despite the consequences, but he knew I couldn't run now even if I wanted to.

I opened the door and he left. I stood there, watching through the screen as he departed, feeling both joy and trepidation. I was going home.

*

I didn't have to return my host to where I'd acquired him, but I wanted to. It would only necessitate a two-hour drive north to Los Angeles, and I knew, from experience, his disorientation would be worse should he awaken in a strange place. I would leave my completed manuscripts with him, to use or not use as he saw fit.

First, I had to tell Mary I was leaving. I found her in the kitchen.

"Oh? I'm sorry to hear that," was all she said. The disappointment on her face spoke more than her words, but I didn't know if it were only the loss income or something more which was the cause.

"You already paid me for next month, so I guess I'd better--"

"You can keep it," I said. "It's only fair since I gave you no notice."

"Alright. Well, good luck to you. Where are you headed?"

"I'm going home."

I could see she wanted to ask more, but didn't.

"Bruce is in the backyard if you want to say goodbye." She hesitated. "I hope everything works out for you at home."

She turned away to continue the work I'd interrupted, but I had the feeling it was only because she didn't know what else to say. I wanted to thank her for her kindness, to tell her part of me didn't want to leave, but I stayed silent. It was best if I said nothing.

I looked for the boy, but heard him before I actually found him.

"Spooky . . . here kitty kitty kitty kitty!" He saw me and asked, "Have you seen Spooky?"

"No, I haven't."

"He usually comes when I call him, 'cause he knows that means it's time to eat. I guess he's out roaming around again."

"I'm sure he is," I said, even though I wasn't certain what had become of the cat, now that my pursuer had no need of it. If he'd returned it to where he'd found it, Bruce might never see Spooky again. I imagined he would handle the second disappearance more easily than the first.

When I told him I was leaving, he didn't seem too concerned, but he did ask, "Why you leaving?"

"Well, I'm a traveler, you know, like those two fellas in *Route 66* who drive all around. But now it's time for me to go home."

"Kind of like Spooky," he responded after thinking about it. "Spooky must have been traveling around until he decided to come home."

"Yeah, kind of like that. Spooky and I are both lucky we have places to go home to."

"Why'd you decide to go home now?"

I wondered how to explain something that occurred so far away, in a place

110

so strange by his perceptions, he couldn't begin to imagine it. To him my contravention would be an abstract concept. So I attempted to describe it in words he would understand.

"I wrote something other people didn't like, and didn't want anyone to read, and now I have to go back and try to convince them people should be able to read whatever they want."

I saw he was thinking about what I said.

"I think people should be able to read whatever they want," he said as if he'd tossed the idea around in his head and reached an obvious conclusion.

Then, as though the conversation hadn't even taken place, he said, "Well, goodbye. I gotta go to baseball practice." And, just as the words were out of his mouth, he was gone. And so was I.

f

My mother, born Mary Ellen Reiner, did rent a room to a science fiction writer when I was young, and to the best of my aging recollection, his name was Richard Matheson. However, that memory is more than a half a century old, and I've found no evidence that the Richard Matheson, noted science fiction writer, ever lived in San Diego. It's possible he looked for a quiet retreat from his home in Los Angeles to work on something (even if his body wasn't possessed by an alien entity), but it's more likely my recall files have been corrupted.

The true story of Spooky is a strange one. As a kitten he appeared on our doorstep one Halloween day, and years later vanished for about a year before returning. Even stranger, years after his return he vanished again. Several years later I recognized him by his torn ear, several miles away from our house. He came to me when I called him, and, after a brief reunion, sauntered away. Part of me wanted to take him home, but I figured he'd been gone for so long, he probably had a new home somewhere nearby. So, reluctantly, I said goodbye and left him there.

111

Ark Angel

November 22, 1633

It was not planned so, but, finally, after years of preparation and several delays, the *Ark* and the *Dove* departed England today. The unforeseen nature of our departure came about after we took shelter from high winds in the harbor at Yarmouth. A small ship, a French bark said our captain, was overcome by the wind, causing it to drag its anchor and dislodge the *Dove* from its mooring. That forced her to set sail into the sea. The *Ark* had no choice but to follow.

We'd left London a month earlier, bound for the Isle of Wight, but were turned back by the Royal Navy in order that every man could swear an oath of allegiance to King Charles as their true religious leader. I'm still uncertain where the order came from, but the delay cost us weeks. I only hope there will be no further delays that might prevent us from arriving in time for spring planting.

As we sailed out of Yarmouth Harbor, one of our Jesuits reminded me it was St. Cecilia's Day, as if it were a good omen. She being the patron saint of music, I see not the significance, but hope it bodes well.

There are more than 300 souls on board our two ships, both gentleman emigrants and those selected for their particular skills--farmers, carpenters, brick makers and such. We brought with us winter and summer clothing, cannon and firearms for protection, food and water. The food was stored carefully so as not to spoil, as were the plants and seeds needed to grow more once we reach our destination.

I'm confident my brother and I planned the voyage as well as could be expected, but I'm apprehensive as well. Our father knew when he selected me to lead this expedition, that my older brother Cecil would inherit his title and businesses (I desired neither), and that managing them would not permit him to leave England. So it was, after our father's death, that Cecil, the new Lord Baltimore, named me governor of the province which King Charles had earlier granted to our father (with the royal suggestion the territory be named for his wife, Queen Maria). We will be the first to settle that region of the New World, and, despite my misgivings regarding religion, I pray I'm up to the task of leading these people into the wilds of Maryland.

November 23, 1633

Come daylight the harsh winds died, and we could still see the shore of England in the distance.

Captain Lowe greeted me in a jovial mood.

"A bright and beautiful day to begin our voyage, wouldn't you agree, Governor?"

"I'm not governor yet, Captain."

"Aye, I'm master as long as we're at sea, but you should get yourself used to the title. And the others should get used to you as their leader. It'll go easier for you later if you take charge now. Whenever possible, we should be seen making decisions together . . . as long as you remember who's captain."

He winked and I took his meaning clear enough. He was right, of course. I would be wise to listen, as he had years of experience leading men, while I had none.

A gentle west wind blew us past a number of jagged rock formations Captain Lowe called the "Needles," and told me, stern-faced, to keep an eye out for Turks and other pirates. I scanned the horizon and saw nothing but our pinnace, the *Dove,* its two masts and flat stern looking so much different from our own much larger vessel.

Glancing off the port side I spotted a group of seals that had apparently followed us. I'd seen them playing offshore near Yarmouth the day before, and the sight reminded me of a memory I preferred remain buried. Of course, traveling across the sea, it was impossible to forget I had a fear of the water. Not an intolerable fear mind you--I could venture into a lake, swim to a degree. But the ocean, with its waves and currents and unseen inhabitants, left me uneasy.

I had, as a young boy, nearly drowned. I was at the shore with my family, but had wandered off alone. I was only waist-deep when I was overcome by a large wave, and drawn under by an overwhelming current that pulled me further and further from the beach no matter how I struggled. At some point, I imagine from lack of air, I passed into unconsciousness.

When I awoke I was being laid on the sand by a woman I'd never seen before. We were both dripping wet. She'd obviously rescued me from the depths.

I remember she had a strange look about her, like a foreigner, and eyes as black as coal. But, of course, I was in no condition to observe, and began spitting up the sea water I'd swallowed. There was one thing, even in my dazed condition, I couldn't fail to notice. She was absolutely naked.

I coughed and spit up more water, and when I turned over to thank her, she was gone. I sat up, looked around, and saw no one. The only movement was a seal that had surfaced directly in front of me, and was slapping the water with its flippers. The seal submerged as I stood and went in search of the woman. But I never found her.

As I've written, my fear of the ocean is ever-present, but not overwhelming. I've traveled across the breadth of the Atlantic before. Once with my father and the rest of my family when we voyaged to Newfoundland, where his attempt at colonization ultimately failed due to the harsh weather and England's hostilities with France, and, of course, the return trip to England. I can make such a voyage . . . I just don't like the idea of being in the water itself, as the sight of the seals reminded me.

November 24, 1633

Late in the day we came upon a large, well-armed merchant vessel, the *Dragon*, traveling our way. It was a fortuitous happenstance which pleased our crew, because it meant, in her company, we were unlikely to be chosen as a target for pirates.

November 25, 1633

I find I have much useless time on my hands, so I will endeavor to update this journal with regularity.

November 26, 1633

A fierce storm overtook us midday and the clouds ahead were fearful to behold. I could barely hear myself think over the berserk howl of the wind. The turbulent sway of the ship was more than most stomachs could take. My younger brother, George, was among those who forfeited his breakfast.

I spotted one of the seals that had been following us, though I didn't see any of its companions. This singular beast was off the bow, slapping the water with its front fins. I stopped momentarily to watch as it swam forward several yards, then began slapping the choppy waters again. It was as if the creature were trying to communicate--as if it wanted us to follow it.

I ventured to the bridge where Captain Lowe told me, shouting above the wind to be heard, "The *Dragon*'s hold is full--she's too heavy. Her captain is turning back, away from the storm. It might be best if we do the same. What

114

say you?"

He stared at me as though the question were a test of sorts. I didn't know what answer he was looking for, but I'd had enough delays, so I said, "Let's stay on course."

For a moment I thought he would argue the point, but he just said, "As you like."

As soon as he said it, I doubted my decision. Surely he wouldn't continue on my say so. He was the experienced seaman, not I. Maybe he'd already made the decision, and only wanted to see what I'd say.

However, the tempest worsened as night approached, and, as prearranged, the captain of the *Dove* hung a second light from her mast, signifying the ship was in trouble. With the winds and the waves tossing us about, there was little we could do to aid the *Dove*. Keeping the *Ark* afloat was task enough for the crew. I was certain we'd be swallowed up by the sea at any moment. At one point, both lights aboard the *Dove* vanished.

Throughout the night we tried in vain to sight her.

November 27, 1633

Morning has come and the storm is quelled, but there is no sign of our sister ship. Thus my day begins with more doubts. Not only have we lost the *Dove*, but our own mainsail has been ripped. My mind is ripe with misgivings and apprehension.

Captain Lowe must have read the look on my face when he told me about the sail.

"We'll be alright," he said. "We're not dead in the water. The winds are favorable, and we've still got the foresail and the mizzen while we mend the mainsail."

Neither of us mentioned the *Dove*, for there was nothing to say. Word had already made its way through the crew and the passengers. Prayers were said and no more was spoken of it.

Using Captain Lowe's spyglass, I scanned the horizon and saw a pod of dolphins in the distance, but no sign of the *Dove*. I kept looking, longer than I should have, and we were soon joined on the forecastle by Father Andrew White, one of our Jesuit priests, and two other gentlemen, Robert Vaughan and John Neville. They're all older and more seasoned than me, and I can't help but worry they might harbor doubts about the ability of a 23-year-old to lead them--especially in light of our loss. I try to put those doubts out of my mind.

"See any mermaids, Governor Calvert?" asked Master Vaughan, a hint of humor in his question.

I didn't bother to reply, but nodded and said, "Afternoon, gentlemen."

Captain Lowe, however, replied to his query.

"I saw a mermaid once."

"Surely you jest," responded Neville.

"I do not," said the captain in all seriousness. "I was just a lad, working aboard my first ship under Captain Richard Whitbourne, more than a score of years ago. We were sailing out of St. John's Harbor in Newfoundland when a few of us spotted this woman swimming towards us. Only it wasn't a woman, because though her skin was white and she had the breasts of a woman, her hair, if that's what it was, was blue-green like sea grass, and from the navel down she was more fish than human, with a tail like a broad-hooked arrow. She was both beautiful and strange."

"You saw her yourself?" asked Vaughan.

"I did."

"Mermaids are demons," said Father White. "They provoke men with temptations of the flesh, and lure them to their doom with lustful songs."

"I heard no song," said Lowe. "The creature did not speak nor utter any sound before my shipmates scared it off."

"Mermaids, sea nymphs, sirens, undines, selkies, they're all myths as far as I'm concerned," said Neville.

"What's a selkie?" I asked, never having heard the term.

"Just another creature of legend," responded Neville. "Supposedly they're seals who can change themselves into women."

"Seals?" Straightaway the notion skewered me.

"Aye, but they're as fanciful as leprechauns and banshees."

They began discussing other mythical beings and the likelihood of their existence, but my thoughts were of the woman who rescued me as a boy, and the seal I saw. I was left to wonder whether or not my long-ago savior had indeed been a magical creature of the deep.

December 3, 1633

When I reached the bridge this afternoon with my brother George and Father White, Captain Lowe greeted us by saying, "We've got trouble."

He handed me his spyglass and pointed off the starboard side.

"It's an Algerian vessel," he said. "Probably pirates."

"Pirates?" responded George in a tone that said he was both excited and fearful.

The Jesuit crossed himself.

I looked and saw the ship--so far away I wondered how the captain could distinguish it.

"Are you sure it's not the *Dove*?" I asked.

Captain Lowe gave me a look that shamed me for doubting him.

"Flank speed," he called out, and the crew began to scurry.

I handed the spyglass to George, and as I did I spotted the seal in the waters near us. I couldn't say for certain it was the same one I'd seen before, but I believed it was. Almost as I spotted it, the animal turned tail and headed for the Algerian ship.

"Can we outrun it?" George asked the captain.

"Not likely," he replied, "but we're not waiting for them either."

For a brief time that afternoon, it looked like the Algerian was gaining on us. Then, without a reason Captain Lowe could deduce, it turned away. There were shouts of elation and relief from both the crew and the men among the passengers who'd been armed in preparation for battle. Under his breath, Father White muttered, "For He will command His angels to guard you in all your ways."

December 25, 1633

Christmas came and, at the suggestion of Father White, wine was given out to celebrate the day. I abstained, but many drank of it too freely, and by nightfall the foredecks were strewn with those who'd passed out of consciousness.

I went to the stern to be alone and spent some time staring up at the crescent moon. I heard something, turned, and saw a woman standing near the railing. She was naked and wet, and I knew immediately she was not one of our passengers. For though it had been more than a dozen years, I recognized her. With those indelible dark eyes and tanned skin she could be no one else.

I approached her slowly, for she seemed apprehensive.

"Mistress, you must be cold," I said as I unfastened my cloak and covered her with it, for both her sake and mine. For she was beguilingly winsome, in an exotic sort of way, and her state of undress had stirred my attraction.

She nodded and smiled, but said nothing.

Even so covered, I found her alluring--her smile entrancing. I took it as no

117

strange coincidence that her hair, still damp, was the glossy dark brown color of the seals I'd seen. It did not occur to me to doubt my sanity or question the strangeness of her sudden appearance. For she was there. I saw her plainly enough.

Despite the evidence of my eyes, I asked her, "How can this be? How can you be here, now, looking exactly as you did so long ago? It is you, isn't it? You're the one who saved me when I was but a boy."

She seemed to understand me, for she nodded again.

"Are you a selkie?" I asked.

She looked at me as if the term had no meaning to her, so I tried something else.

"My name is Leonard," I said, placing my hand on my chest. "What is your name?"

I turned at the sound of someone approaching. George staggered up the stairs towards me. Like many of the others, he'd drunk too much wine.

I heard a splash, turned back, and she was gone. I stepped over my cloak as I hurried to the railing and looked down. But I could see nothing in the dark.

December 26, 1633

Many of those who overly indulged in wine are sick today. Dr. Edwards, the ship's surgeon, says some have a fever, but he doesn't believe their illness is serious.

I'm still obsessed by thoughts of the strange woman who came to me from the sea. I can't explain her existence, much less her appearance before me, but I do not believe I was hallucinating or delirious, as I did not imbibe of the wine. Nor am I ill. But I haven't told anyone what I saw, as I'm certain they would think me deluded, thus eroding my status as leader of this expedition.

December 30, 1633

Twelve of those who fell sick after the Christmas celebration have died. Despite some objections, they were all given burials at sea. When questioned by a woman grieving for her husband as to why God would do such a thing, one Jesuit priest said simply the deity's reasons were mysterious and above the reproach of man. She was not satisfied with that answer and told him so.

December 31, 1633

Despite the eve of a new year, the mood aboard ship is somber, and some have begun to question their decision to embark on this voyage to the New World.

I've seen no sign of my sea maiden, though I'm constantly looking for her. Neither have there been any sightings of seals near the *Ark*. I must assume she, whatever she may be, is gone.

January 3, 1634

The new year came and went without incident or celebration, as no one was in the mood for such. But there was great jubilation when we spied land for the first time today. The sighting came none too soon, as our rations of both food and water were running low.

It was late afternoon before we anchored in the harbor of Barbados, and Captain Lowe began to prioritize who would go ashore first. Everyone wanted their chance to walk on land again, myself included.

January 8, 1634

I had hoped to be underway by now, but Captain Lowe says we will be here for at least a fortnight, because most of the sails need mending to some degree, and it will take time to replenish our stores. There is no beef or mutton to be had at any price, so we've had to make do with smoked fish and whatever other foodstuffs will last the journey to Maryland.

The captain also wants to delay our departure in the unlikely event the *Dove* may have survived the storm, and could be right behind us. I want to believe that, to have faith, but my faith is lacking, even though Father White says he prays every night for the souls aboard the *Dove*.

Many of the passengers of means have taken up lodging at an inn located on the island, but the weather is so temperate one could sleep outside, which I've done several nights after spending long evenings prowling the beaches. I still hold out hope of finding my mermaid, my selkie, my sea maiden--whatever she may be. But my hope fades with each setting sun.

January 13, 1634

The joy I feel this night might be sinful, but if it is I will gladly pay whatever penance is necessary. For my lady of the sea returned this evening, striding through the surf even as I stood on the beach in disbelief. She walked straight up to me, dripping sea water, as bare as before, put her hand on my chest and said, "Len-ird."

119

I placed my hand over hers and said, "Yes, my name is Leonard."

I reached out and lay my hand on her chest. The swell of her breasts stirred my lust, though I tried to ignore it.

She didn't respond, so I touched my own chest again and said, "Leonard," then reached back to touch her.

This time she seemed to understand, and replied, "Suire."

Her voice had a whimsical quality I found enchanting. Everything about her was captivating, intoxicating.

Before I even realized it, she was in my arms and we were kissing. It was rapturous--spellbinding. There, on the sand, we consummated the act of love in a way so much more splendid than I'd ever experienced in the brothels of London, that I will not attempt to describe it, except to say that when her pleasure soared to its pinnacle, she cried out in a voice that was otherworldly, as if calling to all the denizens of the ocean that lapped at our feet.

Afterwards we lay there in the sand and talked. At least I talked. She said nothing, and I wondered what language, if any, she spoke, though she appeared to understand at least some of what I said.

I told her about our journey, about where we were going and why, and how we hoped our lost ship might still be found. At some point, no doubt spent from our activities, I fell asleep. When I awoke, she was gone.

January 17, 1634

Dutifully I've wandered the beaches of Barbados every evening since Suire's disappearance, falling asleep on the sands. Last night George followed me and insisted I return with him to the inn. He tells me my nocturnal wanderings are beginning to stir talk amongst the colonists.

January 18, 1634

Preparations for continuing our voyage are almost complete. No sign of Suire.

January 19, 1634

I was aboard the *Ark,* speaking with Captain Lowe, when someone called out, "Ship ahoy!"

The captain used his spyglass, then handed it to me.

"It's the *Dove*," he said.

Indeed, I saw it for myself. The *Dove* had survived the storm and was about to rejoin us. I watched the ship approach through the spyglass. Swimming before it was a seal. At that moment my heart ascended to heaven.

January 20, 1634

We learned the *Dove* had turned back, finding refuge from the storm in an English port, and once the weather cleared, set out again. She sighted the *Dragon* once more, and sailed in its company to the Canary Islands before turning west to Barbados.

Captain Wintour of the *Dove* told us he'd briefly lost his bearings in another storm two days out, but spotted a seal which he followed, guessing it would lead them to land.

I didn't say anything, but I'm certain I know the source of that fortuity.

January 24, 1634

Though I've kept daily watch, Suire has not visited me again, and today the *Ark* and the *Dove* depart Barbados, bound for Maryland and the New World. I'm both anxious to reach our destination and melancholy that I may have seen the last of my sea maiden.

February 2, 1634

There have been running arguments between our Roman Catholic passengers and those loyal to the Church of England. Nothing extreme, but even the minor spats are beginning to wear on me. Despite the quarrelling, or maybe because of it, I've never been so certain my father was right to insist upon religious tolerance as a founding principle for the new colony.

February 3, 1634

I must admit I find it difficult to keep this journal, as each day falls into the monotony of the next.

February 5, 1634

> *To where I watch on the yellow sands,*
> *And they pluck sweet music with sea-cold hands.*
> *They bring me coral and amber clear.*
> *But when the stars in heaven appear,*
> *Their music ceases, they glide away.*
> *They swim for their grottos across the bay.*

121

> *Then listen only to my shrill tune,*
> *The surfy tide, and the wondering moon.*

Standing over my shoulder, Captain Lowe asked what I was writing in my journal. I told him I was trying to remember the lines from a play by William Shakespeare. He said he was familiar with some of the bard's works, and asked me to read it. I was surprised a seaman would know of such, but I complied.

"I believe that's from *A Midsummer Night's Dream*," he said. I nodded, and he asked, in jest, "What are you dreaming of, Governor, mermaids?"

I feigned a laugh, but said nothing else, and the captain left me to my thoughts.

February 13, 1634

I've neglected this journal for too long, having been tangled in so many petty squabbles and my own apathy. I can't get Suire out of my mind, though I try to keep it occupied with more mundane matters.

February 27, 1634

Today we reached the New World--specifically the colony of Virginia. Everyone rejoiced.

Over the last month, we sailed past St. Lucia, Montserrat, St. Christopher's, round Cape Hatteras, through Chesapeake Bay, and onto Point Comfort, where we anchored today, full of apprehension, not knowing how the predominantly Protestant inhabitants will greet us. Years ago, radical Anglicans forced my father to leave Virginia because he wouldn't swear allegiance to their Protestant faith.

However, I carry letters from the king and the high treasurer commanding the colonists' assistance, as well as personal correspondence they should be grateful to receive.

March 3, 1634

Our fears of mistreatment by the Virginia colonists were for naught. We've been kindly treated during our stay. Some of our passengers have chosen to leave the expedition and settle in Virginia, while a handful of those already living in Virginia have decided to go on with us to Maryland.

We set sail today up the Patawomeck River, which will lead us to our final destination. Never have I beheld a larger or more beautiful river. The Thames seems a mere stream in comparison.

At the mouth of the river we got our first look at the natives, who stood on shore and watched our ships pass by, I imagine, with every bit of curiosity for which we held for them.

Father White suggested we name the first island we came to "St. Clement's," for a martyred pope. Why that name occurred to him, I have no idea. I would have preferred something not related to religion, but conceded when others agreed it would be a good name.

March 11, 1634

We've spent the last several days sending out parties of exploration, looking for a suitable place to start our colony. While in Virginia I secured the services of one Captain Henry Fleet to serve as guide and interpreter, as he spoke, after a fashion, several native languages. His assistance has proved invaluable in dealing with the *Yaocomaco* tribe that claims the lands on which we intend to settle.

March 25, 1634

To celebrate the Feast of the Annunciation, and at the zealous request of our Jesuits, everyone went ashore today, onto St. Clement's, where mass was held.

The island itself is too small for our needs, but we've found another parcel of land further downriver. Our negotiations with the *Yaocomaco* continue, and I'm optimistic we'll reach an agreement.

March 27, 1634

Our efforts to purchase the land we selected for our settlement were successful, and those aboard the *Ark* and *Dove* have been given the word to begin unloading the ships.

After years of planning, exploration, and negotiation--all begun by my father--we're finally here. His dream will be fulfilled.

March 29, 1634

We've named our new town St. Mary's, in honor of the Virgin Mary.

April 12, 1634

Our voyage now over, and all of my time devoted to establishing our settlement, I've abandoned any attempt at keeping this journal with regularity. However, something both unexpected and incredible happened yesterday that

I must relate.

In a small native canoe, Captain Fleet, myself, and one of our native friends were exploring a rivulet that feeds off the Patawomeck. Our friend, who was guiding the canoe from the rear, began chattering alarmingly. Captain Fleet and I turned in time to see him struck by an arrow in the back. Behind us by some 50 yards was another canoe, this one with four other natives I immediately assumed must be Susquehannock, the enemies of our friends the Yaocomaco.

Captain Fleet and I paddled furiously, but it was apparent the belligerent savages would quickly be upon us. Fleet stowed his paddle and grabbed his rifle. I followed suit as another arrow soared past us.

I twisted in my seat to get off a shot, but before I could, the pursuing canoe upended and capsized. Not pausing to question our good fortune, we grabbed our paddles and made quick our escape. However, not before I looked back and saw a familiar sight--my glistening seal, my guardian angel.

April 13, 1634

Though I'd not thought of Suire in weeks, and had even considered the possibility I'd imagined her entirely, I patrolled the riverbanks last night until, indeed, I found her.

My heart leapt with the possibilities, and I couldn't wait to hold her in my arms again. But she didn't leave the river. I walked along its bank, getting as close as I could to her.

"Suire go," she said, uttering the only word other than our names I'd heard her speak.

"No, don't go," I implored her. "Stay--stay with me."

She shook her head and pointed in an easterly direction.

"Suire go."

I guessed she intended to go home, back to England or Ireland or wherever she hailed from.

Despite my longing, she was right. She had to go. What was I going to do-- bring her back to the settlement and make her my wife? I understood, but I wanted one last kiss.

I stepped into the river, gingerly testing the footing, and moved towards her.

She must have thought I was trying to capture her, for she quickly disappeared beneath the surface. I knew, even then, it would be the last I ever saw of her.

Leonard Calvert, son of George Calvert, the first Lord Baltimore, would sow the seeds of religious freedom in Maryland that his father wanted, thereby helping to lay the foundation of one of America's most cherished principles. He oversaw the creation of Maryland's first assembly, and would remain governor until his death in 1647. The selkie in this tale is purely speculative, but the rest of the story is drawn from historical accounts. Leonard Calvert is my great (x10) grandfather.

Syncopation in Time

January 30, 1946 - Allied Headquarters, Paris, France

"What is it, Captain? I'm very busy."

"Sorry to disturb you, Colonel, but you said you wanted a report as soon as I completed my investigation."

Colonel Washburn searched his desk muttering, "Yes, yes. I'll read your report as soon as you've filed it."

Captain Mercer didn't move. He was hesitant to annoy his superior officer when the man was so obviously distracted by other concerns, but he was convinced it was necessary.

"Pardon me, sir, but I know the directive for this investigation came from the top, and I believe you should hear my findings before any official documents are filed."

The colonel looked up at his subordinate for the first time. "What do you mean? What did your investigation reveal?"

"Well, sir . . . ." Captain Mercer hesitated. He'd rehearsed this, but now wasn't certain where to begin.

"Come on, son, I don't have all day. Major Miller's plane went down somewhere over the channel--correct?"

"Well, yes . . . and no." Mercer cringed at how it sounded.

"What do you mean yes *and* no? It can't be both, Captain. What *exactly* did your investigation conclude?"

"My investigation reached no single definitive conclusion, sir."

Colonel Washburn sat back in his chair as if making himself comfortable. "You'd better explain yourself, Captain."

Mercer took a breath. "Colonel, I was unable to conclude, with any certainty, what happened to Major Anton Glenn Miller, because of the number of conflicting reports."

Colonel Washburn just stared, waiting for him to go on.

"It's been assumed Major Miller took off from Twinwood Airfield on December 15th. However, no flight plan was ever filed, and there is no written record of any such departure.

"Disregarding that for the moment, the most disturbing report I've come across originates from an RAF navigator who says that, while returning from a

126

mission, his bomber jettisoned its unused bombs over the channel, and that he saw one of the bombs hit a small plane. He's certain the plane was a single-engine Norseman, the same kind of plane Major Miller was supposedly aboard. The navigator insists the date was December 15th, however the only official document I can find states that a Norseman was lost to a bomb drop on the 16th.

"It could have been an entirely different aircraft, or there could be a mistake concerning the dates." Colonel Washburn stood and looked through the window behind his desk.

"Troubling news, Captain. If we have to report that America's most beloved bandleader was killed by our allies . . . ." The colonel turned back to Mercer. "You said there were conflicting reports."

"Yes, sir. There are several. Despite the fact there is no record of a Norseman landing in Paris on December 15th, there are eyewitness reports that Major Miller was seen at a party thrown by General Eisenhower at the Palace of Versailles on December 16th."

Colonel Washburn said nothing, but seemed to contemplate this as he fiddled with a pencil.

"I've also learned the officer who authorized Miller's flight, and was reportedly aboard the plane, was a Lieutenant Colonel Norman Baessell, a rather shady character with a reputation for black-market dealings. He was known as a reckless operator who ordered his pilots to fly in bad conditions." Mercer cleared his throat. "There are other accounts. One states Miller was accidently shot by a U.S. Army MP in a Paris brothel. Another says he was shot by a Frenchman, who, after being freed from a German prison camp, came home to find Miller in bed with his wife. Still another account--a rumor really--suggests he was a Nazi spy who met in secret with Gestapo chief Heinrich Himmler."

"Is that it, Captain? Don't you have any *positive* scenarios?"

"There is one more, sir, but it's just hearsay. An infantry officer told his men he found Miller's body outside of Bastogne during the Battle of the Bulge campaign. However, the officer was killed soon after, and no such body was ever identified."

"No tag was recovered?"

"Apparently Major Miller suffered from a skin condition that prevented him from wearing dog tags."

Washburn grumbled something Mercer couldn't make out, and turned to stare at him. "That's it? That's the sum of your findings, Captain?"

"Without going into more detail--yes, sir. To be honest, Colonel, I doubt we'll ever know exactly what happened to Major Miller."

December 13, 1944 - London, England

He was glad to get the letter from Bing, but jealous the crooner was back in the good old U.S. of A. He wished *he* was home. He was proud of what he was doing, even if it was just boosting morale, yet he missed Helen and the kids.

His door opened and his aide, Lieutenant Haynes, stuck his head in.

"Colonel Niven is on his way up, sir. He said he needs to speak with you right away."   "Thanks, Don. Did you get that new arrangement out to the band? I want to be able to surprise Helen on the special holiday broadcast."

"They're already going over it, sir."

"How many times have I told you to knock off that 'sir' crap? I don't remember you ever calling me 'sir' stateside."

"Sorry, Glenn, there are so many sirs around this place it's become a bad habit."

"I know you what you mean," said Miller, taking off his glasses and wiping the lenses with a rag. "I hate all this GI stuff."

"If I didn't know better, I'd think you and the Army weren't getting along. You're looking mighty thin these days, Glenn. You've been working too hard. You need to take a break now and then. Let me get you something to eat."

"Just because you used to be my personal manager doesn't mean I need you managing me," barked Miller with a smile. "I'll get something later."

"He's here."

Haynes opened the door and Colonel Niven walked through, looking every bit as dashing in his uniform as he did acting the part of an officer in *Dawn Patrol* and *Spitfire*. Though he was a bit of a stuffed shirt, Miller considered him a friend.

The colonel closed the door behind him. "I've new orders for you, old boy. They come straight from Ike."

"Eisenhower?"

"Yes. You're acquainted I believe."

"Not really. We met once--briefly. Where are the orders?" Miller asked, hand outstretched.

"Sorry," replied Niven. "Nothing on paper this time. This is strictly secret stuff, Glenn. Unofficial as it were. *I* don't even know what it's all about. I only know you're to catch the next available flight for Paris. Your cover story, should you be asked, is that you're going over early to complete preparations for your Christmas concert. A Lieutenant Colonel Norman Baessell at Milton Earnest Hall will arrange your transportation."

"I don't get it, David. What could the Supreme Allied Commander possibly want with me that's so secret?"

"I haven't the foggiest, old man."

December 15, 1944 - Twinwood Airfield, Bedfordshire, England

"Where you from, Private?" Miller asked their driver, trying to be friendly.

"Heyworth, Illinois, sir."

"I grew up in small Midwestern towns myself--in Iowa, Nebraska, Missouri--we moved around a lot. You ever milk any cows in Heyworth?" "Yes, sir. Quite a few."

"Milking cows is how I saved up enough money to buy my first trombone," said Miller, remembering how happy he was the day he brought the instrument home.

"Don, here, is a city boy," said Miller, gesturing at his aide. "He wouldn't know one end of a cow from another."

"I don't know," said Haynes. "I know a horse's ass when I see one."

They all laughed.

"We're here, sir," said their young driver as he pulled the jeep to a stop.

"Doesn't look like a very good day to fly," said Haynes.

He was right. It was cold, wet, and foggy, and Miller wasn't fond of flying on the best of days.

"You want us to hang around in case they cancel?"

"No, Don. Go ahead and get back. I want you to make sure the band is rehearsing. Colonel Baessell assured me we'd be taking off today. 'Weather be damned' I believe were his exact words."

"Alright then, Glenn. Have a good flight. I'll see you in Paris in about a week."

"See you then."

"You take care of yourself . . . was it PFC Golden?"

"Yes, sir. PFC Robert Golden," he replied, unloading Miller's duffle, "though everyone calls me Bob."

"You stay safe, Bob. I'm sure there are plenty of cows back in Heyworth just waiting for you to come home."

"I will, sir."

The jeep pulled away and Miller watched them go. Despite his nonchalance, he *was* worried about the weather. He'd heard someone say all flights were grounded today. His apprehension rose an octave when he saw the plane Colonel Baessell was stepping out of.

"It's only got one engine," said Miller.

"What the hell," responded Baessell, "Lindbergh had only one motor, and he flew clear across the Atlantic. We're only flying to Paris."

"You flying this thing?"

"Nope. I'm just along for the ride. The pilot will be here in a minute."

Baessell picked up one of two cases sitting next to the plane and put it aboard.

"What's that?"

"Empty champagne bottles."

"Empty bottles?"

Baessell grabbed the other case. "Bottles are scarce in Paris these days. You can't buy champagne unless you trade in some empties."

"So is that your *only* cargo this flight?" asked a fellow in a flight jacket who came up behind Miller.

"I've a got few other baubles," said Baessell. "Here's your pilot, Miller. John Morgan, meet Glenn Miller.

Miller shook hands with the newcomer, then put his duffle and trombone case aboard. Morgan slipped right into the pilot's seat and began checking his controls, while Baessell buttoned up the plane.

"You sure you want to go up in this soup?" Morgan asked, continuing his pre-flight check.

"Supposed to be clear over the channel," replied Baessell, sliding into the co-pilot's seat. "Besides, only a pansy would let a little rain and fog stop him."

"Baessell, you're as subtle as a loaded .45."

Miller took the bucket seat behind Baessell and fastened his belt. "It *is* awfully nasty weather," offered Miller, "maybe we should--"

"Don't sweat it, Major," declared Baessell. "Morgan here's a helluva pilot. Flew 32 missions in B-24s without a scratch. He's used to weather like this."

Morgan made a noise that was part disgust, part laugh. "This isn't exactly a Liberator."

Miller looked around. "Where the hell are the parachutes?"

"What's the matter, Miller," jibed Baessell, "do you want to live forever?"

December 15, 1944 - Over the English Channel

He didn't so much wake as become fully conscious of his new surroundings. His terrifying last memories were of panicked shouts and a profound sensation of falling. The plane was going down--that much was clear. Morgan had lost control. Yet he had no memory of the crash, and here he was. But *where* was here?

He was lying on the floor of a small compartment, devoid of furnishings and dimly lit by a source he couldn't determine. His trombone case was next to him, but not his duffle bag. He touched his face to see if he was awake--make sure he was real. It seemed so, yet his inner voice was singing off-key, saying it couldn't be. Had he been taken prisoner?

As he stood, an opening appeared in the wall and a man stepped through. He was a small fellow, almost a good foot shorter than Miller's six-foot frame, and his clothes were rather odd. He wasn't wearing any kind of military uniform, Miller was certain of that, but he'd never seen an outfit quite like it.

"Mr. Miller," said the fellow, "I realize you must be experiencing a certain sense of disorientation. But if you will follow me, I will attempt to explain."

He had to stoop, but he followed him through the hatch into a larger compartment. He felt dizzy and readily accepted the stranger's invitation to sit on a cushioned bench. In the background he caught a glimpse of lights and gauges that made him think of a plane's cockpit, yet were unlike anything he'd seen.

"My name is Quay," began the little man, who remained standing. "I know what I am about to tell you will seem strange--maybe even incomprehensible--but I am a traveler in time. I have come here from, what would be to you, the distant future."

The stranger paused as if to let him absorb what he'd heard.

The future? A traveler in time? Time travel?

"Do you mean . . . " Miller began, then hesitated, "you mean like H.G. Wells? You have a time machine?"

"Yes," he said, raising his hands to signify the hull around them, "this vessel *is* a time machine--and more. Much more than Mr. Wells ever imagined."

"Are you . . . from Earth, or . . . ?"

"Yes, in a manner of speaking, I *am* from Earth. I am a descendent of terrestrials, of Earth men," said Quay, "but my people, the progeny of this world, no longer live on Terra--Earth, as you call it."

It was all a bit much for Miller. The fellow *looked* human enough, though

131

Miller couldn't pinpoint his nationality, or his odd accent. He didn't really understand, much less believe, but still he asked, "What are you doing here?"

Quay let out a sigh. "I am, in my world, somewhat of an outcast, Mr. Miller. The reason for this has been my lifelong fascination with ancient forms of music. I have studied and enjoyed everything from classical European symphonies to 21st-century electropop."

"*Electropop*?"

"You will be pleased to know your own music has survived the ages. I have long been enamored with your indelible tunes. My favorite is 'Moonlight Serenade.' Indeed, it is because of my deep affection for your swing music that I am here."

"What do you mean?"

"I am here to save you, Mr. Miller--at least save you for my time."

"I don't understand."

"I know this may come as a shock," said Quay, "but, by most historical accounts, you died on terrestrial date December 15, 1944, when the small airplane carrying you and two other military officers disappeared over the English Channel."

Miller reconciled what he was being told with what he already suspected. His plane *did* go down--*was* going down. He wasn't dreaming. Or was he? Was he dead? Was this . . . ?   "Am I dead?"

"No, Mr. Miller, though it is very likely you would have been, had I not intervened. Because of that, I have committed a crime--a crime which now brands me an outlaw among my people."

"What do you mean it's very *likely* I'd be dead?"

"Historical accounts of your death are incomplete and in conflict. The only certainty is that after December 15 of 1944 you never again performed with your band, and a few days later all reports of your whereabouts ceased."

Miller shook his head and dropped his face into his hands.

"I understand it must be hard to accept this--to comprehend what I am telling you. Believe me though, I would not be here if it were not the only way to preserve your genius."

"My genius?" growled Miller, feeling at once both bitter and perplexed.

"My definition," said Quay, "of what you have accomplished--what you can still accomplish."

"So now what?" asked Miller, still not buying all he was hearing. "I go home with you?"

"Not yet, I am afraid. History must be played out, as inconsistent and paradoxical as it is. I must interfere as little as possible with historical accounts. You must continue on and meet with General Eisenhower."

"I don't get it. If I crashed in the channel, how would I have ever met with Eisenhower?"

"Understandably confusing, but, as I said, the accounts of your disappearance vary. It is possible your pilot, at the last moment, was able to recover control of the aircraft and that it never crashed. However, I could not take that chance. My trip through time and space is limited logistically. My access to this craft allows me to be here *now,* at this time only, and to return-- that is all. If I had waited to confirm your demise, I would not have had a second chance. It is very likely you *would* have crashed, and by rescuing you and taking you to meet with Eisenhower, *I* am responsible for the discordant historical accounts. Such is the paradox of time travel.

"So, we must play out the chronicled accounts, be they authentic or apocryphal."

Miller was still absorbing what he'd heard when he blurted out, "Can I see Helen? Before we go, can I visit my wife and children?"

"I am sorry, Mr. Miller. The constraints of history do not allow for that."

December 16, 1944 - Versailles, France

It was quite a little shindig Eisenhower had thrown to celebrate his promotion to General of the Army. Any other time Miller would have waded in with both hands. Right now his mind wasn't on celebrating. Too many other concerns dominated his thoughts. Besides, he'd barely made his way into the Palace of Versailles ballroom when one of the general's aides nabbed him.

Now he was on his way to see the newly-christened five-star general with no idea why.

Once inside the general's expansive office he stood at attention and saluted.

"Sit down, Major, sit down," said Eisenhower, not bothering to return his salute.

Miller sat, admiring the overstuffed antique chair the general had designated. It wasn't just the chair. The entire room was decorated like something straight out of the 17th century--which it probably was, he concluded.

"Major, I have a special assignment for you. A very important assignment. However, it's not your usual bailiwick." The general moved thoughtfully around his massive oak desk. "Here it is in a nutshell, Major. My Ardennes Campaign is not going particularly well. Not that we won't win out eventually. Victory is only a matter of time now. But the cost in lives . . . ." His voice trailed off as if he didn't want to think about the numbers. "I want to end this war sooner rather than later. You understand, Major?"

"Yes, sir."

"To that end, we've been in contact with someone in the German high command--Heinrich Himmler. Heard of him? He's the chief of the Gestapo, and he's tight with Hitler. He's gotten word to us that we might be able to broker a peace agreement. He's likely only looking to save his own skin, but if it will spare lives I'm not going to look a gift Nazi in the mouth, if you know what I mean."

Miller nodded.

"This could be our last chance for peace without fighting all the way to Berlin and paying for every inch. So here's the deal. Apparently Himmler is a music buff. In particular, I'm told, he's a huge fan of yours. So I want you to be my representative. I want you to go speak with him, see what he has in mind, see if we can end this thing now."

"Sir? Uh, I mean . . . I wanted to make a contribution to the war effort, but this . . . ?"

"I know this isn't something you've been trained for. However I believe you're the best man for the job. If the fact that Himmler's a fan can help us at all, then I want to use it."

"Yes, sir. I'll . . . I'll do my best, sir."

"One more thing. This mission is strictly unofficial. There's no paperwork on it, there'll be no record of it. Only you, myself, my chief aide, and the OSS agent who will take you to meet with Himmler know about it. You're not to tell anyone--before or after the fact. No one can ever know I made overtures to the head of the Gestapo. I'd be crucified in the press. You understand?"

"Yes, sir, I understand completely."

December 18, 1944 - Basel, Switzerland

The stranger from the future had not reappeared since leaving him in Paris, and Miller was beginning to think the fellow was an hallucination. Maybe he'd bumped his head during the flight over, and it had affected his mind. Maybe it *was* just a dream. It had all seemed so real. The odd little fellow Quay had certainly seemed real.

Now he stood in a hotel parlor in Switzerland, waiting for an audience with a member of the German high command. Was this another delusion?

"Herr Miller, it's an honor to meet you." A fellow wearing a crisp SS uniform and glasses not unlike his own strode towards him, hand outstretched in greeting. "I am a devoted follower of your music. I listen to it whenever I get the chance."

The Gestapo chief had an extremely firm handshake.

"I must tell you," continued Himmler, "I especially love that one 'Chattanooga Choo Choo.' Am I pronouncing that correctly?"

He wasn't, but Miller nodded.

"I admit I need music like some men need women. I'm sure you understand what I mean." Himmler removed his crested military hat. "May I get you a drink?"

"Sure, yes," replied Miller.

"Nietzsche was never more astute than when he said, 'The universe without music would be madness.' Don't you agree, Herr Miller?"

"Well, music is my life."

Miller took the glass handed him.

"I think you'll appreciate this. Even though we no longer hold France, we have access to some excellent French wines. This one's from the Bordeaux region I believe."

Himmler sipped his drink and Miller did likewise.

"Ah, but you haven't come here to discuss wine *or* music, have you? You're here as Eisenhower's representative, concerning a proposition I recently made."

"Yes," responded Miller, happy to get on with it. Something about Himmler made his skin crawl. "General Eisenhower would very much like to see the conflict end as soon as possible--saving lives on both sides."

"Yes, yes," Himmler replied in an offhand manner, "however I'm afraid circumstances have changed since I first contacted your general. I no longer have the Fuehrer's ear. I know Germany is destined to fall--I believe even the Fuehrer knows this, deep in his heart--but he is too willful, too far gone. He will never agree to surrender."

"There's nothing you can do?"

"We can discuss the terms of our capitulation, and the day the Fuehrer no longer breathes, they can be implemented. Until then . . . I'm afraid the war must run its course."

December 19, 1944 - Over Southern Belgium

"So it was all for nothing. You're from the future, you must have known it was all for nothing."

"Yes, I knew," said Quay. "But history had to be played out. At least the fragments of history as we know them."

"Now what?" Miller wanted to know. "Now what do I have to do?"

"There are no reliable reports, no credible evidence, of you ever being seen again. So now we return to my time. If my breach has been discovered, I will face the appropriate punishment. You, however, will be free to continue making your music."

"I don't want to sound ungrateful, but what if I don't want to go?"

"I am afraid that is not an option at this point in time, Mr. Miller. Surely you would not have preferred death?"

Miller thought it over. "No, no I guess I wouldn't."

"I am glad to hear you say so. If not, then my violation would have been for naught."

"I *would* like to see this future world of yours," said Miller. "And there are so many more arrangements in my head that I never got the chance to put down on paper. You use paper don't you?"

"You can if you would like."

"But . . . are you certain I can't visit my family before we--"

Quay's craft rocked suddenly, violently.

"What was that?" asked Miller.

The man from the future scrambled to his controls.

"The time wardens have found me. They are trying to seize control of the ship."

"What will they do?"

Miller saw the first sign of overt emotion in Quay since they'd met. It was fear.

"We must get away. I must get you back before--"

The ship jerked, seemed to accelerate free of whatever was holding it, then plunged.   Miller struggled for a hold as the ship appeared to lose power. He saw Quay working frantically to regain control. The sensation of falling swept over him--the same feeling he'd had just days ago. He started to say something, to ask if they we're going to crash, but before he could get the words out the ship lurched, then bucked in violent collision.

f

Consciousness was slow to return. His left arm hurt. He was sure it was broken. He struggled to get up.

The man from the future lay nearby, not moving, his body contorted in an awful way. If he wasn't dead, he was in bad shape.

There was an enormous rip in the bottom of the ship, which had come to rest on its side. Miller stooped to a crouch to get through the tear in the hull.

It was night outside and snowing. He stood and got his first look at the craft. In the moonlight it appeared more like an oversized carton of cigarettes than a plane. He wondered how it flew with no wings. However it worked, he doubted it would ever fly again.

An explosion rocked his reverie and sent him diving for cover. His arm squawked in pain. He looked up. It wasn't Quay's ship that had exploded. The burst was several yards in the other direction. Another blast annihilated a treetop. By the time the ringing faded from his ears, an erratic serenade of gunfire had erupted all around him.

Miller didn't know where he was, but he realized they'd come down in no man's land. He heard a moan and saw someone lying in the open several yards away. In the dark he couldn't tell whether the man was ally or enemy, but realized the fellow was in a dangerous spot.

Without thinking, Miller ran to the man, hoping to drag him to safety. All around him strident bursts of light arms fire crackled in uneven syncopation. He reached the wounded soldier and bent down to grab him with his one good arm. Even as he did he heard the cacophony of a machine gun, and felt the bullets rip through him.

*

From where he lay in the snow he could see the wreckage of the time ship, but the pain made it difficult to keep his eyes open. The sounds of battle continued, though fainter than they had been. The pain, too, soon diminished, replaced by numbness. His vision blurred, so he couldn't be certain, but he thought Quay's ship began to shimmer. He heard the pristine thrumming of a clarinet in C minor, and watched as the ship vanished in a golden flare of light.

January 30, 1946 - Allied Headquarters, Paris, France

"There's one more thing, sir."

"Yes, what is it, Captain?"

"I have no evidence it's related to Major Miller, or even that it's anything more than battle fatigue. However, members of a 4th Infantry Division patrol reported seeing an aircraft of a type they couldn't identify. They described it as box-like with no wings."

Colonel Washburn made a noise of disbelief. "No wings? What kind of aircraft doesn't have wings? What does this have to do with the case anyway?"

"Nothing, sir. Just that this unidentified flying thing was spotted in the same area outside Bastogne where Major Miller's body was allegedly discovered."

The colonel rose from his chair.

"You were right to come to me first, Captain. In two weeks the brass is going to present a posthumous bronze star to Miller's widow, and the last thing we need is to have this matter confused with conflicting, not to mention embarrassing, reports. You will excise all these baseless rumors from your official report and conclude Major Miller's plane went down somewhere over the English Channel due to unknown reasons. Is that clear?"

"Yes, sir. But what if--"

"No buts, Captain. I want this matter officially closed. Unofficially, I'd say you're right. We'll likely never know the truth of it."

f

To this day there are many theories about the demise of Major Anton Glenn Miller, none of which have been proven. This story is based on both what is known and what is theorized about his mysterious disappearance.

My dad, Robert Bruce Golden, like Miller, served in the Army Air Corps' 8th Air Force. He was part of a bomber group that flew B-15s out of England, and his commander was another celebrity--one who would go on to star in the movie, The Glenn Miller Story-- *Colonel Jimmy Stewart.*

Ascension

Since arriving at Nottingham Castle, Edward had been planning on confronting his mother and Lord Mortimer about his wife's finances. He and Philippa had been married almost two years, and her rightful dower had been deferred too long. He was determined to do something about it.

He held his wife's hand as they descended from their bedchamber. It was an ancient castle, and he likened the way down the spiral stone staircase to sinking into the maw of some great beast. Each step was taken with reluctance and dread. Were they not swallowed up, they'd reach the great hall, where he expected to find his mother and Roger Mortimer, as well as members of the regency council, all busy with matters of state. Most likely it was the trepidation of confronting his mother and her lover that laced the descent with apprehension.

Philippa only occasionally alluded to her household finances. She'd been neither insistent nor vexed. In fact, she'd been all but complacent about acquiescing to the wishes of his mother, Isabella, the queen dowager. But now that Philippa had given birth to England's future king--now that they had a royal child, Edward was resolute.

Philippa knew what he was about and was visibly nervous. He squeezed her hand and smiled. She smiled back, but her winsome blue eyes couldn't mask her anxiety.

She was almost as tall as he, a buxom beauty he'd desired from the first time he'd laid eyes on her--long after the marriage had been arranged by his mother and approved by the Pope. He'd been lucky the woman he'd been told he would marry was his own age and so pretty, and luckier still she possessed a sweet disposition.

He'd quickly fallen in love with her, and now that they'd had their first child, the future king of England, he felt even more protective of her.

Arriving at the great hall, they had to pass by a pair of Mortimer's wild Welshmen who stood guard. There were dozens throughout the castle, as Mortimer never went anywhere without them. Edward didn't like the way they looked at Philippa, but said nothing.

Inside he found his mother, Mortimer, and a contingent of royal officials, including Chancellor Burghersh, Sir Oliver Ingham, and Sir Simon de Bereford,

Mortimer's puppets on the council. Most were seated at the grand table, busy in discussions, various papers splayed out in front of them.

When Edward entered, Burghersh and the others rose from their seats as was customary.

"Good day, Your Highness," greeted the Chancellor.

Only Lord Mortimer didn't stand. The slight was obvious, but not wholly unexpected. It wasn't the first time Mortimer had made plain his disrespect for the young king.

"Please, sit," said Edward. "Continue with thy business."

Edward saw his mother standing near the glazed window, looking bored with the proceedings. Even just standing there, hardly moving, there was an elegance to her. She was still the most beautiful woman in whatever room she graced, despite her 38 years. Edward admitted to himself she was even more lovely than his own, much younger, wife. He marched over to her, Philippa still in-hand.

"Good day, Mother."

She simply nodded as if her thoughts were elsewhere.

"I want to speak with thee about Philippa's household expenses, and her rightful dower. 'Tis time she received it."

Isabella, known by both friend and foe as the "she-wolf of France," turned, seeming to notice her son for the first time.

"Thy wife's dower is in my care, Edward. She will receive it soon enough. As to her household expenses, was she not granted the sum of 1,000 marks per annum?"

"Now that she has a child to care for, 'tis not enough," said Edward.

"What's not enough?"

It was Mortimer, who'd chosen to quit his seat at the table and intervene, as though nothing concerning the young king would escape his purview.

He let go of Philippa's hand and turned to face Mortimer. "I was discussing the queen's dower with my mother," said Edward in a tone suggesting it had nothing to do with Mortimer.

"The dower will be presented to the *queen* in due time." The way Mortimer said *queen* revealed he didn't recognize Philippa as such. "In the meantime, quit thy sniveling. Thou will be king soon--act like it."

"I'm already king," responded Edward, standing his ground.

"By blood, yes," replied Mortimer. "But not by ascension. Until then, thou will do as thee are told."

With an air of condescension, Mortimer took Isabella by the arm and led her away.

Edward stood rock still, fists clenched, his rage building until it he felt his reddish gold hair would burst into flame.

Philippa put her hand on his shoulder. Her touch calmed him, and he composed his bearing enough so his ire didn't reveal itself. Yet, inside, he still seethed.

What the despised Mortimer said was true. Until his 18th birthday, he wielded no real power. He was king in name only. It was the regency council that ran the government, and it was Mortimer, with the help of Edward's mother, that ruled the regency, though neither was an official member.

That it had all come to pass had left Edward with many regrets. One of which was that his father had been deposed by politics and warfare. Taken to France by his mother when he was still very young, Edward had little chance to know his father. Though he'd been told awful stories about the man by his mother and Mortimer, he'd had nothing to do with the rebellion that removed his father from the throne of England,

When it seemed most everyone in England had turned against Edward II, he, the heir to the throne at age 14, had finally stood up to his mother and Mortimer, refusing to accept the crown unless his father abdicated it willingly to him. How they'd be able to secure that abdication, Edward didn't know. But his father had indeed relinquished his crown, so Edward had become Edward III.

His father had died soon after, while a prisoner in the castle of one of Mortimer's allies, and Edward had endured years as a powerless king, at the whim of the regency--at the whim of Baron Mortimer, the Earl of March. Mortimer had used the influence garnered in the bed of Edward's mother to acquire many noble estates, secure his position as overlord of Wales, and increase his personal wealth many times.

Yet, in less than two months, Edward would celebrate his 18th birthday, and the regency council would be dissolved. On that day, Lord Mortimer would no longer rule him--no longer disrespect him. It was a day he longed for.

/

"He treats me like a child, not like the man who will soon wield the scepter of England."

Edward paced as he spoke with his friend and confidant, Sir William Montagu. Though ten years his senior, Montagu had been a member of the royal household since they were both boys, and was like a big brother to Edward. Now he was a sounding board for the young king's frustrations, as well as the captain of his personal guard.

"I tell thee, Will, Mortimer's impudence is galling."

"Calm thyself, Edward," said Montagu. "I'd worry more about his intrigue than his impudence."

"What does thou mean?"

"I mean, be careful what thou says, and who thou says it to. Lord Mortimer has spies everywhere."

"But I am king," said Edward, finally ceasing to pace. "I can say what I want."

"Thou can say what thee wants, but petulance will get thee nowhere. Thou must bide thy time. Meanwhile, Mortimer is his own worst enemy. His plundering, his audacious political moves, have alienated noble families across the country. There are many who can't wait to support thy ascension to the throne. When the time is right, they will rally to thy side."

"As always, thy counsel is sound, Will. I will chew the bit with forbearance."

As he said it, Edward knew, in his heart, patience was not among his virtues. He could ride a horse, parry with a sword, and had even learned to speak three languages, but his equanimity was tested by the plodding nature of politics.

f

Though he told Sir Montagu he would proceed with caution, it wasn't in his nature to do nothing. So he crawled through a dust-ridden recess to the hidden alcove where he knew he could overhear Lord Mortimer and his mother in her bedchamber. Mortimer wasn't the only one who could spy.

" . . . and he never would have abdicated the throne if I hadn't threatened it would go to someone other than thy son." It was Mortimer's voice. "But even so, something had to be done. Thy husband still had supporters, and their numbers were growing every day. They were preparing to mount a counter coup against us, and put him back on the throne."

"But did thee have to do *that*?" asked his mother.

"It had to be done," replied Mortimer.

Edward wondered what he meant. *What had to be done?*

"I've heard ghastly things about the way 'twas carried out," said Isabella. "Is it true? Was he--"

"Don't concern thyself with such lurid rumors," said Mortimer. "'Tis over.

'Tis done."

"What about Philippa's finances? Thou knows we spent her entire dowry on the mercenary army we used to overthrow my late husband. We'll have to concoct her dower in some manner."

"Let's not worry about that," said Mortimer. "Thy son remains under our control for now. Thou should continue thy deceptions with him."

"But he will soon ascend the throne, and deceptions will no longer be enough."

"Who knows how the future will unfold."

What did he mean about the future? What will unfold?

Edward wasn't sure what Mortimer was speaking of, but the confidence of his tone did not bode well. Edward was certain he must do something--but what? What *could* he do?

f

Edward was restless that night. He was afraid his tossing and turning would wake Philippa, so he dressed and ascended the stairs to the castle's parapet. There, alone, his restlessness and boot leather wore at the stone battlements. He considered his situation as he paced--considered the possibilities--relived the impertinence of Lord Mortimer and fumed again. No resolutions came forth, and even the wind seemed to mock him.

"Father," he finally said out of frustration, "if only thee were here to guide me, to tell me what I must do." He spoke to the clouds looming in the night sky. "How shall I be a king, as thou were?"

Edward dropped his head, staring at his hands--his smooth, uncalloused fingers, and considered how childlike he felt--how ineffectual. But he wasn't a child, and he knew raving against the night like a madman would do no good. He must use his mind, not his unbridled emotions.

The wind surged against him, billowing his cloak. He looked up to see the clouds swirling with an angst matching his own. The moon appeared where it had previously been hidden, and with its light he witnessed a shape materializing in the firmament. The silhouette was ill-defined, wavering in a state of flux, but gradually congealing, taking the shape of a man--a bearded man familiar enough to tickle the hairs on the nape of his neck.

"Father? Father, is that thee?"

He couldn't be certain of the apparition's identity. He'd seen little of his father for several years. Only on the day the former king abdicated his throne, looking gaunt and weary, had Edward seen him. Whether this ghastly vision

143

was his father, he didn't know, until it spoke.

"*Edward . . . my son . . . thou . . . are troubled.*"

Edward staggered back, ready to take flight. But he held his ground, staring in disbelief at the phantom form.

"Father, since thee died, I have been beset by all manner of travails."

"*I did not die,*" bellowed the ghost, "*I was . . . murdered.*"

The word echoed down the parapet--"*murdered . . . murdered . . . .murdered.*"

"Was it Lord Mortimer who killed thee?"

"*He bears . . . the guilt.*"

"When I ascend the throne, I will punish him for his foul deeds," declared Edward.

"*The throne . . . may not be thine . . . if vile Mortimer has his way.*"

"What does thou mean? How could he prevent--"

"*There is a passageway . . . known to but a few . . . from the castle rock . . . near the* Jerusalem Inn. *It leads . . . to the kitchen. Unlock the door . . .* " As the words reverberated around him, the specter of his father faded. " *. . . unlock the door . . . unlock the door.*"

"Father, wait! What does thou mean? Father!"

The ghost was gone, and Edward had no idea what his last words meant. *Unlock which door . . . and why?*

ʃ

At the first opportunity to catch her alone, Edward confronted his mother.

"Did thee and Mortimer murder my father?"

She was caught off guard, stricken either by his accusation or by her own guilt.

"What say thee, Son? Of course I didn't murder thy father. He died untouched except by his own illness."

Edward stared at her, his penetrating eyes searching hers for the truth . . . for deception.

"Would thee even know if thy lover had ordered the deed?" accused Edward. "Thou who concede to his every whim."

"I shall not listen to such insolence from my own son," replied Isabella, turning to leave.

Edward grabbed her arm and pulled her back. "And I shall not be thy puppet forever, Mother. Be forewarned."

She stared at him, seeing the blaze of determination in his eyes, then pulled away and fled the room.

Edward watched her go. He knew she'd run straight to Mortimer. He didn't care, but decided to use that time wisely. He made his way to the kitchen and ordered the servants there to clear the room.

It didn't take long to find the door of which his father spoke. It was at the rear of a dusty pantry, hidden behind bags of grain and onions. He moved the bags enough to reach the door, unlock it, and look behind.

A fetid odor assailed his nostrils. The air behind the door was rank with mold and other scents he had no wish to identify. But there was indeed a passageway, dark and dank, and slanted downward as if into the bowels of Hell. He shut the door and replaced the bags, but left the door unlocked as the haunting words of his father commanded. How that would help him, he had no idea.

*

Philippa, Edward, Sir Montagu, and a pair of young nobles of their acquaintance were listening to the coos and cries of the infant Prince Edward when a royal clerk appeared in the nursery, followed by six armed men.

"What's the meaning of this?" demanded Edward.

The clerk stuttered as he said, "The Council of Regents requests thy presence, Your Majesty."

"For that they sent these guards?"

"They also request the immediate presence of Sir William Montagu, Sir Ralph de Stafford, and Sir John Neville," stated the clerk.

Philippa looked worried. Montagu only smiled.

Edward turned to his wife. "I'll return shortly. There's nothing to fear."

Edward and the others followed the clerk to the great hall, their guards trailing. He wondered how the council had known the friends of Montagu were in the castle, and then he remembered. *Mortimer has spies everywhere.*

The regency council was arranged behind the large oaken table, facing the entrance to the hall. It was all too formal a setting. Edward wondered what they were up to, and what they wanted. Lord Mortimer, meanwhile, was on his feet, treading back and forth behind the table, until he saw them enter. This time no one stood to recognize the young king's entrance. It was not a good sign.

"Evidence has come to the attention of this council of a plot against the crown," said Mortimer. Edward recognized the man was barely holding back his rage.

"What kind of a plot?" asked Edward.

145

"A plot against me," raged Mortimer, "and thou are so accused."

Edward wasn't certain if he meant Montagu or himself, or all of them, but he saw Chancellor Burghersh flinch at Mortimer's words.

"Thou speaks as if thee and the crown were same, Lord Mortimer," said Montagu defiantly. "The crown is the king, and his regency--of which thee has no standing."

"My standing is not thy concern," snapped Mortimer. "'Tis thy allegiance which the regency questions."

"I've done nothing to break my allegiance to the king. I've obeyed his every command. And I defy anyone on this council to call the king a traitor against himself."

Several council members looked flummoxed by Montagu's undeniable logic, but Mortimer was still angry.

"When the king's wishes are in conflict with my own," said Mortimer, "my commands take precedent."

The audacious statement caught the council off guard. They appeared embarrassed, even stunned, by Mortimer's words.

Chancellor Burghersh said, "Of course no one is accusing the king of plotting against the crown, but the regency council's authority cannot be usurped by anyone." He flashed a disapproving look at Mortimer. "To deny such allegations is thy right as nobles of the land, but know thee the council will examine the evidence Lord Mortimer has provided, and thee may be called before us again."

"I wish to see such evidence thee speaks of," said Edward.

"In due time, Your Highness," said the Chancellor. "We are not certain it yet merits thy attention."

"Inform me when it does," said Edward, using the most imperious tone he could muster. Turning from the council table he left the great hall, followed by Montagu and the other two young nobles.

When they reached the king's bedchamber, Edward was still fuming. His anger was so obvious, the young nobles held their tongues.

"The council may have the power now, but in two score days I'll turn 18, and the regency will be disbanded," said Edward with authority.

"If Mortimer lets thee," responded Montagu.

"What does thou mean?" Edward turned angrily and stared at his friend. "What does thou mean *if he lets me*? How could he stop me?"

"Thou can't be king if thee are dead," said Montagu, his expression matching the seriousness of his words.

"What are thee saying, Will? First thou counseled patience. Now thee believes Mortimer will have me killed?"

"Something has changed," responded Montagu. "Something has driven Mortimer to act, and act rashly if all is as it appears."

"I confronted my mother about my father's death," said Edward contritely. "I vowed vengeance."

"That could be the dagger which prodded Mortimer," said Montagu.

"Possibly," spoke up Sir Stafford, "but there has been speculation for some time among noble families that Mortimer plans to take the crown for himself."

"His position is even more precarious, now that thou has a male heir," said Sir Neville. "If he indeed plans to be king, it would be foolish of him to let thee live to see thy next birthday."

Edward looked stunned by the notion. Would Mortimer really go that far? Would his mother be complicit in such a scheme? He'd never considered the possibility. Yet, looking at the faces of his comrades, he saw they believed it.

"Could this be true, Will? Should I fear for my life?"

"'Tis a real possibility. Not only is *thy* life in jeopardy, but that of thy wife and son."

"What should I do?"

Philippa and her servants entered the bedchamber, laughing about something. Montagu stepped closer to the king and said quietly, "'Tis better thou should eat the dog than the dog should eat thee."

*

Dusk crept slowly across Nottingham Castle, both driven and waylaid by Edward's eagerness. As soon as night fell, he made his way to the parapet. He'd already planned to meet with Montagu later, but first he hoped for the reappearance of his father . . . or at least the spirit of his father.

He didn't have to wait long.

The apparition appeared in the identical spot it had before, and this time Edward held his ground without fear.

"Edward . . . my son."

"Father, I'm beset by enemies. I know not if I will live to be king. Tell me what the future holds. Tell me what I should do."

"Thou will . . . be king . . . if first . . . thou acts like a king."

"Act like a king? How? How did thee?"

"I was not . . . a great king. I had . . . faults. I failed . . . as often as not. Thou must

147

be . . . better . . . a better king . . . a great king."

"But how? If I don't act now, I may not be king at all. What should I do?"

"Do what needs be done."

"What?" asked Edward, desperate for an answer. "What must be done?"

The apparition began to wane. Edward cried out, "Wait! Don't go!" As the image of his father evanesced, the ghost's final words echoed across the castle heights.

"Unlock the door . . . unlock the door."

"I already unlocked the door!" shouted Edward at the empty sky. He slammed his fist against the gray stone. "What else am I to do?"

Frustrated, alone once again, he turned and slid down against the wall, plopping forlornly on the cold, rough pathway. The specter's cryptic words had been of no help. How was he to be a great king, much less ascend the throne, if he didn't know what to do.

He sat for a long time, thinking, weighing alternatives, mustering his courage, before he left to meet Montagu. Though there was no sudden realization on his part, something manifested within him. Something changed. When he pulled himself up and made his way down the parapet, a new determination varnished his manner. There was a resoluteness to his stride, a look in his eye that was more predator than prey.

At the appointed hour, he met Montagu in the kitchen. At that time of night, most servants were asleep and the kitchen was empty. Even so, they spoke in low tones to guard their words.

"Mortimer must be stopped--now," stated Edward with assurance. "He must be arrested for his crimes, including the murder of my father."

Montagu nodded. "It won't be an easy task. We can't just march through the castle gates and into the great hall with a troop of knights and arrest him. He won't allow that. He's surrounded by a well-armed retinue at all times, and has some 200 men guarding this castle. 'Tis locked tight, with sentries at every gate."

"Yes. My mother sleeps each night with the keys to the gates under her pillow in their tower stronghold."

"Mortimer is no fool," said Montagu. "He suspects treachery at every turn."

"Because he's so treacherous himself," said Edward.

Montagu nodded again. "It would take thousands of men to storm Nottingham Castle, and I fear thee would not survive its taking, even if we had the army."

"We have something else," said Edward. "That's why I wanted to meet thee here. There's a secret passageway from a cave just outside the castle, near the *Jerusalem Inn*, that leads to this room."

"What?" Montagu was taken aback. "Does Mortimer know of this passageway?"

"I doubt it. 'Tis unguarded. Let me show thee."

Edward led him into the pantry, moved the sacks, and opened the door. It was too dark to see much, but Montagu was intrigued.

"Has thou gone inside to see where it leads?"

"No, not yet."

"We'll have to be certain. But if, indeed, this is a way out of the castle, we can use it to move thee, thy wife and child, to safety."

"No," said Edward without hesitation. "I will not flee. I will not give Mortimer what is mine. If I were to go, the regency could declare me abducted or in exile. They could crown someone else, and I would be unable to ascend the throne which is my birthright."

"But that would give us time to build an army," encouraged Montagu, "to topple Mortimer's already unpopular regime, and thee would be safe."

"I seek not safety, but a kingdom," stated Edward. "If I want it, I must take it. I must do what needs be done." Edward smiled at his friend. "I must eat the dog."

*

After dinner, Philippa left to check on the baby, but Edward stayed in the great hall. A pair of troubadours his mother had invited into the castle were playing a lute and a gittern, and singing songs of chivalry and courtly love, so Edward pretended to listen. What he was really doing was waiting.

Between songs, Lord Mortimer asked Edward, loudly enough for everyone to hear, "Are thee aware thy captain of the guard is no longer in Nottingham?"

"What does thou mean?" replied Edward, though he knew full well.

"Sir Montagu and his cohorts have fled the castle, obviously fearing prosecution for their treasonous plots."

"'Tis not true," said Edward.

"But it is," responded Mortimer with arrogant assurance. "Thou would be wise to better choose thy allies in the future."

As the music continued, Edward began showing signs of illness. He grabbed his stomach, bent over, and seemed ready to vomit. Isabella immediately called for the royal doctor.

149

"It might have been something he ate," said the doctor. "I'd better see him to his bedchamber."

It didn't matter to Edward whether Mortimer and his mother thought it was something he ate or the word of Montagu's flight from Nottingham that had made him sick. Yet, as he left the great hall, he heard Mortimer jest about the "king's weak stomach." It provoked laughter from his confederates.

If Edward needed to boost his courage, Mortimer's disparaging remark was just the medicine. It fortified the young king, who soon dismissed the doctor, saying he was going to sleep.

First, he put on a servant's robe to both disguise himself and conceal his sword. When the time was right, he made his way to the kitchen, keeping his head bowed as he passed a contingent of guards. Once there, he made certain the hidden door was still unlocked. Then he waited.

The minutes passed at a snail's pace. Edward began to doubt Montagu and his allies would ever arrive. He knew his friend wouldn't let him down, so he suspected something must have happened to him. *Were they captured trying to enter the passageway? Did Mortimer have them arrested before they ever left Nottingham Castle?* These and many other thoughts gnawed at Edward's courage as he waited.

He opened the door and took another look. He saw torchlight.

Montagu and some two dozen men were making their way up the narrow passage. Among them Edward recognized Sir Stafford and Sir Neville. They were all heavily armed, wearing grim faces, ready for a fight. All except Montagu. He smiled and grasped Edward by the forearm.

"Are thee ready to claim thy crown, Sire?"

"I'm ready."

With Edward and Montagu leading, they made their way up the winding tower stairs to the floor of the queen dowager's bedchamber. There they were spotted by a small group of guards and servants.

"Traitors! Traitors!" shouted one of the guards.

Montagu's men rushed forward, weapons in hand. Sir Neville's mace bashed the head of the guard who was shouting. Montagu stabbed another. The rest were overwhelmed and surrendered, as the interlopers burst into the bedchamber.

They found Mortimer armed with his sword and ready to fight. Less ready to resist against such odds were Mortimer's accomplices, Sir Ingham, Sir Bereford, and Chancellor Burghersh. They'd been plotting, no doubt.

Mortimer managed to stab one of Montagu's men with a quick thrust. But he was overpowered and knocked to the floor. Ingham and Bereford surrendered without a fight, and the chancellor was apprehended trying to escape down the privy shaft.

Montagu stood over Lord Mortimer and said, "I arrest thee in the king's name."

Isabella rushed forward from where she'd cowered when the intruders broke in, and threw herself at her son's feet.

"Fair Son, have pity on noble Mortimer. Do him no harm."

Edward ignored his mother's pleas and looked at Montagu.

"Now what? The castle is still brimming with Mortimer's men."

"By now they've likely spotted the Earl of Lancaster's troops," said Montagu. "He's surrounded the castle and awaits thy orders, my king."

"Have some of thy men take the keys from my mother's bed down through the passageway and give them to Lancaster, should he need them." Edward gestured to their prisoners, who were being bound and gagged. "To the dungeon with them, and bring me the captain of Lord Mortimer's guard. We'll see if we can end this without further bloodshed."

"Yes, Sire. And thy mother?"

"She's not to leave her chamber."

The prisoners were taken, Isabella was left locked in her room, and Edward and his cast of young nobles started down the tower to take command of the castle.

"I don't know about the rest of thee," said Sir Neville, "but fighting makes me hungry."

"When the castle's secure, we'll have a great feast," said Edward. "Whatever thee wants."

Montagu smiled at the young king and said, "I'm so hungry I could eat a dog."

*

After a short trial, Lord Roger Mortimer was hung at Tyburn Tree--a gallows for common criminals. Sir Bereford was also executed, but Sir Ingham and Chancellor Burghersh were pardoned, and went on to serve King Edward. Isabella would live out her life under house arrest, but in a gilded cage--a castle where she had a pension and plenty of servants.

Those who helped Edward ascend to the throne were all rewarded, including several earldoms for the young nobles who came up through the secret passageway to confront

Mortimer. Sir William Montagu would become the Earl of Salisbury, but would be killed not long after in a jousting tournament.

During his 50 years as king, Edward III would guide the nation through the hundred years war and the plague of the black death. With unprecedented popularity, he would increase the role of parliament; create, with chivalry as its founding principle, the Order of the Garter for the nation's most illustrious knights; and transform England into one of the world's greatest military powers.

The appearance of Edward II's ghost is pure speculation, but the man himself, his son Edward III, Philippa, Isabella, and Sir Ralph de Stafford are all my direct ancestors (Edward's great granddaughter would marry Stafford's great grandson). Sir John Neville was the brother of another direct ancestor.

Wanderlust

The juncture of coalescence is akin to a sun going nova . . . a bud opening to flower . . . a cell propagating through binary fission. It's all that and more. But that exquisite instant always gives way to territorial reality. On one new world, joined with one unique entity, I found it a harsh reality.

My first moments of shared awareness were filled with abrupt, brutal violence fed by a profusion of savage emotions, the likes of which I'd never experienced in all my travels. I was used to the extreme variety and volatility of alien perceptions and sensibilities, organic drives to procreate, to feed, to survive. I'd joined consciousness with life forms both high and low, though I normally gravitated toward the former. But no creature I'd ever merged with prepared me for the onslaught of barbarism which overwhelmed me that first day.

Typically it doesn't take long to exert at least a modicum of control over my host entity. The first step is always to establish a link with the organism's sensory receptors and neural pathways. But the emotional chaos I experienced from first contact left me a powerless observer, for, while I had no control, I could see what my host saw.

What I saw, what I heard, what my olfactory connections sensed, was bloody carnage. I'd left my ship and joined the body of a creature engaged in mass conflict. There was no bridling the feral nature of the entity. It struck its foes again and again with a weapon grasped by one of its appendages. I could only hold on and watch as bodily humors and limbs scattered in its wake. The sounds were horrid. The screeches of agony, the ignominious cries of jubilation, the finality of the death rattles, all layered into a non-stop symphony of slaughter.

I wondered if this was truly the planet's most intelligent life form, as my preliminary assessment of the world revealed. If so, I was concerned about the effect such vicious psyches would have on my own identity. For the longer I shared consciousness, the more I took control of the organism, the more of its id I would absorb, the more its instincts, its drives, would become a part of me.

As I analyzed the creature to determine the risk, I felt intense pain. It was sharp, unyielding, spreading throughout the body. I knew almost instantly my host had been mortally wounded. I jumped.

153

Over the briefest of periods I went from one combatant to another, pain and anguish prodding me to withdraw before each host's life force completely ebbed. The continuous transference was dizzying. I would barely establish a presence when I'd be forced to flee.

Finally I jumped into a creature whose raw emotions weren't quite as chaotic, whose savagery seemed more directed. I had time to establish a sensory link, to become fully aware of the being's physical strength and relative calm, even in the midst of the turmoil raging around it.

It was a superior being. I sensed it, and sensed that it knew it was . . . at least in some respects. I discerned, through both its manner and its consciousness, that it was a leader among these creatures. From the vantage point of its visual receptors I determined it stood at a greater height than its fellows. In its limbs I felt immense physical power--much greater than those I'd previously inhabited. I hoped that strength signaled an end to my too-rapid staccato shifts of perception.

/

Hrolf knew the battle couldn't be won--not this day. He was covered in the blood and entrails of his enemies, but the Franks' position was too strong. His forces had briefly breached the castle walls, only to be beaten back. As much as it galled him, he called for his men to retreat. Whether the other chieftains would do the same he didn't know. Each would make his own decision, and their men would live or die with it.

For his part, he'd had enough of this foreign land. It had been an ill-advised venture, costing more lives than it was worth--Sigfrid be damned for convincing them to follow him here. The fortifications surrounding the great city of Paris were too strong.

Hrolf would advise the other chieftains to convince Sigfrid to accept the payment of silver offered by the Franks to leave them be. He would have his men collect what plunder they could as they returned to their homes in the north, and thank the Norns they lived to tell their families the tale of their quest to Francia.

He couldn't wait to feel the rolling sea under his feet again, and smell the salt air. He missed the taste of properly brewed *skyr* and the soft skin of a willing woman.

Francia was a rich land with much potential, but Hrolf wanted to go home.

/

My new host was an uncommon amalgam of barbarity and intellect. A combination that proved an impediment to my influence. Its mind was open to me, but not immediately subservient to my commands. I knew it was going to take longer than usual to gain even partial control over the organism. Much longer than I first estimated. I would have to be patient.

Over the planetary rotations that followed my joining with the creature, I learned many things, first of which was that it had a rudimentary language it used to communicate with its fellow beings. Its designation was *Hrolf*, but it was also known as *Ganger*, a term in its language meaning the *Walker*, but was somehow a reference to its great size, compared with others of its kind. It thought of itself as a *vikingr*, defined as a sort of sea-going warrior. Indeed, its first course of action was to lead a swarm of like creatures onto a vessel constructed for traveling on a liquid surface--a river it knew would lead to a much larger body of water.

It was then I realized my misfortune to have selected a traveler. My concern its journey would take me far from my own vessel ultimately proved correct. Yet I had little alternative but to bide my time until I gained full control of the entity's complex neuro system.

I'd learned, through my many joinings, the quickest, most efficient way to gain control of an alien organism, was to understand its motivations, its desires, and augment them with my own. With a creature as intelligent as this one, that would take not only time, but guile. It couldn't be forced. I would need to gradually meld its aspirations with my own.

In the case of this *vikingr*, this *Hrolf*, its ambitions were simple . . . primitive. It wanted riches, which it thought of in terms of property--specifically vast amounts of land. It wanted power over its fellows--which it already had to some degree. And it had an overriding lust to procreate with the female of its species--any female.

These were all desires I could build upon, over time, to gain the control I would need. Yet its immediate yearning was to return home, to whatever land had spawned it. I knew from my host it would be a long journey, but I had no idea how long.

∫

It was good to be home, to feel the biting wind of Thor's breath against his skin again, to taste *lutefisk* and *hakikarl* the way it was meant to prepared. But Hrolf couldn't shake the notion of his disappointment over the raid against the Franks. The walls of Paris had withstood their assault, and though he returned home with a bounty of treasure, it was not enough. All he could think of was

Bruce Edward Golden

how rich the lands of Francia were, and how someday he would sail back and carve out a kingdom there for himself.

*

Timeless as my essence was, I eventually grew weary of my host's limits. I'd remained joined with it for many revolutions of the planet around its star--far longer than I'd ever merged with any other life form. Far longer than any of my kind had ever coalesced. I considered jumping to one of its fellow creatures for sheer variety, but chance had given me a leader among these beings--one with the power to make decisions for the others. I didn't want to lose that.

My influence with the creature continued to grow. I was making progress, becoming attuned to its primitive yet driven mind. But I was also weakening. Alien forms could only sustain me for a time, and my fundamental vitality had never been so weak. I relied heavily on the strength of my host, yet I needed to return to my ship to replenish my energy reserves in a way no foreign energy source could.

The weaker I became, the more susceptible I was to the organism. I was adapting to the creature more than I wanted. For some time I'd felt the pleasure of its mating practices, the satisfaction of its feeding, the bloodlust of its combat. All of its emotions, its sensory patterns, were becoming intertwined with my own. I feared total immersion.

It was an old fear of my kind, never tested to this extreme, that lengthy contact could result in an unwanted symbiosis--a permanent symbiosis. I feared that outcome. But more than the fear was the longing. I longed to return to my own world.

*

Hrolf couldn't say why he was so driven to revisit the land of the Franks. When questioned by doubters he spoke of riches, of adventure, of the *vikingr* spirit. Yet deep within himself he knew there was more. He couldn't explain it-- not even to himself--but it was there. It was an itch he couldn't scratch. Not until he stood outside the walls of Paris once more.

It took years of beating the drums of war, but he'd finally convinced enough of his fellow chieftains to attempt another invasion of Francia. With their help he'd gathered more than a hundred ships, and thousands of willing warriors. But this time *he* would lead. This time *he* would be victorious.

He made an offering of a calf to Aegir to protect them on their long journey across the sea, prayed to Wotan, Thor, and every other god he could think of, and set sail. Never for a moment did he doubt his decision. Even in the roughest of seas he never considered turning back.

ʄ

I was close now--close to my vessel. As long as it had been, as tightly knit as I'd become with the id of my host, I could still sense its presence. Soon I would be close enough to return to my sanctuary . . . return to my own.

I'd been away too long. I'd learned much more than I ever cared to about this world's highest form of life. What I'd learned had both impressed and disturbed me. The primal drives of the creature were frighteningly savage and raw. Its self-destructive propensity for violence and brutality surpassed any creature I'd previously shared awareness with. Yet I was impressed by its perseverance to strive against often impossible odds, by the creative spark of its problem-solving. Its vital core had promise. The promise of fellowship, of compromise, of a yearning for more. It was this yearning, I believed, that would continue to elevate the organism from the primordial soup from which it evolved--would continue to augment its intelligence, its willingness to learn, to develop.

All that would take time--hundreds of lifespans, if not thousands. Whether I'd ever return to witness such an evolution, I didn't know. At the moment I had only the desire to be quit of it, to cleanse myself of its corporeal animal nature.

I waited as Hrolf led his fellows to within sight of their objective. I was so close--so ready to be alone again. Yet a disturbing fraction of my being didn't want to separate. It yearned to stay, to remain aligned with the perceptions of the alien entity. It lusted for its sensory impulses, its physicality, its raw sensations. I fought for my identity--for my very essence. I grappled with my consciousness using my host's inner strength, the same fortitude and resilience it had used against its enemies.

When Hrolf reached an area close enough to my ship, I posed the suggestion he halt and consider his next move. When he did, I jumped.

ʄ

When his siege of Paris resulted in another stalemate, the Viking chieftain Hrolf, better known to history as Rollo, made a deal with King Charles III of France. He was made Count of Rouen, married to one of the king's illegitimate daughters, and given lands on the west coast of France in return for his homage to the king, his conversion to Christianity, and a sworn oath to prevent further Viking attacks against Paris. Hrolf's descendants would become the dukes of Normandy, which got its name from Hrolf's "Northmen" who settled there. His great, great, great grandson, William,

157

conquered England in 1066, and his descendants have occupied the throne ever since. Legend has it Hrolf was called the "Walker" because he was too large to ride a horse. His great grandson by way of 32 generations is not so large, but is the author of this tale.

Whether it was an alien entity that influenced Hrolf to return to France, or just his own wanderlust, is a matter of speculation.

A Song for Senescence

They'd put her rocking chair under the old elm, the one she and Joseph had planted more than 50 years ago. So much had happened in those years, as they'd watched it grow higher and higher, spreading its branches out in all different directions just like their family. But today, on her special day, most all of her scattered kinfolk had gathered here to celebrate with her.

There were so many children running about, she couldn't begin to count them. She just sat in her rocker, in the shade of the old elm, enjoying the breeze and listening to the children laugh and play. The only thing missing was Joseph. She wished he was here to celebrate with her, but he'd been gone some 20 years now.

A semi-circle of picnic tables, dozens of them, had been assembled and placed around the elm just for this occasion. While the children played, the adults talked and ate, and every once in a while some would come up, bring her something to eat, wish her happy birthday or just ask how she was doing. Rarely did she recognize any of them. Her eyes were so bad, their faces were a blur. She knew the voices of those she lived with, like her son Isaac, but she had no idea who any of the others were unless they introduced themselves. It didn't matter. A minute later she'd forget the names. There were just too damn many of them.

"If I could have your attention everyone." She recognized Isaac's voice. "Please, everyone, if you could gather round. You kids over there. Hush up and come over here and sit on the ground around your great grandma."

"Don't you mean great, great grandma?" said someone else.

"Guess it depends," said Isaac with a laugh. "Come on now, everyone."

When everyone had settled, and the children had hushed, Isaac walked over and put his hand on her shoulder.

"I want to thank everyone for coming today. I know some of you had to travel quite a distance. But it's nice to have the whole family here to celebrate the 100th birthday of Martha Clarke Willard, the woman who gave birth to this family . . . my mom."

A spontaneous burst of applause broke out. Martha blushed. All this fuss just because she'd lived so long. The way her body ached these days, she wasn't sure it was worth it . . . living so long that is. Nothing worked right any more. She couldn't really walk without help, her hands were all crippled, she couldn't hear talk more than ten feet away, and could only see half as far. But though she told everyone who'd listen she didn't need a birthday party, she was secretly happy her family had shown up from parts unknown, and proud she was the matriarch of such a considerable brood.

When the applause died down, she looked up at Isaac and said, "Well, you ain't no spring chicken yourself."

Everyone laughed.

"It's true," responded Isaac, "I'm an old man of 70."

"That's nothing," said Martha. "My father lived to be 102, despite spending a good part of his life fighting Indians."

"I guess that's why I didn't have to fight any," said Isaac. "He took care of all them hostiles himself."

There was more laughter, though Martha failed to see the humor. She'd been there for the Indian wars. There'd been more than one. She'd seen people die. She couldn't remember all the details, but she remembered that.

"I know the Willards came from Kent in England," said someone, "but where was the Clarke family from?"

"My father's family came here from Ireland," said Martha. "I don't know about my mother's."

She remembered that because her father used to tell her stories about Ireland that his father had told him.

"As most of you know," began Isaac, "Martha raised all of her 12 children in a one-room house. That small house back yonder." He turned and pointed.

"That's right," said Martha. Though she couldn't see where he was pointing, she knew her old house wasn't far away. "Joseph built that house after he and a bunch of others bought the land hereabouts from the Nipmuc Indians in . . . 1735 I think it was. All of us got together and formed the town of Grafton that some of you still live in today.

"Where's Sarah?" Martha asked suddenly. "Where's my Sarah?"

An old woman sitting at one of the tables didn't move, but called out, "I'm right here, Mother."

"Sarah was the first white child ever born in these parts," said Martha.

"From Sarah," said Isaac, "and Martha and Joseph's 11 other children, grew the family of more than 300 who've gathered here today . . . along with assorted wives and husbands."

160

There was more applause, but Martha was confused.

"Three hundred?" she said in disbelief. "That can't be right. There can't be that many."

"Sure there can, Mother." Isaac pulled a piece of paper from his pocket and read from it. "You've got 12 children, 90 grandchildren--none of whom are children any more, 226 great grandchildren, and 53 great, great grandchildren."

"Imagine that," said Martha, still unable to comprehend the numbers.

"We're a very prolific family, Grandma," called out a voice she didn't recognize.

Everyone laughed.

"Tell us a story about the old days, Grandma," said another voice.

"Tell us about that time you were in Boston, when the Sons of Liberty started up," said a third voice.

"Well," began Martha, "we went to Boston to see a special doctor 'cause Joseph was ailing. We hadn't been to Boston since the end of the French and Indian War, so it had been many years, and we were surprised at how much animosity there was towards the king and his British troops. Anyway, I remember it was just before Christmas, 'cause we wanted to get back home for the holiday. There was this group of rebels calling themselves the Sons of Liberty, and I guess they'd had enough of the king's laws and taxes and such, and they dumped a shipload of tea right into the harbor."

There were cheers and more applause from her family. They were proud Americans now, no longer just colonists or rebels. Martha remembered Joseph supporting the rebels, thinking the Sons of Liberty were right. But then it all led to those fights at Lexington and Concord and Bunker Hill, and all the years of war that followed. During those bloody years, after Joseph had passed, she had her doubts about the fight for independence. So much death and destruction. So much worry when her sons and grandsons had joined the fight. Isaac, who was more than 50 at the time, left his blacksmith business and joined Colonel Chandler's Continental Regiment, fighting the British in Connecticut and New Jersey. It was pure luck none of her family died in the war.

Yet, when it was all over, she'd gotten to see the first American president elected, and fellow Massachusettsan John Adams become vice president. She'd even lived to see the Bill of Rights ratified, though it didn't give women the right to vote, and she was still angry about that. After all, women worked as hard as men, and most of them were smarter.

Once the gates to her memory opened, an onslaught of recollections washed over her. Martha closed her eyes, sorting the half-remembered from the distant and the fuzzy. So many years . . . so many good years. Though she and Joseph had been married for 60 of them, it hadn't seemed like enough.

Seeing his mother's eyes closed, Isaac thought she'd fallen asleep, as she had a habit of doing without notice. So he put his finger to his lips to alert the family, then walked away to join them at the tables. The talk continued at a lesser volume.

Martha was still awake, but she ignored the voices and concentrated on trying to remember what she could.

The warbling of a thrush finally broke her reverie and she opened her eyes. She knew it was a thrush because she used to love to go into the woods and search for birds. She even had a picture book to help her identify them. And though she could no longer see them, she knew them by their songs.

Her thoughts drifted once more, and she might have even dozed once or twice, until the sounds of the cleanup brought her back. Most of the gathering had likely either departed for their own homes or wandered over to the big house by now, though groups of children still played here and there. She delighted in their laughter, their screeches of frivolity. How wonderful it would feel to be a child again, to be able run and play without pain, without a care in the world.

One little girl ran up and stopped in front of her. Martha couldn't make out her face. All she could tell was that the girl was wearing green, had long dark hair, and was holding her hand behind her back.

"Hello," said Martha. "Who are you?"

"*Nikommo*," said the little girl.

"Nikommo? That's a funny name. I don't remember it."

"You can call me Niko if you want."

"Okay. Are you one of my great, great grandchildren, Niko?"

"I'm *nikommo*."

Martha wondered if the child were playing some kind of game, pretending she was someone or something else.

"What have you got behind your back, Niko?"

"You have to guess," the little girl replied. "It's a riddle."

"Oh, I like riddles," said Martha.

"First you see me in the grass, dressed in yellow gay. Next I'm in dainty white, then I fly away. What am I?"

She was certainly well-spoken for such a little girl thought Martha as she considered the riddle. It seemed familiar, but she just couldn't remember.

"I give up. What is it?"

Niko brought her hand forward, but Martha still couldn't see it.

"Bring it closer, child. I don't see as well as I used to."

The little girl moved it right in front of Martha's face.

"It's a dandelion," said Martha. "I should have known."

Her fondest memory of a dandelion was when she married Joseph, and her mother added a single dandelion to her wedding bouquet for luck. Maybe it was that luck that had kept her and Joseph together for six decades, and kept her family safe in the wars against the Indians and the British.

"Make a wish," said Niko, "then blow on it. If you blow it all away in one try, you get your wish."

She hadn't made a wish on a dandelion since she was a little girl herself. It was so long ago, she couldn't remember what she had wished for. She wished she could remember what it was like to be that young again.

Martha took a breath, as deep as she could, and blew with all the breath she could gather. The white puffball dissipated into the wind. But she'd blown too hard. Her head began to spin. She couldn't catch her breath. She heard music . . . or was it birdsong? Dizziness faded to blackness.

f

The first thing she noticed when she woke was that she could see clearly. She was sitting on the ground in the middle of a great field of purple and white flowers. She didn't recognize the place, but more than that, she was struck by the clarity of her vision. There was no blurring, no blind spots, everything was as clear as day. And it was a beautiful day--the sun was high in the blue sky, with only a few delicate clouds meandering by. But the sun should have been lower. It was almost twilight as she recalled.

Where was her family? What had happened to them? Where was she?

She stood, not even realizing she'd done it without assistance, and looked around. There was nothing but open fields and trees as far as she could see . . . and she could see as far as the horizon. It occurred to her that she felt no pain, no aches in her old bones, nor rheumatism in her hands. She looked at her hands . . . at what was her body but wasn't.

Her hands were tiny and smooth--not a wrinkle on them. Slowly, full of disbelief, she realized the body she inhabited was that of a little girl. A girl wearing a prim white dress and little white shoes.

She must be dreaming, but she didn't feel like she was dreaming. Had she died and gone to heaven? Yet everything was so real. She reached out and touched a purple flower. She bent down and sniffed it. It was real. She was real--a real little girl.

The thought was intoxicating. She began walking, testing her legs, gingerly at first, but soon she was running through the field of flowers. It was so easy, so carefree, like she was being carried along by the wind. She spotted a butterfly and chased it. She'd never realized how good it could feel just to run.

When she finally stopped, it wasn't because she was tired. Instead, she began wondering how it had happened. How had this miracle occurred? Then she remembered her wish--her dandelion wish.

"Hello."

Martha flinched at the sound, startled momentarily. Behind her was another little girl, with long dark hair, wearing a green tunic of a sort Martha couldn't identify. The girl was shorter, and Martha wondered at her age until she looked closely at her face. It wasn't the face of a little girl at all, but that of a grown woman.

"Who are you?" asked Martha.

"I'm *nikommo*."

Her old eyes hadn't been able to focus on the girl's face before. She'd just assumed she was a little girl--one of her great, great grandchildren.

"You're Niko?"

The little person nodded.

Martha remembered the stories of her father, about the wee people who granted wishes. "Are you a leprechaun?"

She shook her head. "I'm *nikommo*."

"How did this happen?" asked Martha, gesturing at her own body. "Did you do this?"

Niko shook her head again. "You made a wish, now you're here and we can play. I'll hide and you find me. Close your eyes."

"Wait--wait. I want to know what happened . . . how . . . ?"

"You have to find me first. Close your eyes."

Martha closed her eyes but said, "How will I know where to look?"

"I'll tell you a riddle," said Niko. "If you can answer it, you'll know where to look."

"Okay," said Martha hesitantly.

"What always runs but never walks, often murmurs, but never talks, has a bed but never sleeps, has a mouth but never eats?"

"Why would you have a mouth but never talk or eat?" Martha opened her eyes and looked all around. Niko was gone. "Niko?" she called. "Niko?"

She had no idea where to begin looking, but decided to head for the closest stand of trees. She figured that's where she would run to hide. But soon after she walked into the trees she was lost.

A host of dark clouds abruptly rolled across the sky, blotting out the sun. An icy wind blew through the trees, giving her goose bumps. She rubbed her arms to keep warm.

"Niko!" she called desperately. "Niko!"

She heard something behind her--part growl, part snicker. She turned and found herself face-to-face with a hobgoblin out of her worst nightmare.

It was no bigger than her, but it had the ugly face of some storybook troll, with an oversized dog-like nose, long pointy ears, and thick black hair. Its body was more porcupine than human. The quills running down its back were as sharp as the claws on its gray hands.

She let out a little girlish scream. The thing flinched at the sound, then snarled at her. "You're no *Tei-Pai-Wanka*," it said with a hiss, baring its jagged teeth.

"What . . . what are you?" stammered Martha.

The creature didn't reply. It charged straight at her, emitting a light as bright as the sun. Martha tried to run, but she couldn't. She was blinded and paralyzed at the same time.

She braced for the thing to crash into her, but it didn't. She couldn't see or move, or even hear a sound. There was no pain--she felt nothing, sensed nothing. Consciousness slipped from her.

/

When she woke, she was still blind. She still couldn't move, nor hear anything. Gradually she realized there were fingers on her face. Someone helped her to sit. Her hearing returned enough to take notice of the breeze in the trees and the song of a marsh wren. The paralysis that held her body faded, and her vision gradually cleared.

What she saw she couldn't believe. The hands that had touched her, the face now looking down at her, belonged to Joseph. Not the Joseph she remembered lying on his deathbed, nor a childish Joseph. Instead he looked exactly as she remembered he did on the day of their wedding. He was even dressed in the fine suit he wore that day.

"Joseph? How are you here? Am I dead too? Are we in Heaven?"

"I'm here because you want me to be."

Martha stood and looked around. She was still in the same spot where the ugly troll had accosted her. She was still a little girl.

"Where's that thing? Where did it go?"

"What thing do you speak of?"

"It was awful, it was hideous. I thought it was going to hurt me. It blinded me . . . I think."

"There's nothing here, Martha. Nothing that can hurt you."

Martha threw herself at Joseph and hugged him. "I've missed you so much. There's so much I've wanted to share with you all these years. Our family has grown so large."

"I'm here now," he said, stroking her hair.

"But where are we?"

"Does it matter? We're together."

Martha released her hold on him and took a step back. "But I don't understand how. How--"

Before she could finish, the hobgoblin came racing out of the brush, straight for Joseph. Before he could move, the snarling creature tackled him. They went down in a heap of grappling limbs, and Martha scooted away. When she looked back, Joseph was no longer there. Instead it was Niko who stood opposite the enraged creature, its quills bristling.

"Run, Martha!" yelled Niko. "Run! Solve the riddle!"

Martha ran. Behind her rose the sounds of a fight, of inhuman voices. She ran until she could hear no more. She stopped and listened. All she heard was the warble of another marsh wren and the trickling of running water.

Water! That was it! The answer to the riddle came to her. It was a river that runs but never walks, murmurs but doesn't talk, has a bed but never sleeps, has a mouth but never eats.

She followed the sound to the river, and there she found Niko waiting for her.

"Niko, are you alright? I thought that creature would hurt you."

"It tried."

"What was it?"

"A *pukwudgie*," responded Niko. "It's a demon, an evil spirit that preys upon the weak, the helpless. It devours flesh, imprisons souls. It can change shape, become whatever it wants."

"What about you, Niko? Can you change shape? Was that you that looked like my Joseph?"

"Yes."

"Why?" asked Martha angrily. "Why'd you deceive me like that?"

"Because that's what you wanted," replied Niko. "I heard you think so. You wished you could be with Joseph again."

Martha knew it was true. She had wished it. Her anger waned, only to be replaced by fear.

"Will the *pukwudgie* return?"

Niko looked around and replied, "It might. It thought you were one of the souls it commands. It was angry to learn you were not. It might try to take you."

"What about you? Did it try to take your soul?"

"I am *nikommo*. It cannot take mine."

"What exactly is a *nikommo*," asked Martha. "What are you, Niko?"

"I am *nikommo*. I bring joy, peace, love, unity, and good fortune. I am the spirit of celebration, of dancing, of selfless generosity. I answer wishes for those deserving."

"And you found me deserving?"

Before Niko could answer, a tiny arrow sprouted from her chest. She gasped and pulled the arrow out. "*Pukwudgie* poison," she said as if barely able to speak. "Run, Martha, run."

Another arrow flew into Niko's shoulder. A third thudded into the ground at Martha's feet. She ran. She kept running until even her girlish body was out of breath. When she finally had to stop, she was afraid to breathe too loudly. She was certain the *pukwudgie* would hear her and reappear at any moment. But it was Niko she saw.

"Niko, I thought you were dead."

"*Pukwudgie* can't kill me, but I fear for your soul. It will hunt you."

"This isn't Heaven, is it?"

Niko shook her head.

"Wherever it is, I don't belong here," said Martha. "I need to go back, back to where I belong. Back to my family."

"What about Joseph?"

"It wasn't really Joseph," said Martha. "Not my Joseph. It was only you, pretending to be him. It's not the same."

"If you go back, your time will be short," said Niko. "Here there is no time, only being."

Martha knew what going back meant, but she couldn't stay here, even if she could be young forever. Even if going back meant returning to the worn-out shell that was her body. She'd had her time. Her time to strive, her time to live, had come and gone.

"Even if you could protect me from the *pukwudgie,* I need to go home"

The *nikommo* nodded and pulled a dandelion from behind her back.

"You must wish it."

Martha took the dandelion and wished with all her youthful vigor to return to the ancient soul that was Martha Clarke Willard, to the bountiful family that was her legacy. Then she blew as hard as she could.

The dandelion seeds shot into the breeze, rising higher and higher. Martha watched in amazement as each little seed puff transformed, becoming a white-throated sparrow, happily chirping its song as it flew away.

∫

"Mom? Wake up, Mom."

"It's time to go in."

First she heard a man's voice, followed by a woman's. It was Isaac and Sarah.

"It's late, Mom," said her son. "Let's get you inside where it's warm."

"Is it over?" asked Martha.

"Yes," said her daughter, "your birthday party's over."

Martha realized she was still in her rocking chair . . . still under the old elm. As real as it had all seemed, she concluded it had been nothing but a dream. She'd fallen asleep and dreamt of being a young girl again. The white dress and the little white shoes were gone. Her hands were shriveled with age and rheumatism once more, though in one hand she clutched something.

It was a dandelion stem, long and bare. If it was a dream, where had she gotten it? Someone else must have given it to her and she just didn't remember. There was no Niko, no *nikommo,* no *pukwudgie.* It all must have been something out of her imagination, something she'd been told about once upon a time. Then she heard the twitter and chirping of birds.

Martha looked up. Her vision was as poor as it had been for years, and though she couldn't see them, she recognized their song. Above her, in the old elm, was a flock of white-throated sparrows, singing unusually late in the day.

She looked back at what she held in her hand and wondered.

Her life was like that dandelion, she thought. One day you're a beautiful flower, the next your beauty is gone, but your seeds have dispersed upon the winds, flown far and wide, eventually to land and become beautiful flowers themselves.

"We're going to get a couple of your strong young grandsons to come out and carry you back into the house, rocking chair and all," said Isaac.

"No," said Martha sternly. "Get me my cane. I'm feeling spry today. I want to walk."

*

Martha Clarke Williard died a week later, but her family would continue to grow, continue to fly far and wide. Eight generations later, one of her direct descendants, living some 3,000 miles away from where she was born, would write this story.
The original one-room house, in which Martha and Joseph raised their 12 children, still stands today. It's the nucleus of the Willard House Museum in Grafton, MA.
The nikommo *and* pukwudgie *are of Native American folklore, shared by the Nipmuc, Wampanoag, Algonquian, and Narragansett tribes of the Northeastern United States. While Martha's encounter with these mythical creatures is purely speculative, the remainder of this tale is based on historical records.*

Man of Sorrows

It was dark. Not the absolute darkness of night, but as if everything were bathed in shadows. Dusk had fallen with a fitful mantle of gloom. He could feel it as much as see it. The prevailing mood was one of overbearing silence . . . until he heard the sound of running feet. He looked around. He could only make out vague shapes. Nothing moved, nothing stirred, just the sound, coming and going.

Then it was no longer feet. Whether it evolved or his perception of it changed, he was now certain it was the flapping of wings. Still, he saw no birds. He saw nothing of any substance, until flashes of bright white light began to score the periphery of his vision and the sound transformed again.

Screee-ahhh! Screee-ahhh!

He kept turning, twisting, trying to find the light's source, the sound's cause, but each time it retreated just beyond his range of perception. He listened more closely. It sounded like a bird in distress. He listened longer and it became something more human--almost a wailing.

Cal-verrrt.

Another flash, but this time he watched it take form. It coalesced in seconds--a winged woman, dressed all in white--so white she seemed to glow. Even her long hair was white as milk, and it blew with a wind he couldn't feel.

Cal-verrrt.

He thought she must be an angel of God, but his certainty clouded as the wings took on the manifestation of a cloak blown by the wind. He couldn't see her face, but her plaintive call was clear enough. She was calling *him*--speaking to *him*.

Cal-verrrt.

She started to turn so he could see her face. There was something familiar . . . .

He sat up.

He was in bed, his nightclothes drenched in sweat. Daylight seeped into the familiar surroundings of his chamber. It had been a dream--just a dream.

Yet the sounds were real. They were coming from outside the manor.

He threw aside the bed covers and got to his feet. He was still shaky from sleep, weak from illness, and his troubled knee pained him with each step, yet he managed to limp to the window.

By the way the subdued light fell against the patches of days-old snow he could tell it was late afternoon. A gaggle of townspeople were gathered outside his gates, ranting and cursing his name. He couldn't make out much more of what they were saying, but their tone was clear. They were angry, and maybe a bit fearful.

"Your Lordship, you shouldn't be out of bed."

The voice startled him, but he realized it was only Mrs. Quinn. When he turned he noticed someone behind his head housekeeper.

She hurried over, took his arm, and led him back to bed.

"I've brought your physician, so back to bed it is for you, so he can divine what ails you."

"God sakes, woman, I'm not a magician, just a scholar of the healing arts."

He recognized the voice immediately, and his eyes confirmed the physician Mrs. Quinn had found was his old friend, Liam. They'd known each other some two score years, since they were both students at Oxford. They not only studied together, but caroused as well. He remembered they once attended a performance at the Globe Theatre by that upstart playwright Shakespeare, whose play, he recalled, took liberties with the actualities of history. *Macbeth* it was. He remembered Liam drank too much at the Mermaid Tavern that night and heckled the actors.

Funny he could remember that, but not the last time he'd seen his friend.

"Liam, how came you here?"

Liam's hair was longer than he remembered and shot with gray. He was dressed rather formally in a white linen shirt with a ruff collar under his doublet.

"I was visiting my youngest brother and his wife, who's about to give birth," said Liam, sitting on the bed and taking his hand. "They live not far, in the village of Ardagh. There was talk of your illness, so I came forthwith. What's wrong with you, George?"

Mrs. Quinn frowned at the physician's familiarity. He noticed her scowl.

"Excuse me," said Liam with a smile. "I meant to say, 'What ails you, Lord Calvert?'"

"I've been ill since I returned from London. I had business there with my eldest son, Cecil."

"The people think he's brought the Black Death back with him," said Mrs. Quinn. "But don't mind them, your Lordship. Just a few noisy troublemakers."

171

"We did have a few cases of the plague last year," said Calvert, "so it's no wonder they're frightened."

"I doubt that was the plague, or there would have been more than a few cases," said Liam, placing his palm on Calvert's forehead. "Have you had any trouble breathing?"

Calvert shook his head.

"What about vomiting?"

"No."

The physician felt around his neck and his armpits. "There's no swelling. You've no symptoms of the plague I can see, your Lordship. And there hasn't been an outbreak in London since 1603, though I hear it's rampant in Italy now."

"Then what is it, old friend? What ails me?"

"I'd say it's just a case of the sweating sickness. Your humors are out of balance, milord. Mrs. Quinn, see to it he drinks plenty of water, and make him a mixture of molasses, vervain, chickweed, and hawthorn. You should be fine in a day or two."

"If the fair folk of Longford Shire don't burn down my manor first."

Liam laughed and Mrs. Quinn snorted at the absurdity of the idea as she left the bed chamber, no doubt to begin mixing the physician's brew.

"If you weren't a good Catholic, they'd likely have tried to burn you out before," said Liam. "No doubt that's why King James gave you a barony in Ireland instead of England, where Protestants rule."

"No doubt."

"You're surely aware there's much resentment of how the king and his predecessor have given Irish lands to English lords--especially those who swear fealty to the Anglican church. I tell you, George, rebellion is coming. The people of Ireland won't hold still for it."

"I'm aware," said Calvert. "It's one reason I've been attempting to regain a foothold for my family in the New World."

"Yes, I heard about the misfortune of your Avalon colony. You haven't given up?"

"No, the land there is rich with promise. I aim to fulfill that promise before I die."

"The good news is you won't be dying anytime soon."

"Blesséd be God for He hath preserved me now from shipwreck, hunger, scurvy, and pestilence."

"And I'll do my best to preserve you from the wrath of the townspeople. I'll tell them you don't have the plague."

"Thank you, Liam. It's good to lay eyes upon you again, and know you're still the man of medicine you studied to be. Now, be a good fellow and help me downstairs before Mrs. Quinn can chastise me."

Lord Calvert sat next to the fireplace, in his padded oak chair, enjoying the warmth of the flames even through the blanket Mrs. Quinn had insisted on covering him with. He sipped from the warm cup in his hand. He'd come to like this new drink they called "tea." He'd first tasted it during his most recent trip to London, where it was imported by the East India Company, of which he was an investor. He liked it so much, he made certain to take some home with him. However, it didn't taste nearly as good with Liam's concoction mixed into it. He could barely get it down, but that was easier than arguing with Mrs. Quinn. For all her notions of propriety, she often treated him as a child.

Not that she was impertinent. She was just used to taking charge. She'd managed his household here in Ireland for six years, ever since he retired as secretary of state and King James awarded his service with 4,000 acres and the Barony of Baltimore.

Despite the umbrage of the people, he loved Ireland, and did his best to mollify any resentment. Still, he wished he could once again set out for the New World, and carve a home out of the wilderness there. But he knew he was too old for such a journey--such a challenge. Even if the king granted his petition, it would be his children who would have to forge his dream.

Absentmindedly he stroked his chin beard, thinking of how his sons Cecil and Leonard were, even now, making preparations for such a journey.

Two of his other children entered the manor from outside, and a glance told him the sun must have just set. Helen and young Philip had been out with their dog, a giant gray wolfhound that never seemed to leave Philip's side. The dog was a comfort to Calvert, for he knew it was very protective.

"Father! Father!" exclaimed Helen. "I saw mother in the forest."

"What?"

Helen rushed to her father and knelt next to him. "It was mother, I'm certain, dressed in white. I saw her for only a moment, then she vanished in the mist."

Calvert thought of his dream, of the woman in white. No, no, it couldn't be. Still, Helen was 15 now, and not given to figments.

"It couldn't have been your mother. She's still aboard ship, bound for Ireland from the Virginia colony," Calvert told his daughter. "She can't have arrived yet."

"No, no," insisted Helen, "it wasn't Lady Joan, it was my *real* mother."

Helen spoke of her mother, Anne, his first wife. The thought of her struck a hollow place inside Calvert. Anne had died many years ago, but his love for her lived on.

"Now none of that, Daughter. Lady Joan *is* your mother now. And you know Lady Anne is with God, so you couldn't have seen her."

Helen made a stubborn face, as if she were about to object, but replied, "Yes, Father."

Mrs. Quinn shooed the children into the kitchen, but his daughter's words remained in his thoughts.

A woman in white? A woman she thought was her mother?

⨍

Lord Calvert lay in his bed, eyes closed, slumber about to take him, yet with thoughts of his deceased wife roused by his daughter's words. He hadn't thought of Anne in a long time. With a new wife, it wasn't seemly to dwell on his past love.

Outside the manor he heard the wind, hollow and howling, as if blowing through an empty room. Gradually, its bluster took on a more human resonance, a forlorn cry. His first thought was that he was dreaming.

Cal-verrrt.

He sat up with the sudden alertness fear brings. He hadn't been asleep. He wasn't dreaming.

He got up and went to his window. It was closed. No wind intruded there, yet he heard it again.

Cal-verrrt.

He threw open the window and leaned outside. A witches' breath fog shrouded the grounds of the manor, but he saw nothing--heard nothing but the wind, gusting through the treetops, light and inconsistent. He waited and listened.

"Your Lordship, I thought I felt a draft. Whatever are you doing at the window?"

"I thought I heard something."

Mrs. Quinn hurried over to him. "You're still ill. We need to get you back into bed. You need your rest."

She ushered him back to bed and he didn't resist.

"I was certain I heard something . . . or someone."

"What was it you heard?" she asked, pulling the blankets over him.

"It sounded like a wail--like someone was crying out my name--*Calvert*. I heard the same thing earlier, before you brought the physician, but it was only a dream."

"I'm sure you were dreaming again, milord."

"No, no, I don't think so. I didn't see anything. In my dream I saw a woman in white."

Mrs. Quinn gasped, quickly covering her mouth with her hands.

"What's wrong, Mrs. Quinn?"

"You saw a woman in white? You heard her wail?"

"Yes, but, as I said, it was only a dream. Why do you look so frightened?"

"It sounds as if you've seen the *bean sidhe*." She whispered the last two words.

"The *bean sidhe*?"

"The English say *banshee*," she said, looking about as though the mere word would bring some terror forth. "The banshee's lament foretells of death."

Calvert knew of the legend. It was one of many local folktales he'd heard.

"A banshee? I'm surprised at you, Mrs. Quinn. A good Christian woman like you shouldn't believe in pagan myths."

"You're right, sir. Let's speak no more of it," she said hurriedly. "Back to sleep with you now. I must check on the children."

"The children?"

"Aye. Their names be Calvert as well."

The woman seemed genuinely fearful, so Calvert let her go without further questioning. But try as he would, he couldn't fall asleep. He didn't dwell on his housekeeper's fears, because he didn't believe in banshees anymore than wood fairies or leprechauns. There was only one supernatural being--blesséd be Him. But the idea wouldn't be banished from his thoughts. It was still there when slumber finally took him.

*

Calvert was feeling better the next day. He was sitting in his study, looking over ledgers his son Cecil had given him, when Grace and Sir Robert Talbot arrived for a visit. The young Irish noble had married his daughter the previous year, and since then he'd not seen Grace at all.

"How are you, Father?"

"I'm better for seeing your bright face."

175

Grace kissed him on the cheek and he acknowledged her husband.

"How goes life in County Kildare, Sir Robert?"

"Life is good, milord, though maybe not so hereabouts. We heard angry murmurs as we passed through the town. There's talk you've brought the plague to the shire."

"As you can see, the talk is false. My physician assures me it's but a fleeting case of the sweating sickness. However, as you've heard, rumors spread even faster than disease."

"I should go pay my respects to Lady Joan," said Grace.

"My wife stayed behind in the Virginia colony when I left," said Calvert. "She only now voyages home."

"Yes," said Sir Robert, "word came to us some time ago that you'd returned to England and petitioned King Charles for a new land grant."

"Aye, but that wasn't the only reason for my departure. Radical Anglicans forced me to leave because I wouldn't swear allegiance to their Protestant faith."

"Damn Puritans."

"I'm used to them, my boy. I've been wedged between the Catholic/Protestant conflict since I before I left my father's house."

"How goes your petition for land, Father?"

"I've no official word, but I'm confident. Your brother Leonard is in London making preparations for a colonial expedition. He's securing ships, materials, prospective colonists, and gentlemen investors."

"I pray such an expedition will prove profitable for you and your family," said Sir Robert.

"Not only profit, Sir Robert. I envision a land of religious tolerance, where each man would be free to worship as his own faith decrees."

"And each woman?" asked Grace with a wry expression.

"Aye, and each woman, Daughter."

*

In his bed chamber that night, Lord Calvert was on his knees, praying, when once again he heard the mournful keening from outside the manor. In order to quickly haul himself to his feet, he pulled on the bedside bell rope that summoned Mrs. Quinn and rushed to the window as fast as his old legs would take him. When he opened it the shock of what he saw left him stumbling backwards. It was the woman in white, floating in the gloom above the treetops, looking in every aspect the image of his deceased wife. Only the translucent paleness of her skin and her snow-white hair differed from the woman he remembered.

Cal-verrrt," she wailed, "*Cal-verrrt.*"

"Anne!" he cried, reaching out the window in vain. The sallow woman was beyond his
reach--beyond his reason. He collapsed against the sill and slumped to the floor. He was certain his fever must have returned. He was hallucinating.

"Your Lordship!" Mrs. Quinn ran to him. "What is it? What's wrong?"

"I've seen her again."

"The banshee?"

"My wife . . . my dead wife, Anne. It was her."

"It was she who died in childbirth?" asked Mrs. Quinn.

"Yes, yes. It was she." Even as he said it, he didn't believe the words coming out of his mouth.

"It was the banshee, milord. A banshee is most often born of the spirit of a murdered woman, or one who has died in childbirth. She keens for a coming demise."

"Why would she? Why would she do this to me?"

"She does not bring death, milord, she only warns of its imminence."

Could it be real? Could Anne be warning me of my impending doom? Would the angry townspeople indeed storm the manor and dispatch me, or was Liam wrong? Have I contracted the plague? Will the Black Death take me? If it's my time, does it matter?

✶

He was rationalizing what he'd seen the night before, blaming it on the last vestiges of the sweating sickness, when Leonard arrived unexpectedly from London. His son fended off several questions from his younger siblings, and made straight for his father, pulling papers from beneath his doublet.

"It's come, Father. The royal decree. King Charles has accepted your petition for a land grant."

Calvert took the papers and began scouring them.

"It's not what you asked for," said Leonard. "The lands you requested south of the James River were promised to others. However, the king has given you the land just north of the Virginia colony--nearly 12 million acres."

It wasn't precisely what he'd hoped for, but it would do.

"The king also had a suggestion for your colony's name."

"A suggestion?"

"Well," said Leonard, "I guess it was more of an informal request. He would like the colony to be named after his wife."

Calvert had planned to name the new colony Crescentia--meaning fertile land--but he knew it would be prudent to acquiesce to the king's wishes in this matter. He'd met Queen Maria when she first arrived from France. She was a good Catholic, so he wouldn't mind naming the new colony for her.

"I've already purchased a ship, Father," said Leonard. "I knew when I heard its name, you'd approve. It's called the *Ark*."

Calvert clapped his son on the shoulder. "Sounds like the perfect ship for a new start."

"I've also made overtures to purchase a smaller second ship."

"Well then, we best get about completing preparations for the voyage, hadn't we?"

Calvert felt a great weight lifted from his shoulders. If, indeed, the banshee had come for him, he could die happy now, knowing his sons would colonize this new land according to his wishes.

He thought of his own father, and how the agents of Queen Elizabeth had harassed him and the entire family, using the Act of Uniformity to force him to deny his Roman Catholic faith and swear allegiance to the Church of England. Many years later, even after he'd become a member of parliament, and then the king's closest advisor as secretary of state, he'd had to hide his true beliefs.

No more. He would create a land where all faiths were equal, and each man could pray to God in his own way.

*

The king's response to his petition had put new vigor in his step. He felt ten years younger, with a renewed faith in God, though a touch blighted by the shame he'd ever considered a heathen myth might be real.

Even as he censured himself, or maybe because of it, she returned--the entity that was his Anne.

This time she wasn't outside, but inside his bed chamber. He sat up and stared at the pale apparition floating above his bed. It no longer occurred to him to doubt his eyes or his sanity.

"*Cal-verrrt.*"

The ghostly woman was beautiful--as beautiful as his Anne had ever been. It *was* her, he saw that clearly now. The idea of her filled him with dread, though not fear of the banshee herself. What terrified him was the loss of faith in God this specter represented. How could this pagan sprite visit him--how could he see it--if he were truly the man of God he thought himself to be?

"*Cal-verrrt.*"

He wanted to talk to her, ask her so much, but acknowledging her presence aloud would be to deny God, to deny his Christian beliefs. At that moment he feared more for his immortal soul than his life.

"*Cal-verrrt.*"

He closed his eyes and prayed to God to vanquish the spirit and protect him. He prayed his faith would be fortified and that when he opened his eyes the banshee would be gone--never to return.

Indeed, when he dared open his eyes, the woman in white was gone.

*

It had been several days since he'd last seen the banshee, and he'd dismissed the visions as residue of his illness. Indeed, all traces of the sweating sickness had left him, and he was hard at work with Leonard, planning the colonization of Marialand.

It wasn't just the supplies and materials that needed their attention. He stressed to Leonard, who would lead the expedition, the importance of selecting the right colonists, and of making friends with the savages they would find there. The hardships of building a new colony were tough enough without creating conflict with the natives.

"I've spoken with enough sea captains to learn we can't travel directly west against the strong currents," said Leonard, tracing his suggested route along the sea chart. "We'll voyage southwest with the more favorable winds to the isle of Barbados, and from there turn north."

"You're going to want to be certain you arrive at the beginning of the planting season."

"A good idea, Father. I hadn't thought of that."

His son, George, chose that moment to enter the study. He stood silently so as not to interrupt.

"What is it, George?" asked Calvert. "Your brother and I are busy."

"Father, I'm not boy anymore," said young George, standing straight, huffing his chest out to accentuate the point. "I'm 17--a man. I want to go back to the New World with Leonard."

Calvert looked his son over. He hadn't really noticed, but the boy *had* become a man. Leonard was only 21 himself--though intelligent and mature for his age.

"What do you think, Leonard? Is he man enough?"

179

Leonard hesitated, as if giving the matter careful consideration, then smiled. "Certainly, Father. I could use a good assistant."

Young George beamed with pride, and made a point of studying the charts the two men had been examining.

Before they could continue, Mrs. Quinn entered.

"What is it, Mrs. Quinn?"

"Milord, a messenger has just arrived, from Galway."

"Show him in."

The messenger, covered with dust, entered the study, offered a quick bow and stood waiting.

"Tell me, my good man, what's so urgent you've ridden the distance from the port of Galway?"

"'Tis poor tidings, milord."

"Out with it then."

"The ship carrying Lady Calvert has been lost at sea. None survived."

Calvert stood motionless for a moment, then suddenly slumped to the floor. Leonard, George, and Mrs. Quinn all rushed to his side. He ignored them.

Was this punishment? Was God angry he'd seen the banshee? Or was the banshee a messenger of God, with a message he'd misunderstood?

He'd been ready for death, but the spirit had not come for him. She'd come to augur the death of Joan.

Now God had taken both his wives, and left him to his sorrows and the burden of his faith.

*

Lord Calvert never fully recovered from the death of his second wife, and would go on to describe himself as a "man of sorrows"--a phrase from the Bible. *He died a year later, before his sons Leonard and George ever set sail for the New World. But their voyage would be a success, and they would sow the seeds of religious freedom their father insisted upon, thereby helping to lay the foundation for one of America's most cherished principles.*

Leonard would become the first governor of what is now known as Maryland. The city of Baltimore would take its name from both the first Baron of Baltimore, George Calvert I, and his eldest son, Cecilius, who inherited the title.

George Calvert came from a family of cattle ranchers and, despite his family's less than royal heritage and the prejudice against their faith, he became one of the most powerful men in England, as well as one of the most educated and wealthiest men of his time. He was also one of the first to invest in the Virginia Company, which financed Jamestown, the initial English settlement in America.

The appearance of the banshee in Lord Calvert's life is sheer speculative fiction, but the rest of the tale is imbedded in history. George Calvert, by way of Leonard Calvert, is my great (x11) grandfather.

Upon a Pale Horse

1087 - France

Smoke billowed above the town of Mantes in the fullness of the sunset. But the sunlight and all its sundry colors were blotted out by the unbridled burning of the hamlet. The battle had raged all day, and yet there were still pockets of resistance where vehement defenders refused to lay down their arms. Their fight was futile. The outcome of the incursion had never been in doubt. The forces of William, King of England, formerly Duke of Normandy, formerly William the Bastard, were too many . . . too strong. They were seasoned, ferocious warriors clashing with uninspired French troops and untrained townspeople.

The brutal sacking of Mantes had begun.

Under normal circumstances, William wouldn't have allowed the pillaging of a town in the region where he was born. But he'd ordered it to make a point to Philip, King of France, as well as to his own son Robert, who'd once more turned against him. Transgressions against his sovereignty would not be tolerated.

No longer the great burly warrior, William approached the smoldering town a rotund old man whose eyesight was failing him. Once unequaled as a horseman, he now kept his pale war horse reined in to an ambling gait instead of a triumphant gallop. He hadn't even worn his hauberk because he'd grown too fat and it made him uncomfortable. He wasn't worried. He would need no chainmail on this day.

Next to him rode his young son, Henry. He'd brought him along with the intention of teaching him the art of warfare, but his heart wasn't in it.

Henry noticed the look of grim dissatisfaction on his father's face.

"What is it, Father? What troubles thee?"

William spit the dust and ash that had gathered in his mouth and replied in the guttural voice he was known for, "I tire of war, Henry. I've been fighting my whole life. It seems so long ago that I took England for my own. Now I'm back in Normandy, the land of my birth, fighting again to retain what's mine. It seems war never ends. Remember that when I'm gone."

"Yes, Father."

One of his captains rode in from the front and stopped next to William.

182

"We've taken the town, sire."

"That of it which does not burn," replied William.

"Those *were* your orders, were they not, sire?"

"Yes, those were my orders. See to it, Captain."

The officer rode off to ensure the king's orders were carried out.

As they moved into the town, the raging flames grew higher, burned hotter. The scarlet glare of the conflagration turned the pallid gray tint of William's horse to a hellish hue. The carnage was all around them. William watched Henry's eyes, his expression. He was heartened to see his son's distaste for the slaughter and destruction.

A structure near the king abruptly collapsed amidst a blaze of sparks and flaming planks. A shower of hot embers splayed out in front of the king. His steed reared violently, kicking its hooves into the air in protest, its amber eyes shimmering with fear.

Instead of being thrown back off his mount, the stirrups that held William, the same stirrups he'd improved his legendary cavalry with long ago, thrust his upper body forward. His gut slammed into the broad pommel of his saddle. So great was the force, even his girth did not protect him.

The pain shot through him like a dozen arrows. He fell. The pale horse did not hesitate. It raced off across a bloody, trampled field with stony indifference.

*

Five weeks passed, and the king's injuries had not healed, even with the ministrations of the priors of Saint Gervase. In fact, William's condition had worsened, and he knew he lay on his deathbed.

Lying there he recalled his wife, Matilda, who'd died years earlier, and his son Richard, who'd been killed in a riding accident when he was not much older than Henry was now. Soon he'd be joining them both.

He called forth his ministers and issued his final proclamations. He would leave Normandy to his oldest son Robert, despite his treachery. But the crown of England would go to his second son, William Rufus. Little did he know this division of his kingdom would create the stage for enmity and conflict for centuries to come. A legacy of violence and strife would haunt him even in his grave.

He ordered large sums to be given to his son Henry and his daughters. Other monies were to be given to the church and to the poor. He also ordered that all of his prisoners be released, including his half-brother Odo, who, in a vain attempt to become pope, had defied William's orders and attempted to corrupt his vassals.

In the king's last moments, his son knelt by his bedside. There were tears in the boy's eyes.

William joked to Henry, "Well, the bastard will soon be dead." He started to laugh, but the pain was too great. "Be not like me," he told his young son. "For war and death have been my standards. Let them not be yours.

"May God forgive me, for I have taken that which is not mine. I am stained with the rivers of blood I have shed."

With that repentant statement still fresh on his lips, William the Conqueror died.

1682 - Maryland

William Calvert was in a hurry. He wanted to reach his home in time for his son George's 14th birthday celebration. His business in Charles County had taken longer than he expected, so he was pushing his horse harder than usual, slapping its flanks with the reins whenever it threatened to slow its pace.

To his left a wall of morning fog had begun to dissipate. Despite the cool air and the patchy clouds, sweat ran down his back and chest. It was warmer than usual for May, and he could feel it would be downright hot before the day ended.

His wife, Elizabeth, had expected him home days earlier, and was likely worried. As the daughter of Governor Stone, she was raised to be punctual, and expected it of everyone else. However, Calvert's position as Secretary of Maryland and member of the House of Burgesses often required him to travel, especially in these times of Catholic and Protestant conflict.

He didn't understand why the zealots of each sect couldn't just live and let live. Religious freedom in this new world had been a dream of his father's, and his grandfather's. It was what drove his grandfather, the original Lord Baltimore, to petition the king for the right to colonize the region he named Maryland. But it seemed some people couldn't be happy if their neighbors prayed differently than themselves.

It had been a long quiet ride, intruded upon only by the staccato beat of his horse's hooves. Soon he'd reach the Wicomico River. Once he crossed it he'd be back in St. Mary's County, just an hour's ride from home and the loving embrace of Elizabeth--that is if she wasn't too upset with his tardiness. She called him Colonel Calvert whenever she was angry with him, though he hadn't used his militia title in years.

He spotted the river ahead of him. He'd find out soon enough if she were glad or mad. He really couldn't guess which it would be.

The Wicomico appeared to be swollen from the recent rains, but he'd forged it before. He slowed his steed as he reached the river's edge, and despite the animal's brief trepidation, guided it slowly into the water.

By the time he reached mid-stream, the river was lapping at his waist. His horse struggled to keep its head above water, snorting its displeasure. The current was as strong as any he'd felt, and when his mount lost its footing and began to swim, he was jerked from the saddle.

He struggled to reclaim hold of the animal, but it kicked away, trying desperately to regain its own foothold. He was close enough to see the fright in the beast's tawny gold-flecked eyes, but not close enough to grasp it.

He tried to swim, but his clothing held him down. The current pushed him further and further away. Just before he went under he saw the pale gray horse reach the river's bank and dash up the slope onto dry land.

1808 - Massachusetts

Solomon pulled the cinch tight to secure his saddle, then led the horse by its bridle out of the barn. The cold morning air blew from the beast's nostrils like smoke. It stamped its hooves restlessly, its gray head high and alert, its bronze eyes rich with anticipation.

It had been a while since he'd been riding. Various health concerns had kept him out of the saddle, but today he was looking forward to it.

His old friend Joseph Varnum was going to be in Worcester, and he hadn't spoken with him since he'd last been in Boston.

Joseph's status had long ago risen from his quiet days as a farmer with little formal education. He'd served with valor in the war for independence from England, eventually rising to the rank of major general in the state militia. Now, 14 years after first being elected to represent Massachusetts in Congress, he'd become the Speaker of the House of Representatives.

Joseph wasn't just an old friend. He'd become a man Solomon greatly admired. As long as they'd known each other, they'd both been vehemently opposed to slavery. And ever since Joseph had entered Congress, he'd been an outspoken opponent of negro servitude. He'd even submitted to Congress a proposition to amend the Constitution--a proposition that would abolish the slave trade. It took him two years, but finally the proposition was passed by both houses of Congress. Now it was up to the states to ratify the amendment.

185

It would take three-fourths of the state legislatures to approve the new law, but Solomon was hopeful it could be done. He wanted to speak with his old friend about the chances the amendment would be added to the Constitution, and to congratulate him.

"Solomon Willard, where do you think you're going?"

It was Lydia. He was hoping to ride off before his wife spotted him.

"I'm riding into Worcester to see an old friend," he replied, pulling himself up onto his mount.

"You're too old to be riding into town like that," said Lydia. "Let me get Micah to hitch up the wagon for you."

"I'm 52 not 82, Wife. I can still ride a horse."

She stood there frowning at him.

"I'll be back before dark."

His youngest sons, Isaac and Archibald, playing with their dogs out in the south field, spotted their father and came running.

"I want to ride! I want to ride!" they both squealed as the dogs barked at the boys' enthusiasm.

Solomon's old pale horse, which surely had heard dogs barking and children shouting before, nonetheless became agitated by all the noise and frenetic activity. It nickered and reared up unexpectedly. Solomon was thrown backwards, landing head first. His neck broke on impact.

1888 - Missouri

It was a long way from Kansas City back to Atchison County. Two riders making the journey had stopped to rest when the sky began to darken and the wind rose up to whistle through the trees. Their horses stood grazing in the nearby meadow.

"You think the Cowboys will ever field a good team?"

"I don't know, Charlie. They sure didn't look too good today. They've been in last place all year."

"The Browns sure beat up on them," said Charlie.

"That's why they're in first place, and are probably going to win the American Association pennant again this year."

"I don't know why St. Louis always has to have such a good baseball team," said Charlie. "It ain't right."

"Right's got nothing to do with it. If the Cowboys had Tip O'Neill and Jocko Milligan hitting, and Ice Box Chamberlain hurling the horsehide for them, they'd be in first place instead of the Browns."

"Look at that," said Charlie, pointing at the heavens. "We'd better get going, Richard." As he said it, the first few drops descended upon on them. "Then again, maybe we should hunker down somewhere until it passes."

"There ain't much shelter around here," replied Richard. "And it don't look like it's gonna pass anytime soon. It's coming in from the south. If we get going we might beat it home. Anyway, I'd rather ride in the rain than sit in it."

They mounted their horses--Charlie on his sorrel, Richard on his pale gray-- and galloped off.

They heard thunder in the distance as the rain gained in intensity. The wind was at their backs, and so was the storm, pushing them, prodding them to ride even faster.

When a bolt of lightning flashed up ahead of them and the thunder cracked loud enough to hurt their ears, Charlie shouted, "Shit! That was close."

Richard didn't respond. He just kept riding.

They'd gone less than a mile when it became obvious they weren't going to outrun the storm. But there was nothing for it save to keep going. By the time they passed into Atchison they were soaked through and through, chilled to the bone.

Richard looked over at his brother-in-law and smiled. Charlie smiled back. They were thinking the same thing.

Richard's wife, Carrie, had warned them about the storm. She had a sixth sense about such things. He and Charlie knew they'd hear it from her to no end when they got home.

The last thing Charlie saw before the lightning flash blinded him, and the force of the electrostatic discharge knocked him from his horse, was Richard smiling.

It had been so close, the thunderous explosion so loud, Charlie's ears were ringing with it. He picked himself up and checked himself for injuries. Finding no broken bones, he looked for his horse. What he saw instead was Richard. Both he and his pale gray were on the ground, smoke rising from their bodies. His brother-in-law was as still as stone, and there was no spark of life in the horse's amber eyes. The streak of lightning that had just missed Charlie had struck Richard and his horse.

History has recorded that Richard Greenville Golden, Solomon Willard, William Calvert, and William the Conqueror, also known as the first Norman King of England,

Duke of Normandy, and William the Bastard, all suffered equestrian-related deaths just as described herein. That it might have been the same horse they were riding is pure speculation.

All four men are also my direct ancestors. As a matter of sheer historical coincidence, when William Calvert married Elizabeth Stone in 17th-century Maryland, it joined two family lines that would diverge over time and then merge again ten generations later, when my mother and father were married in 20th-century Illinois.

I'm no horseman--I've only been on horseback a couple of times in my life. However, I continue to use the same mode of transportation I have for the last 30 years--a 1965 Ford Mustang.

The Dola and the Saint

The storm was relentless. For hours the ship swayed and jerked until she was sure she'd be sick. Her brother and sister had already succumbed to the constant pitch and roll, heaving their suppers across the sodden decks. She was determined not to. There had been lulls in the gale, but each time she thought it might be fading away, the wind resurrected and the sea resumed its onslaught against the battered vessel. She beseeched God to save them from the tempest, and, though she felt guilty for it, she also implored Anya to not let her family's fate be to drown.

She was alone for the moment, uncertain where her mother had gone. Likely Mother was ministering to her brother and sister on the other side of the hold--though the squall was much too loud for her to hear them, or anything else.

It was bad enough they'd had to flee their home in Wessex, but her mother had insisted they must do so right away, in the dead of night. Margaret had overheard her uncle tell her mother and brother that the armies of "William The Bastard" were on the march, and would be at his door the following day. He said it wasn't safe for them. Their royal blood would be sure to adorn the executioner's block if they stayed. William of Normandy had defeated the armies of King Harold at Hastings, and he was not likely to let anyone with a claim to the crown live to stir up rebellion.

So they fled--though her brother Edgar foolishly wanted to stay and fight. Fight with what? The English were a conquered people now. They'd have to bend knee to a Norman king.

Margaret didn't care who was king--even though Edgar thought he had every right to the throne--she only cared that she'd found a home in the court of Wessex. Her family had traveled so much . . . and now they were off again.

Even before she was born, when her father was but a baby, he'd been banished from England by Canute, the Viking who seized the throne when Margaret's grandfather King Edmund died. Canute shipped her father to Sweden where he was to be murdered. But someone took pity on the infant, and spirited him away to Kiev. He grew up there, and spent years traveling across the continent, before finally settling in Hungary where she was born. They called her father "Edward The Exile"--though never to his face.

After Canute's reign ended, England was torn by various factions. When one

189

group of nobles learned her father was alive, he was sent for. His claim to the throne was expected to have a stabilizing effect on the fractious nation. So Margaret and the rest of the family left Hungary and traveled with him, across the continent, to England--which to her was as foreign a place as the godless halls of Persia. But not long after they arrived, her father died. She heard whispers it was poison, but no one would tell her. She didn't think anyone really knew for certain.

The years after her father's death were happy, for the most part. She enjoyed life at the court of Wessex--the pomp, the merriment, the gaudy feasts. However, despite the luxuries of court, she and her sister Christina had vowed to one day become nuns and devote themselves to the church.

Now they were forced to leave--running away like thieves in the night. Her mother wasn't sure where they'd go--Burgundy first, then maybe Franconia where her mother had family. Maybe they'd even return to Hungary. It didn't matter to Margaret. She'd seen the world, and didn't think much of it. It was a man's world. Women weren't allowed much. She wanted to do things with her life--not just become some man's wife.

She wondered if all her childhood friends in Hungary were married now. They probably had children of their own, while she had spurned many a suitor. They all seemed to be dilettantes, philistines, or vulgar boors. Now, more than ever, she was certain the only bride she'd become was a bride of Christ.

"You never know what fate has in store for you."

Margaret turned at the sound of the voice. Sitting next to her, seemingly impervious to the swaying of the ship, was a tiny gray mouse.

"Anya?"

"I see a man, a powerful man with golden hair and a voice rich like molasses."

The voice Margaret heard was that of a young girl, though it emanated from inside her head rather than in her ears. Yet she knew it was coming from the mouse. It wasn't the first time. Anya appeared to her in many forms.

"Oh, Anya. I beg you to save us from this awful storm. Please, at least save my family. Even if I must die, please spare them."

"Their fates are not my concern. I am only for you, Margaret. Your destiny lies not in the sea, but in being seen."

"Seen by who?"

The ship rocked violently and Margaret tumbled over backwards. When she regained her balance, the mouse was gone.

"Anya? Anya, are you there?"

She was alone again, but no longer afraid. Anya had said her destiny did not lie in the sea, and her *dola* had never been wrong--not since she'd first appeared to her those many years ago in the Hungarian forest. But she wondered what Anya meant? To be seen? And who was the man with golden hair and a voice rich like molasses?

*

She woke to a calm that belied her fitful night of half sleep. The deck no longer rolled beneath her. The ship was still.

Margaret rubbed her eyes, pulled off the cloak she'd used as a blanket, and stood. She was sore, bruised by the battering of the storm. She straightened her robe skirt and tied it at the waist with a gold-embroidered silk belt. She threw the cloak over her shoulders and fastened it with her silver brooch--the one her father had given her just before he died. She pulled her wimple over her hair and tied it under her neck before climbing the stairs to the main deck.

The ship was docked to a ramshackle pier. Looking seaward, Margaret spied a number of small fishing vessels already underway, sailing out of the harbor. Inland, a quaint hamlet dotted the coastline, and beyond that was a range of rolling hills so green they might have been painted. In the distance loomed nature's counterpoint, a range of jagged black mountains. None of it was familiar to her.

She spied her mother walking along the pier and wondered where her brother and sister were. A man on horseback cantered down the pier toward her mother. When her mother reached the man, she curtsied--which was not at all like her. Having come within a hairsbreadth of being Queen of England, her mother did not show deference easily.

The rider was a powerful looking man, with a rich mantle across his shoulders, sword at his side, and legstrappings bound at the knee over forest-green tights. Though she couldn't hear his voice, his hair and full beard were indeed golden.

The ship's captain strode up to the railing where she stood.

"Is this Burgundy?" she asked him.

"No, milady. The storm damaged our foremast and blew us off course. It's alright, I've harbored here before. This is Scotland."

Her brother and sister appeared at her side.

"Where's Mother," asked Christina.

Margaret simply pointed.

191

Their mother bowed again and turned back to the ship. The man wheeled his horse and galloped away.

"Who's that fellow on the horse? Why is mother bowing?" wondered Christina.

"I recognize him," said Edgar. "That's King Malcolm III. I saw him at Wessex once."

Margaret had heard of Malcolm, King of Scotland. But all she knew of him was that he was her uncle's ally, and had visited Wessex years ago. Unlike her brother, she had no memory of ever having seen him.

Her mother drew close and called to them.

"King Malcolm has granted us safe haven and invited us to his castle. Come now, he's sending for a wain."

*

Their ride was more rustic than royal, and its driver had to quickly construct some makeshift steps for the ladies. King Malcolm watched the proceedings from his horse, ordering his retainers to load their luggage.

Margaret prepared to follow her mother and sister up the steps to the rear of the wagon while Edgar took his place on the driver's seat in front. As Margaret stepped up, a strange urge overcame her. For a moment she felt as if she had no control over her own body. She pulled her skirt off the ground to step up, but raised it much higher than was necessary, baring a length of her leg. As she did, she looked up. King Malcolm was watching her. She continued up the steps and sat in the wagon, only then feeling as if the loss of control had passed. When it did, she was overcome by embarrassment. What had caused her to do such a thing?

As the wagon pulled away, she chanced a glance. The king was still looking at her.

*

Margaret found the Scottish castle dreary and damp compared to the colorful halls of Wessex. Even Castle Réka in Hungary, where she'd played as a young girl, was a nicer place. Like the rest of the manor, the room where they gathered to eat was less than spacious, poorly lit, and badly in need of a tapestry or two to adorn its colorless stone walls. Much too austere, she thought, for a king's dining hall.

Still, they could be worse off. They could be eating scraps in William's dungeon. She chastised herself for her lack of graciousness. She should be thankful to King Malcolm for taking them in.

The food, at least, was delicious. There were helpings of mutton, pork, and a kind of fish she couldn't identify. The bread was coarse though tasty, but the dates were not nearly as good as the ones she remembered eating in Hungary. She tried the ale in her cup and found it much too bitter.

The king was an older man--she guessed him to be in his late thirties--more than a decade her senior. A touch of gray streaked his beard, yet he was handsome and there was a thick brogue in his voice Margaret found charming. Now that she knew he was a king, he seemed more regal than he had on horseback. A ring of brass fastened a fur-lined mantle across his shoulders, and a single eagle's feather hung from the side of his long blond hair. She'd never seen a man wearing a feather like that before.

The king sat at one end of the table, her mother at the other--which made Margaret wonder where his queen was. Across the table from her, Edgar, and Christina, were the king's three young sons, the eldest of whom was only eight or nine. They did not speak, but demonstrated hearty appetites.

"It grieves me, Lady Agatha, to hear of the bastard William's invasion of England."

"Look to your own borders, Sire," warned her mother, "for he might not be content with the lands he's already conquered."

Malcolm pulled the dirk from his belt and jabbed it more forcefully than was necessary into a serving tray full of pork. "Aye, he may try, milady, but he'll likely find Scottish meat a bit too tough for his liking. So says I, *Máel Coluim mac Donnchada.*"

Malcolm cut off a piece of pork. "Still, it's passing strange that a Norman now sits on the throne of England."

"He's an interloper, not a king," spoke up Edgar. "I'm the rightful King of England."

For a long moment Malcolm regarded the skinny teenager who was her brother. "That may be, young prince, but a man who would be king must have followers, an army. Royal blood isn't everything. Your grandfather Ironside would have told you the same."

Malcolm bit into his hunk of meat. He stared at Edgar as he chewed, waiting for a reply. Edgar looked vexed, but remained silent.

"I was in much the same state as you, Edgar Atheling, when I was a boy. After the betrayer Macbeth slew my father, my mother spirited me away for my own protection. But when I reached manhood I made allies, gathered my forces, killed Macbeth and his son Lulach, and took what was rightfully mine.

193

It wasn't easy, but being a king isn't as simple as saying you're one. What is yours is only yours if you can take it . . . " Malcolm grabbed a fistful of air " . . . and hold it."

Margaret thought it sage counsel, though she doubted her brother would embrace it. She'd had no idea Malcolm had been exiled much like her father. She couldn't imagine what ordeals he must have gone through to regain his father's crown. She glanced at the king. He was staring at her. She averted her eyes and reached for a piece of bread.

"I was sorry to hear of the death of your wife, milord," said Agatha. "She was known in Wessex as a gracious woman."

"Aye, she was."

"It will be lonely for you now, and hard with three young boys to raise."

"They're good lads . . . most of the time." Malcolm stared at his sons as if they'd recently committed some transgression. They avoided their father's gaze.

"When do you think you'll remarry?"

Margaret was appalled at her mother's lack of propriety. The king simply shrugged and took drink of his ale.

Boldly, her mother continued. "What a fine union it would be if the King of Scotland were to marry a granddaughter of King Edmund II. If the royal house of Scotland were to unite with the royal bloodline of England, it would forge a powerful alliance."

Margaret blushed, but kept her head down, eyes on her food. She didn't know if her mother was referring to her or Christina, but the blatant nature of the suggestion was mortifying. It wasn't unusual for her mother to try and find them husbands, but speaking thusly in their presence was outrageous.

"You speak true, milady," responded the king politely. "It would make for a fine union."

Although she dared not look at him, Margaret was certain she felt the king's eyes upon her as he spoke.

f

Margaret was alone in the chamber she and her sister had been given. Christina had gone out riding with Edgar, and she didn't know where her mother was. But that was alright. She was happy propped against the bed, doing her needlework, though she kept thinking about King Malcolm. She tried not to--even to the point of reciting holy verses in her head. But thoughts of the king would not be vanquished.

194

Something brushed against her and she looked down. It was a cat with thick orange fur, purring and rubbing against her. She'd seen this cat before, but that had been a world away.

"Anya? Is that you?"

"You must catch his eye before you can capture his heart." It was the familiar voice of a young girl that Margaret heard in her head, but she wasn't sure who or what Anya was speaking of.

"What do you mean, Anya?"

"The king needs a wife. You need a husband. There are children to be born."

"The king? No, no, I can't," replied Margaret, bemused by the idea. "I'm to be a nun. I am for Christ. God calls me."

"Fate is stronger than faith." The cat rubbed against her once more. "There are children to be born."

Even though her *dola* had never been wrong, Margaret protested. "That can't be, Anya. I've promised--"

"Beg your pardon, milady."

Margaret looked up to see King Malcolm at her door. She hastened to her feet and bowed.

"May I enter?"

"Of course, Your Majesty."

"Who were you talking to, lass?"

"I . . . uh . . . I was just talking to the cat."

"There are no cats in this keep, milady. My dogs would tear it asunder if they saw one."

Margaret looked around, but of course Anya was gone.

"Who is Anya?" asked Malcolm.

Margaret hesitated, wondering what to say, nervous because it was the king who questioned her. However, it was not in her nature to lie.

"Anya is my *dola*, Sire."

"Your *dola*? What, may I ask, is a *dola*?"

"A *dola* is a protective spirit, the embodiment of one's fate. It can take the form of an animal or a person."

"So you pray to this pagan sprite?" wondered Malcolm.

"No, Sire. I am a good Christian. I pray only to the one true God. But Anya has been with me since I was a little girl in Hungary. She guides me. I believe God sent her to me."

"I see," said Malcolm, walking over to her small stack of books and picking

195

one up. "I am not so good a Christian, milady, though I make allowances." He opened the book and looked inside. "I've never told anyone this, but, as a child, I believed in the *Ghillie Dhu*--little folk in clothes woven of leaves and grass. I even saw one of these benevolent forest elves once, or so I thought. But that was before Macbeth killed my father and the world changed. On that day I could no longer lend myself to such flights of fancy."

Malcolm continued to look through the book, once or twice tracing the lettering with his fingers. Watching him, Margaret couldn't help but think about what Anya had said to her.

"This is a work of great craftsmanship," said Malcolm. "I've never seen a book with golden letters and precious stones on its pages."

"I like to embellish my books. Would you care to borrow it?"

"I'm afraid I don't have the knowledge of reading, milady. But I do find books a thing of both beauty and mystery. I suppose if I could read them, they wouldn't be so mysterious, would they?"

Malcolm chuckled, but Margaret was surprised at his admission. A king that couldn't read?

"Reading is not that difficult, milord. I could teach you, if I had time."

"Speak you true?" Malcolm appeared intrigued by the possibility. "Then I pray God grant us the time.

"However, I have other demands upon my time now. I must depart, and beg pardon for interrupting your needlework."

"Not at all, Your Majesty. As your guest, I am at your bidding." Margaret said with a curtsy.

"Your presence in my home does me honor, milady," said Malcolm with a brief bow of his head.

When he was gone Margaret looked for Anya, but she wasn't likely to return now. Yet what the *dola* had said kept returning to her. *There are children to be born.* The king's children? Her children?

*

After supper the second night in Dunfermline Castle, Margaret was unsettled. She begged leave to go to her room as soon as was polite, and stayed there for some time. During the meal, Malcolm had made a point of speaking to her several times, asking her opinion and seeming to gauge her answers. He all but ignored Christina, and did not seem that enthralled with engaging either her mother or brother in conversation.

It was his manifest interest in her that was troubling. Not that she didn't find

Malcolm an intriguing and handsome man. But it was something she didn't want to dwell on. Instead she wanted to pray. She felt the need to commune with the Holy Spirit. However, she found it difficult to clear her mind of the king.

"Go to the chapel."

Startled by the sound, Margaret flinched. She turned to see a familiar face. A young girl of only 12 or 13 years.

"Anya. Oh, Anya, I'm so glad to see you. My mind is in disarray. Tell me what to do."

"Go to the chapel," repeated the *dola*.

"Yes, yes," agreed Margaret. "I'll be able to clear my mind and pray in a house of God."

By the time Margaret had collected her cloak and put on her wimple, Anya was gone. But Margaret hardly noticed. She hurried out, down the stone stairway, and outside the castle. The soldiers there paid her no mind.

The night air was thick with fog, but she knew where the little chapel was. She'd seen it just across the courtyard when she first arrived. Still, she went slowly, careful of her footing, her skirt sweeping the ground with every step.

She heard a noise and discovered a trio of waifs so poorly clothed they must have been chilled to the bone. They were huddled inside a small shed next to the chapel.

"What are you children doing here? You should go home."

The oldest of the three, a boy of maybe ten, replied, "We have no home, milady. We're orphaned, we are."

The poor wretches were as scrawny as scarecrows, and Margaret could only think of feeding them. She reached into her robe and pulled out what coins were there. She gave them to the boy.

"Get yourselves some food. I'll speak to the priest about finding you shelter."

The boy accepted the coins, but replied, "The priest runs us off when he sees us, milady."

Margaret couldn't imagine anyone being so cruel to children, especially a man of God.

"I will speak with the priest. Go on now, feed yourselves."

The children ran off and Margaret found the entrance to the chapel.

She didn't know what she'd expected--certainly not the splendor of the churches in Wessex--but she was surprised by the extravagance of this tiny place of worship. There were rich tapestries of velvet and ermine along the walls and adorning the altar, upon which lay chalices of gold. A golden crucifix hung on the wall above it, with golden candlesticks at each end.

Given what she'd witnessed just outside its doors, the opulence was anything but devout to her way of thinking. Praising God was one thing. Ignoring poverty was another. Someday she would work to change that.

She refrained from approaching the altar, choosing instead to kneel in the rear. She began to pray, asking for clarity to end her confusion. Before long, her silent communion was interrupted by voices coming from the front of the chapel. At first Margaret tried to ignore them, continuing to pray. When the voices grew louder she had no choice but to listen--though she kept her head down and continued to kneel.

"And if I aid you in this plot against the king, what is my reward?"

"My dear priest, isn't the removal of this heathen king enough? He's never been a true Christian."

"That may be so, but neither does he interfere with the church's business. What you propose is for the church to intercede and support your claim to the throne. Some might call that treason."

"Treason to right the wrong? I, Máel Snechtai of Moray, am the rightful King of Scotland."

"Perhaps, but--"

"Don't pretend you have qualms, priest. We both know you can be bought. The only question now is the price."

"Yes, well . . . how much gold are we speaking of?"

The men continued to move as they spoke, and for a moment Margaret was afraid they would happen upon her. She shifted her position, trying to see where else she could hide, and slipped.

"What was that?"

"Someone's in here."

Hearing she'd been discovered, Margaret stood in plain view of the men and ran for the door.

"Stop her!"

She heard them give chase as she pushed open the chapel door and raced through the fog. She was frightened and disoriented. She could only pray she was headed in the right direction, running like she hadn't since she was a young girl.

A voice ahead of her, to her left, called out, "This way, this way." It was Anya.

Her heart pounded as though it would burst from her chest when she reached the castle. One of the soldiers she had passed earlier came running. She could hardly catch her breath to say, "The king . . . I must speak with the king."

The guard outside the king's chamber stopped her.

"I must speak with the king. It's urgent."

"The king has retired for the evening, milady. He mustn't be disturbed."

"He must be," insisted Margaret, "for I have news that is more than disturbing. You must allow me--"

"What's this all about?" bellowed Malcolm, appearing at the entrance to his chamber.

"Sire, I'm sorry. The Lady Margaret insists upon speaking with you."

Malcolm looked at her, and she realized in the moment what an unflattering figure she must present. Between the damp of the fog and the sweat of her own exertion, she must look like so much flotsam.

"Please enter, milady."

Margaret stepped inside, but couldn't contain herself.

"Your Majesty, there is a plot against you."

"There usually is." Malcolm smiled. It almost seemed to Margaret as if he found her state amusing.

"Sire, this is no jest. There are those here in Dunfermline who would see you cast out or worse."

"Did your *dola* tell you this?"

"No, but she led me to where I heard it with mine own ears. Your own priest plots with a man named Snechtai--Snechtai of Moray he called himself."

The name struck a chord with Malcolm. His expression darkened. "Snechtai is the son of Lulach, whom I dispatched to reclaim my throne after I killed his stepfather Macbeth. You say the priest is in league with him?"

"The last thing I heard, Sire, was the priest discussing how much he'd be paid for his treachery."

To his guard Malcolm commanded, "Gather the men and conduct a search. Bring me the priest and Snechtai of Moray if he's still about."

The guard hurried off and Malcolm took Margaret's hand, leading her to a chair within his chamber. By now, several servants had been roused and stood waiting.

"Please sit and rest yourself, Lady Margaret." To the servants he said, "Bring us some warm broth and bread."

Malcolm paced as he spoke, and Margaret saw the concern on his face. "I must thank you for your forewarning, milady. A king must always beware of assassins."

"I simply wanted to pray, milord. It was Anya who sent me to the chapel. I think she must have known what I would hear."

"Then I thank Anya as well as your piety. It is unfortunate that many of the Christian faith only feign to follow their own teachings."

"It is a sorrow, but true, Your Majesty. I have seen such time and again."

Malcolm stopped pacing and looked at her. "Your brother tells me you and your sister are determined to join a nunnery."

Margaret felt herself blush, though she didn't know why. "Yes, Your Majesty. I hope to someday right such wrongs within the church, and to work for the further glory of God."

"A solitary nun would find altering the course of the church quite difficult I imagine. Perhaps you would be in a better position to right those wrongs if you were a queen."

It took Margaret more than a moment to absorb the implication. She blushed all over again.

"Sire?"

"You should know, Lady Margaret, that, with your permission and that of your family, I intend to pursue your hand in marriage, and to make you my queen."

His words left her dazed, speechless. Though her grandfather had been king, and had come from a long line of kings, Margaret had never considered, even for a moment, that she might become a queen. Such fanciful thoughts were for little girls who knew nothing of the real world.

She didn't know what to say--let alone what to think. Malcolm was right. As queen she would be able to help the less fortunate, to change the church for the better. It would not be easy, but at least she could try. Yet she didn't know how to be a queen . . . or, for that matter, a wife. She'd long since given up on the idea. Perhaps it was time to consider new ideas.

ƒ

Less than a year after their chance meeting in 1070, Margaret and Malcolm were married. They would have eight children, including a daughter Edith, who would go on to become the Queen of England when she married Henry I, and three sons who would all become kings of Scotland. Christina would indeed become a nun, but Edgar never became king.

Though Shakespeare's Macbeth *was a work of dramatic fiction, there was, in fact, a real Macbeth. However, he didn't murder King Duncan. The king was killed in battle against Macbeth's forces, and years later, the king's son, Malcolm, killed Macbeth (as King Malcolm relates in this tale).*

Queen Margaret was known to attend to orphans and the poor every day before she ate. She is said to have risen every night at midnight to attend church services, and was known to work for religious reform. She was considered to be an exemplar of the "just ruler," and influenced her husband and children to be just and holy rulers.

Margaret was canonized in the year 1250 by Pope Innocent IV in recognition of her personal holiness, charity, fidelity to the Church, and work for religious reform. The spot where she and her family first landed in Scotland is still known today as Saint Margaret's Hope.

In 1093 Malcolm was killed in battle after reigning as King of Scotland for 35 years. Margaret, who was already ill, died just a few days later--some say from sorrow.

Among the direct descendants of Saint Margaret and King Malcolm were King Henry II, King Edward III, and the author of this tale, who has no title to speak of (royal or otherwise) but is their great (x28) grandson.

The King's Cavaliers

Istepped into the chamber with more than a little trepidation. It wasn't my first jump, but there was much more riding on this trip than pure research. Lives were at stake. How many I didn't know. Thousands? Millions? The truth is, no one could really say what might happen, how events and the course of history might change should I fail. It's more than possible my own existence could be erased, along with so many others. I tried to put that out of my mind the first time it occurred to me. It was better not to worry about the infinite permutations, the possible paradoxes of time manipulation. But ignoring it was easier said than done.

The running joke among agents was *Don't step on a butterfly or you may come back to find Hitler's descendants running the world*. Of course we no longer believed the timeline was that fragile, but who really knew for sure?

How this particular "unauthorized incursion" originated still boggles my mind. When you consider the detailed scrutiny of the background checks, the psych evaluations, the nearly constant security sweeps, it's hard to imagine how a member of the *Opus Dei* could have gotten clearance in the first place. Then, to be able to use that clearance to infiltrate our operation. Somebody somewhere screwed the pooch.

It didn't matter that the *Opus Dei* agent had been captured. He'd already set events in motion. He bragged about it--taunted us with it. So we knew what he'd attempted to do--what he'd already done if you look at it from the perspective of the timeline. We knew approximately when it would happen, but not how. That was my job. To find what exactly he'd done, and stop it.

I had all the training I needed, though I would have preferred more time for dialect reinforcement, and to research the era and culture I was about to insinuate myself into.

Funny I didn't have time. I should have had all the time in the world. But the longer a temporal deviation is in play, the more time it has to become absorbed by the sequential fabric, the harder it is to alter. That's the best I can explain it. Temporal mechanics was not my best subject. I just knew they wanted to send me back as soon as possible.

That was alright with me. I was confident. I was ready for this. I wouldn't have been chosen if I wasn't the best agent for this particular mission. The only thing that really annoyed me was the attire I was encased in for the trip. How women of the time managed to move about and still breathe was nothing short of a miracle.

Not only had my waist been tied down like I was in some kind of S&M film, the gold-thread embroidered stomacher, the full skirt of green silk brocade, and underskirt ruffles weighed me down like I was back in basic carrying a full pack. Not only that, my hair, along with assorted extensions, had been piled so high on my head, it messed with my balance. And, to top it off, I was told by the costume department that women's fashions changed so quickly during the period, they'd taken their "best guess," and "hoped" I wouldn't be committing any fashion faux pas.

I looked in the mirror when they were done and didn't recognize myself. It reminded me of when I was a little girl, always dressing up like one princess or another. I guess I looked pretty, in a very old school sort of way, but it wasn't practical for my purposes. At least the long dress trailing my every move was good for one thing. My feet were hidden, so I was able to wear my light boots so I could move about and run if necessary. I hate to even imagine what archaic footwear women's feet were forced into back then. I tell you, it was a barbaric time for female fashion.

I was about to ask what the hold-up was when I heard the slight vibration signaling the chronovectinator had activated (we just called it "Cranky"). When I began to feel the tell-tale sensation of ants crawling across my skin, I was certain I was on my way. Then came the part most agents dreaded, but I always enjoyed--I guess because my dad used to take me on all the scariest rides even when I was little.

The air in the chamber seemingly became substantive and started to spin around me. It took on a sheen of subdued coloring I always found beautiful, but made many would-be agents puke, thus eliminating them from the program.

Next came the feeling my body was rising above the floor, and that the chamber had become so immense in size I could no longer see the walls. My senses told me I'd been engulfed in a typhoon that had swallowed a rainbow. Scientifically, I knew that's not what was happening, but, visually, it had a virtual reality feel to it.

While it seemed to go on and on for several minutes, I knew it was actually only seconds before everything faded to black.

ʄ

203

Thanks to the reconnaissance of a previous agent, I knew exactly where to find my contact. Of course he didn't know he was my contact. Nor would he have any idea of the centuries-old bond we shared. That proved to be coincidence--though my old chronology professor always used to insist there was no such thing as coincidence. After several fruitless debates on the subject, we had agreed to disagree . . . well I had anyway.

My contact had been selected because he was one of the king's cavaliers--a sort of elite unit of bodyguards--and because he had ready access to the palace and the king himself. The idea being my mission was more likely to succeed if I wasn't immediately arrested as an interloper myself.

I heard the noise of a raucous crowd as soon as "the lights came on"--as we agents liked to call our materialization in a new time. I headed straight for the clamor. That's where I was told I'd find him.

He was as easy to spot as a signal flare, surrounded as he was by an unruly crowd. He was engaged in a duel with another fellow. And by duel I mean old school, with swords--rapiers to be exact. I recognized him right away, but only because of the covert photos the previous agent had taken. There was no family resemblance I could see, but then the bloodlines had gone off on several diverse tangents over the decades that would follow.

I pushed my way to the front of the crowd to get a better look, all the while trying not to gag at the smell of body odor that enveloped me. Good hygiene was not a strength of the early 18th century.

"I beg thee to reconsider thy actions, my good man. There's no reason one of us must bleed this day." It was my designated contact who spoke. I saw him clearly now.

"Thee will not only bleed, thee will die, William Deatherage," said the other man. "The honor of my sister will be avenged."

"Thou hast me confused with another, sir. I know not of the lady of which thou speaks, but I'm certain her honor is intact, if not her maidenhood."

This enraged the apparently offended party to an even greater degree, and he lunged wildly, thrusting left and right without effect. As cool as frozen yogurt, the accused philanderer sidestepped each thrust, then parried and spun about with such panache you would have thought he was dancing.

"I entreat thee to withdraw, sir, as to continue in this vein can have but sour consequences. Thy sister can ill afford to lose such a protective brother in these dangerous times."

I had to admit my target was quite the sight. Never had I seen a man dressed so colorfully, so flamboyant . . . well, maybe in a circus. The cuffs of his royal blue jacket were as heavily-embroidered with metallic gold threat as was my own outfit, and the collar of his shirt was trimmed with white lace. A gold baldric--a diagonal sash like beauty contestants wear--was emblazoned across his chest. He wore black velvet breeches, black leather gloves, also embroidered in gold, and high-rolled tawny leather boots. Shoulder-length curly brown hair framed his face, which was further adorned by an upturned mustache and a soul patch on his chin. Atop his head was a royal blue hat--the kind with the brim folded up on one side. Protruding from the back of the fold was a resplendent white feather.

The best word I could think of to describe his countenance was *dashing*.

"I will not withdraw, sir. If thee thinks I fear thee simply because thou are one of the king's cavaliers, thee can ponder thy poor judgment on the end of my blade."

The angry fellow launched a new attack--more measured this time. He initiated a *balestra*, feigned a lunge, side-stepped and executed a *redoublement* and lunged for real. Deatherage parried the attack, smiled, riposted, disengaged, feinted an attack, smiled again, and employed an *attaque au fer*, obviously toying with his adversary as opposed to trying to harm him. My fencing master would have been impressed . . . and he wasn't easily impressed.

It was quite apparent my contact was in no danger. He was a superior swordsman, and he knew it. I think the infuriated brother knew it as well, but his anger wouldn't let him back down.

As they spun and whirled back and forth, Deatherage happened to look into the crowd, right at me. There was a devil-may-care glint in his eyes. He smiled and winked in a manner no woman could misunderstand. Before I even had time to process this, he'd disarmed his attacker, wounding him only slightly.

I backed out of the crowd, but kept my eye on him. I needed to approach him, but not then, not there.

*

I followed the cavalier, managing to keep my distance most of the way. But just before we reached the palace gates, I lost him, cursing myself for being too careful.

On reflection, however, I discovered I hadn't been careful enough. Someone came up quickly behind me. I whirled around, ready to defend myself, only to find my target had turned the tables on me.

He smiled and fingered his mustache like I remembered my grandfather always doing when he was thinking. Yet, by the spark in his eyes, I could tell his appraisal of me was anything but fatherly.

"No need to be coy, milady. If thou wishes to engage me, thou only has to ask. Such a clandestine approach is wholly unnecessary."

"Forgive me, milord, but I must speak with thee on an urgent matter."

"I'm no lord. That title went to my older brother, Thomas, along with the family estates. I am William Deatherage Esquire, at thy service." He doffed his hat and executed a flawless bow before returning hat to head. "But thou must call me Will."

"As thou wishes."

"But milady has me at a disadvantage. By what appellation are thee known?"

I'd already decided there was no reason not to use my own name, so I told him.

"Savannah."

"Ah, Lady Savannah. Such an exotic name, as is thy accent. Are thee French?"

That caught me off-guard. I didn't know if being French in this period was a good thing or a bad one. The conflicts between France and England were so many over the centuries, I couldn't recall.

"Do I sound French?" I asked, giving myself time to think.

"Not entirely," he responded. "I'm not quite certain I've heard such an accent before."

"'Tis likely because my family traveled so much when I was younger," I said. "We spent much time in France, as well as Espana, Prussia, Hungaria."

"That explains it then," he responded. "So pray tell, Lady Savannah, what is so urgent that thee follows one of the king's cavaliers to the gates of the palace?"

"The king's life is in jeopardy," I blurted out, not knowing how else to broach the subject. "We must see to his safety at once."

"How know thou this?" He looked at me suspiciously.

"I overheard a group of men plotting to kill the king this very night."

"What men were these?"

"I know not their names, but they were desperate fellows, full of confidence in their scheme."

"Enemies of the crown are always threatening the king, milady. Most often those threats carry all the substance of windblown curses."

I knew I had to get him to take me seriously, so I called upon the brief research I'd been able to conduct.

"But they were Jacobites, milord--I mean, Will. I'm certain they meant to assassinate the king this night."

At the mention of the Catholic cabal, he frowned, obviously taking the threat more seriously.

"Those papists will do anything to put their Scottish king on the throne," he said angrily. "How do they plan to kill the king?"

"I'm sorry, but I heard not those details of the scheme. I only know it will happen sometime tonight."

"Then I must go directly to the palace and see to the king's safety. King George is a douchebag--and even more so a Prussian douchebag obsessed with all manner of frippery--but 'tis my duty as a cavalier to protect him."

"Thee must take me with, Will," I said, moving close enough to embrace his arm. I batted my eyelashes just enough, I hoped, to encourage him.

"'Tis too dangerous, milady."

"But some of the conspirators may have infiltrated the palace. I might recognize their faces, and thee could apprehend them before the deed is set into motion."

He considered this briefly, obviously conflicted with the idea a woman should be any part of such an endeavor.

"Alright, milady. But stay close to my protection."

"Of course, Will," I smiled up at him in the most demure, helpless female way I could muster--all the while thinking how I could have knocked him, or any assassin, into unconsciousness with one quick move if necessary.

∫

The palace guards looked me over as Will ushered me in, but the look was more of a smirk than one of suspicion. I gathered this wasn't the first time he'd brought a woman to the palace. But it also meant he had enough rank he wouldn't be questioned. I knew we'd need that kind of authority if we were going to succeed.

"We're going to need the help of those we trust if we're to protect the king," said Will, hurrying through the corridors. "I must find my brothers."

I nodded and tried my best to keep up with him, despite the cumbersome nature of my garments. He knew where to look, for shortly we turned into an alcove and came upon a couple engaged in a bit of amorous play.

"My brother, John, with Petra, one of the king's illegitimate daughters," he whispered to me as we approached them. "John's the real cocksman of the family, and the most devout.

"John!"

The pair looked up from the divan they were stretched across, ceased their frolicking, but didn't look a bit embarrassed. I noticed brother John was wearing the same bright blue embroidered costume as Will, and guessed it must be a uniform of sorts.

"What is it, Brother? Can't thou see I'm ministering to the spiritual needs of Lady Schulenburg?" He both looked and sounded perturbed.

The Lady Schulenburg's bodice was askew, and, upon seeing us, she began buttoning up, though in no particular hurry. How long it would have taken her to become completely free of her apparel, I had no idea. I would have thought that task alone would deter most men.

"I'm afraid Petra's needs must wait, John. There's a plot afoot. The king is in mortal danger."

John grabbed his sword and cavalier hat, and leapt to his feet. "By God, we must hurry then!"

"Where is Georgie?"

"Last I saw, he was headed for the kitchen to visit his scullery maid," said John.

"Let's fetch him."

The brothers took off, with Lady Schulenburg and myself hurrying to keep up. It wasn't easy, for she was dressed much like me, only her stomacher was embroidered with what looked like diamonds. My theory over women's footwear of the period was confirmed when, while trying to maintain my pace, her feet flew out from under her and she slid on her backside a good 20 feet across the polished palace floor. It was so comical, I couldn't help but chuckle.

I didn't want to fall too far behind the men, but I stopped to help her up.

"If you're going to keep up, milady," I said, foregoing dialect and with more of a scolding tone than I meant, "you might want to get rid of those shoes."

She frowned, giving me a look like *Who was I to talk to her so?* I ignored it and kept moving.

We made our way to the palace kitchen, where we discovered brother number three entangled with a servant girl. He was smaller and younger than both Will and John, didn't have their facial hair, but was strikingly handsome.

"Georgie, there's no time for that now," said Will. "The king's life is in jeopardy."

"What has happened?" asked Georgie, re-fastening his trousers.

"Nothing yet, but Lady Savannah here was privy to a conspiracy of treason and assassination. She says there will be an attempt on the king's life this very eve. We must act."

"Must we?" asked Georgie. "After all, the king *is* a douchebag."

"And a Prussian douchebag who doesn't even speak English," added John.

"Still, he is the king," replied Will. "And 'tis our duty as cavaliers to protect him from the Jacobite threat."

"Jacobites?" exclaimed Georgie. "Why didn't thee say such?"

"We can't let those filthy apostates kill our king," proclaimed John. "How will this wicked plot be carried out? Poison? Daggers?"

"We know not," said Will. "Only that they strike tonight."

"By the seven veils of Salome, we must rush to the king's side," declared John.

"Wait," said Will. "We should be wary of threats both within and without. John, thou goest with Lady Schulenburg and warn the outer palace guards of the danger. Georgie, thee and Bess search the kitchen and warn the king's cooks of the possibility of poison. Lady Savannah and I will see to the inner sanctum guards and warn the king. When the palace has been alerted, join us outside the king's chambers."

"God's will be done," said John as he and Lady Schulenburg hurried away.

Georgie and his servant girl scurried off in a different direction, and I followed Will to the king's chambers. He alerted each pair of palace guards we passed, and we both kept our eyes open for any threat, searching every alcove and chamber on our way.

"I believe thy words are true, Lady Savannah," said Will as we inspected the premises. "Yet I can't help but feel thou has not told me the entire story of how thee *just happened* to overhear this plot, and where thee really hails from."

"Thou must trust me, Will. What I say is true. And if I were to tell thee more, tell thee where I come from, thou wouldn't believe me. Thou would think me mad."

"I've been to an asylum before, milady. Thou are nothing like the poor creatures there. I will not think thee insane if thou tells me the truth. I will know it if I hear it. Besides, I like a good tall tale."

I considered fabricating something he could comprehend, something I might want to hide but was believable, but then I thought, *What the hell*.

"Okay, Will. The truth of the matter is, I'm from the future."

As I suspected, he stopped in his tracks and gave me the strangest of looks.

"Someone else from my future traveled back to this time to set in motion an assassination. He is a member of a Catholic cult in my time similar to the Jacobites. I was sent back to prevent the assassination from occurring, because it would change history, and result in unimaginable ripples in time."

He was still looking at me as if trying to decipher the words of an ancient text when he said, "Alright, maybe thou are a bit touched in head. Yet the king must be protected, and I still believe thou overheard the would-be assassins. Either that, or I'm blinded by thy beauty."

"Thank thee, Will," I said, reaching up to peck him on the cheek. "Thou won't regret it."

"Let us be quick. King George's chamber is near."

∫

Though I'd failed to read it in my research, it turned out what John had said was true. King George I of England didn't speak English. I knew he was actually German-born, and that he'd come to the throne after Queen Anne died because he was the closest relation who wasn't a Catholic, and the *Act of Settlement of 1701* prohibited Catholics from inheriting the throne. It was ludicrous logic as far as I was concerned, but when it came to religion, I knew logic wasn't a prized precept.

So I stood there while Will tried to communicate with the king in French. Unfortunately, Will's French was only slightly better than the king's English. I put my hand on Will's shoulder to silence him, dropped into my best curtsey, stood back up and said, *Votre Majesté, votre vie est en danger. Vos cavaliers doivent prendre des précautions supplémentaires pour assurer votre sécurité. Vous devez rester ici, dans votre chambre, jusqu'à ce que les assassins sont traitées."*

Basically, I told the king his life was in danger, and that he should stay in his room while his cavaliers dealt with the threat. He tut-tutted the whole idea with disdain and a wave of his hand, said he wasn't to be disturbed any further, and dismissed us as though he hadn't a concern in the world. I thought "douchebag" was putting it politely.

Once we were outside the royal chamber, we checked the terrace overlooking the palace grounds. The sun was nearing the horizon, but I saw no obvious threats.

John, Petra, Georgie, and Bess joined us.

"The palace guard is on alert for the heretics," said John.

"The royal chef is aware of the threat, and will personally prepare all the king's meals," added Georgie.

"And I've doubled the king's personal guard with men I know to be loyal," declared Will.

"An imminent threat to the king's life at this point is highly implausible," said John.

"Quite impossible," added Georgie.

"Certainly improbable," agreed Will.

"Maybe," I said, not sounding so sure, "but there must be something we haven't thought of. What else can we do?"

"Let us pray," said John.

"No time for prayer, Brother," said Georgie, gesturing. "Look there."

On another terrace to our right, a rope was hanging to the ground, and several armed men were helping the last of their group complete his climb.

"Unholy assassins!" cried out John.

"We must intercept them!" commanded Will. "Ladies, go quickly to the king's chamber and warn the guards there. Come, Brothers."

Bess and Lady Schulenburg took off, but I wasn't going anywhere except with the cavaliers. They were in such a rush, they didn't even notice I followed.

We came upon the half dozen assailants in the corridor leading to the royal chamber, and the cavaliers clashed with them there. I marveled at the expert swordsmanship displayed by all three Deatherage brothers, as well as their banter.

"May we see thy tickets, gentleman," said Georgie politely as he ducked under an oncoming blade into a *passata-sotto*, then used the flat of his own blade to slap his attacker on the *derriere*. "Naughty, naughty. There's no admission without a ticket."

John rushed two of the assassins at once, forcing them back with a furious compound attack. While his movements were so quick they were hard to follow, his punditry was delivered with calm rectitude. "There is a way that seems right to a man, but its end is the way to death," he said, executing a <u>croisé</u> against one man while looking sternly at the other. "I tell thee, there is joy before the angels of God over one sinner who repents."

Meanwhile, Will had dispatched one man quickly with a *raddoppio*, and engaged another saying, "It seems thy comrade wasn't up to the task. I hope thee will prove a better amusement."

I stepped forward, picked up the sword of the man who was writhing in pain on the floor, and checked its balance. It wasn't a particularly well-crafted weapon, but certainly deadly in the right hands.

"Do not fear those who kill the body but cannot kill the soul," said John, pressing his opponent back against the corridor wall while delivering another bit of scripture. "Rather fear him who can destroy both soul and body in Hell."

My attention turned back to Will in time to see his frivolity lead him astray. As he let his obviously lesser-skilled opponent press the attack, pushing him back, he tripped over the man he'd already downed. Seeing the opening, the assassin came in for the kill, using a two-handed thrust aimed at Will's chest.

I stepped forward, slapped his blade away, and disarmed him with a *coup d'arrêt*. He stared at me in disbelief, then, seeing the rest of his fellows down or disabled, he took off, running right into an oncoming group of palace guards.

I reached down and gave Will a hand up.

"Lady Savannah," he said, looking at me with both amazement and respect, "thou saved my life."

I'd been wanting to tell him the "Lady" designation wasn't necessary, but I was beginning to like the sound of it.

"Thou would have done the same for me," I said, realizing as I did, that if I hadn't saved his life--had he died on that corridor floor--I would no longer exist. At least the person I knew as myself wouldn't exist . . . which means I could never have saved his life in the first place . . . unless that was one of the serpentine paradoxes of time travel that would let me live in the past but disappear from the future. It could all get very confusing, so I reverted to my training which directed *just don't think about it.*

With the assassins dispatched, or in the hands of the guards, Georgie and John approached and raised their swords. Will's blade joined them and he looked at me. I raised mine as well, and all four clashed overhead in a sort of antiquated high-five. It was so gloriously camp--right out of an Alexandre Dumas novel--it got me thinking. It had all been a little too easy. Could this be all there was to our time intruder's plot? My chronology professor had another saying, that seemed apt at the moment. *If everything seems to be going well, you've obviously overlooked something.*

I shrugged off my paranoid concerns and let my smile join those of the Deatherage brothers. I was about to say something poignant, when a flare of light blinded us all. When my vision cleared, I saw him standing there, not ten feet from me. It was Troy.

f

"Another assassin!" called out Will, gallantly stepping in front of me and readying his blade.

"No!" I yelled, grabbing Will's arm. "He's no assassin. He's my brother."

Will turned and whispered to me. "Thy brother from the future?"

I nodded and knew by the look on Will's face that the flash of light and sudden appearance of Troy had him re-thinking the whole time travel aspect of my crazy story. John and Georgie just looked confused.

I walked around Will and straight to Troy. He looked me up and down.

"Wow, they really dressed you up for Halloween, didn't they?" he said with that familiar Troy smirk of his.

"I see you didn't have time to bother. You know you're breaking regs looking like that don't you?"

Not having troubled himself with a period costume, he shrugged off any worry over regulations. He was attired in his usual shorts and sandals, topped off with a blue and gold Chargers lightning bolt T-shirt. Well, at least his colors matched the cavalier uniforms.

"I don't know why you're here, Baby Brother," I said, using the endearment that always pissed him off. "But the plot's been foiled. We stopped the assassins."

"That's why I came back," said Troy. "To warn you. The assassins were just a feint. We duped our time trespasser into thinking his scheme had worked, and found out the assassins were a ploy to keep us occupied. The real threat is a bomb he built. It's likely crude, but effective."

"A bomb?" I was flabbergasted.

Will stepped up next to me. "Lady Savannah, what is this 'bomb' thy brother speaks of?"

"It's an explosive device." Will's expression remained blank, so I explained. "A bomb is made from compacted gunpowder. It's like the power of a canon-- thee has canons, right?" He nodded. "Well, it's like that, only smaller, and likely much more powerful."

"This *bomb* must be close to the king, must it not?"

It was my turn to nod.

"Then we must find it with all haste."

"Yes, we must," I said. "I have no idea how large it is, or what it might look like, but start in the king's chamber and look for anything unusual."

The Deatherage brothers ran off toward the royal chamber and I looked at Troy.

"*Lady* Savannah?" he asked with a double dose of smirk.

"Come on," I said, ignoring his tease, "we've got to find that bomb."

213

ʃ

It didn't take long. Only a few minutes after escorting a very annoyed king out of his chamber, Will asked, "Is this it?" He held it up to show me. "Thou said to look for anything strange. I know not what this is."

What he held was indeed strange looking, with leather strips and gold wiring built around a woven basket that might normally hold produce.

"There are numbers flashing inside of it," said Will. "They appear to be counting backwards--14, 13, 12, 11 . . . ."

"It's a on a timer!" I yelled. "Get rid of it! Throw it out the window!"

He ran to the nearest balcony and hurled the basket out as far as he could. The instant I joined him, the bomb detonated.

I pulled him down in case of shrapnel, but the only thing that landed on the balcony looked like mud . . . very smelly mud.

"Was there anyone down there?" I asked. "Did anyone get hurt?"

"I think not, milady. I threw it in the direction of the royal cesspit."

We stood and scanned the blast site for casualties. I didn't see anyone who was injured, though there were plenty of befuddled faces, and several who'd been showered with dung.

"That's unfortunate," said Will.

"What is?"

"Does thou see the lady there?" He said, pointing down. "The one dressed so finely, but now covered in shite?"

"Yes, I see her. She doesn't appear injured."

"That may well be," said Will with a distressed look. "But she is Petra's mother, the Lady Melusine von der Schulenburg, the king's mistress."

I couldn't stop the smile forming on my face. "Well, at least it's royal shite."

Despite his anxiety over soiling the king's mistress, Will broke out in laughter so infectious I was induced to join him.

ʃ

"Come on, *Lady* Savannah," said Troy with more than a touch of sarcasm, "we've got to go."

I was saying goodbye to Will, while trying to ignore my little brother, who exemplified the adage, *We never really grow up, we just learn how to act in public.* Only he was still learning.

"I have never known a lady such as thyself," said Will. "Must thou return to thy future time?"

"Yes, I'm afraid I must. Now that the threat to the king has passed, I've got to leave. I can't risk any other fluctuations in the timeline."

"But there will be other threats."

"Yes, and I'm certain thee and the other cavaliers will be up to the task."

Without warning, he took me in his arms and kissed me as well as I'd ever been kissed. If he was trying to get me to stay, it was an excellent effort. But there was a reason other than possible paradoxes of time that prevented me from taking him up on his implied offer. Not a logical reason, but a cultural one ingrained in me and still hard to shake.

"There's something I should tell thee before I go, Will," I said once I'd steadied myself. "Something which will help thee understand why I must leave."

"What could that possibly be, milady?"

"I'm thy great, great, great, great, great, great, great granddaughter."

Brothers George, John, and William Deatherage, members of the king's cavaliers, immigrated to America in the early 18th century. Some sources say they were forced to leave England by King George I. Whether the reason for that was an incident involving the king's mistress, is only speculation. However, nearly two decades later, the new king, George II, who was often in opposition to his father, granted 950 acres of land in Virginia to the Deatherage brothers.

This tale is a little different than those that have preceded it, in that it not only features one of my direct ancestors, my great (x5) grandfather, William Deatherage, but also two of my descendants, my granddaughter Savannah Presley Golden and grandson Troy Conner Golden.

Of course I'm not really predicting time travel will be developed some time in the next 20 years, but what if?

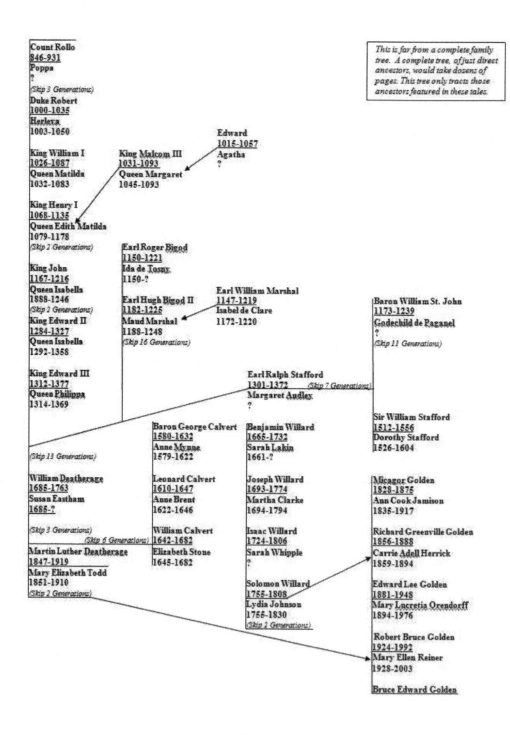

This is far from a complete family tree. A complete tree, of just direct ancestors, would take dozens of pages. This tree only tracts those ancestors featured in these tales.

Count Rollo
846-931
Poppa
?
(Skip 3 Generations)
Duke Robert
1000-1035
Herleva
1003-1050

King William I
1026-1087
Queen Matilda
1032-1083

King Malcom III
1031-1093
Queen Margaret
1045-1093

Edward
1015-1057
Agatha
?

King Henry I
1068-1135
Queen Edith Matilda
1079-1178
(Skip 2 Generations)

Earl Roger Bigod
1150-1221
Ida de Tosny
1150-?

King John
1167-1216
Queen Isabella
1888-1246
(Skip 2 Generations)
King Edward II
1284-1327
Queen Isabella
1292-1358

Earl Hugh Bigod II
1182-1225
Maud Marshal
1188-1248
(Skip 16 Generations)

Earl William Marshal
1147-1219
Isabel de Clare
1172-1220

Baron William St. John
1173-1239
Godechild de Paganel
?
(Skip 11 Generations)

King Edward III
1312-1377
Queen Philippa
1314-1369

Earl Ralph Stafford
1301-1372   (Skip 7 Generations)
Margaret Audley
?

Sir William Stafford
1512-1556
Dorothy Stafford
1526-1604

(Skip 13 Generations)

Baron George Calvert
1580-1632
Anne Mynne
1579-1622

Benjamin Willard
1665-1732
Sarah Lakin
1661-?

William Deatherage
1685-1763
Susan Eastham
1685-?

Leonard Calvert
1610-1647
Anne Brent
1622-1646

Joseph Willard
1693-1774
Martha Clarke
1694-1794

Micagor Golden
1828-1875
Ann Cook Jamison
1835-1917

(Skip 3 Generations)
                    (Skip 6 Generations)
Martin Luther Deatherage
1847-1919
Mary Elizabeth Todd
1851-1910
(Skip 2 Generations)

William Calvert
1642-1682
Elizabeth Stone
1645-1682

Isaac Willard
1724-1806
Sarah Whipple
?

Solomon Willard
1755-1808
Lydia Johnson
1755-1830
(Skip 2 Generations)

Richard Greenville Golden
1856-1888
Carrie Adell Herrick
1859-1894

Edward Lee Golden
1881-1948
Mary Lucretia Orendorff
1894-1976

Robert Bruce Golden
1924-1992
Mary Ellen Reiner
1928-2003

Bruce Edward Golden

ACKNOWLEDGMENTS

I want to thank Carolyn Crow, my editor, for all of her suggestions and her work in finding those hundreds of typos that got by my own eyes. For help with my research, both ancestral, historical, and cultural, I'm grateful to my aunt, Barbara Jean Reiner, my sister Rebecca Anne Golden, Glenda Dawe of the Centre for Newfoundland Studies, and my good friend Stephen Gregory Vaughn, without whose family volume I may never have discovered the improbable connection between our ancestors.

While the cover design was my own, I needed the assistance of others to complete it. I'm grateful to Mike Watts for his fractal art piece *Wave Curl*, which provides the background for both the front and back covers, and to Phil Nenna for his technical assistance in creating the cover art. In Frogner Park, Oslo, Norway, Jinah Kim-Perek took the photograph which I used for my ancestral monolith. The monolith was designed by Gustav Vigland in 1924 in Norway, which makes it particularly appropriate, as Norway was the birthplace of Hrolf "Rollo," one of my oldest known ancestors. The monolith took three stone carvers 14 years to complete.

And, lastly, I want to thank my mother, Mary Ellen Reiner, who encouraged my creativity; my dad, Robert Bruce Golden, who helped mold my sense of humor; and all my ancestors, without whom I wouldn't be here to write this book.

Mary Ellen Reiner singing aboard cruise ship (1968).

PFC Robert Bruce Golden in England (1946).

ABOUT THE AUTHOR

Novelist, journalist, satirist . . . Bruce Golden's career as a professional writer spans almost four decades and more endeavors in more media than you can shake a pen at. Born, raised, and still living in San Diego, Bruce has worked for magazines and small newspapers as an editor, art director, columnist, and freelance writer; in radio as a news editor/writer, sports anchor, film reviewer, feature reporter, and the creator of *Radio Free Comedy*; in TV as a writer/producer; as a communications director for a non-profit; and as a writer/producer of educational documentaries on public health for the state of California.

In all, Bruce published more than 200 articles and columns before deciding, at the turn of the century, to walk away from journalism and concentrate on his first love—writing speculative fiction. Since devoting himself to that end, he's seen his short stories published more than 120 times across 15 countries and a score of anthologies. Along with numerous Honorable Mention awards for his short fiction, including those from the Speculative Literature Foundation and L. Ron Hubbard's Writers of the Future contest, he won Speculative Fiction Reader's 2003 Firebrand Fiction prize, was one of the authors selected for the Top International Horror 2003 contest, and won the 2006 JJM and the 2009 Whispering Spirits prizes for fiction. *Tales of My Ancestors* is his sixth book. You can read more about Bruce's books and stories at:
http://goldentales.tripod.com/

Other books by Bruce Golden

MORTALS ALL
BETTER THAN CHOCOLATE
EVERGREEN
DANCING WITH THE VELVET LIZARD
RED SKY, BLUE MOON

Made in the USA
Charleston, SC
23 February 2016